DONNY BROOK

DONNY BROOK

THE OZARKIAN FOLK TALES TRILOGY
—BOOK THREE—

BY TODD PARNELL

P
Pen-L Publishing
Fayetteville, Arkansas
Pen-L.com

BOOKS BY TODD PARNELL:

THE OZARKIAN FOLK TALES TRILOGY
Skunk Creek
Swine Branch
Donny Brook

The Buffalo, Ben, and Me
Mom at War
Postcards from Branson

DEDICATION

The Ozarkian Folk Tales Trilogy is dedicated to my wife who challenged me to write fiction.

When I asked how, she advised, " . . . start with something you know and understand—the Ozarks, small towns, creeks and rivers, float trips . . . then make it a mystery, add a little violence, sex, humor, exaggeration, and even a hint of the supernatural, and have fun." I am grateful for her recipe and can only hope that this celebration of life amidst chaos and confusion entertains as well as frames a fictional village and her colorful citizens as heroic, resilient, and deeply rooted. It has been fun to try!

AUTHOR'S NOTE

A brook is a look at history's flow.

This is a third novel about the Ozarks, that vague notion of geography and culture tucked into southwest Missouri and northwest Arkansas. I was privileged to grow up here and I treasure the history, the beauty, the humor, the toughness, the kindness, the independence, the gentleness, the lore and the legend, the bonds that bind us.

Donny Brook is an Ozarkian folk tale* featuring the village of Hardlyville as hero, beautiful Skunk Creek as backdrop, and a large support cast of colorful Hardlyvillains facing grave natural, unnatural, and environmental threats to their way of life. It is a mystery grounded in Ozarks waters, culture, and history, and set in the tragedy, love, lust, and resilience of a fictional Ozarks village. Crafted in the long tradition of Ozarks storytelling, *Donny Brook* is bawdy, irascible, and irreverent. Its reach extends far beyond city limits to centers of government and distant foreign cultures. It is a sequel to *Swine Branch* and the third volume in the Ozarkian Folk Tales Trilogy.

The Hillbilly caricature of bibs, corncobs, white lightening, ignorance, and bliss is often a self-inflicted and profitable iteration of the hardscrabble life many of our forefathers lived in forging an existence in a beautiful but unforgiving landscape.

Dark tales of violence, drugs, and abuse are but one side of the Ozarks. Herein I have sought to meld the tragic with the exaggerated to honor the mythical Arcadia of ancient lore and the dogged resilience of a people and place beset with myriad contemporary challenges. Humor underlies it all as it has served as an antidote for tough times and rough lives throughout Ozarkian history. And yes, the threats to tradition and precious natural and water resources are real and ongoing.

I was raised in a giving and extended family and community, short of perfection, but long on love. Characters and locales featured within are fictional, but grounded in the imagination and tall tales of my youth. At the same time, jabs at prevailing political and moral hypocrisies play out every bit as well alongside a beautiful Ozark stream as in a teeming metropolis. Earthy and ribald moments are meant to soften body blows and bring an occasional chuckle, not to offend. Beyond all, I smile at my homeland, its rugged elegance, its many special characters real and imagined, fond memories, and huge hopes.

Todd Parnell
SPRING, 2016

* Folk tale: A tale or legend originating and traditional among a people or folk having to do with everyday life, and frequently featuring wily peasants getting the better of their superiors.

CONTENTS

CAST OF PLACES, CHARACTERS, AND INSTITUTIONS

PLACES
Hardlyville—Fictional Town
Hardlyvillains—Residents of Hardlyville
Skunk Creek—Fictional creek
Swine Branch—Fictional tributary to fictional creek
Donny Brook—Fictional new name for Hardlyville

CHARACTERS: (CURRENT)

Pierce Arrow—Editor, *Hardlyville Daily Hellbender*, Congressman
Lettie Jones—Genuine Hero, partner of Pierce Arrow, wife of deceased Lucas Jones
Lucas Jr., Vixen, Mona, Peli—Young children of Lettie
Lucas Jones—Genuine Hero, deceased
Jimmy Jones—Entrepreneur
Sally Boswell Jones—Wife of Jimmy Jones
Sheriff Sephus Adonis—The Law
Pastor Pat—Minister
Dylan "Ol' Dill" Thomas—Deaf owner of family still
Tiny Taylor—Owner, Greasy Spoons, girlfriend of Ol' Dill
Muffle—Ol' Dill's Dog
Donald "Dinky" Doodle—Village Jester, aka "The Donald"
Sisters Sledge—The Donald's girlfriends
Doc Karst—Town physician
James Bond (PB)—Postmaster, civic leader
She—Demon Lady, Devil Woman, Evil One
Chuck Hendricks—Hot Shot CPA
Billious Bloom—Executive Director of Rosebeam Foundation

Pres Bloom—Illegitimate son of Billious Bloom, Mayor
Rifleman and Steele—Small business owners
Li'l Shooter Abdul—Rifleman and Steele's daughter
Booray Abdul—Li'l Shooter's husband
Abdul Abdul, Kiri, Obi, Uvi—Booray Abdul's family
Jamin Bennell—Banker
Mabel Bennell—Banker's wife
Captain Happy—Banker's best friend
President—The President of the United States
Paul Michael Peters (Pomp)—Hardlyville high-schooler
Aimless Bevel—Really Bad Guy
Freeload Twins—More Bad Guys
Clyde Shade, Esq—Hardlyville attorney
Sarcoxie Combs—Lead tracker
Sadie Sally Mae—Pierce Arrow's old girlfriend
Abraham Isaac Joseph Smith—Science teacher

CHARACTERS: (HISTORICAL)

Thomas Hardly—Founder, Hardlyville
Petunia Perfidy Hardly—Thomas Hardly's second wife
Hardlita Hardly Rosebeam—Thomas and Petunia's daughter,
Ms. Octavia Rosebeam's mother
Octavia Rosebeam—Bequeather of Rosebeam Foundation

INSTITUTIONS

Hardlyville Daily Hellbender (Newspaper)
Bank of Hardlyville
Skunk Creek Church of Christ

PROLOGUE

The small green sign read:

> # DONNY BROOK
> ## (FORMERLY HARDLYVILLE)
> ## POPULATION 277*
>
> *Civic leaders have agreed on this population estimate as a compromise between competing numbers on prior city limit signs at opposite ends of the village.

A simple average trumped accuracy in the interest of harmony.

A larger sign in red and black trumpeted:

> **WELCOME TO THE ONLY GENUINE WORKING VILLAGE IN THE OZARKS DAILY ADMISSION $10 PER GUEST. COME GET TO KNOW US . . . AND OUR WAY OF LIFE.**

TO ROB A BANK

Jimmy Jones had taken wife Sally and toddler daughter Girl Jones to Tiny Taylor's Greasy Spoons Grill and Bar for a fried squirrel and scrambled egg breakfast before dropping off his large aromatic cash deposit at the bank. Jimmy was a leading local weed grower and the bank's largest depositor. As Jimmy carefully counted each fragrant dollar bill for the bemused teller, Girl Jones walked straight into President Jamin Bennell's office for her standard morning sucker. Banker Jamin obliged and sat on the floor next to Girl with ten silver dollars asking her to help him count them. If she got to five, she got one Jamin promised. Jamin was good with numbers and probability theory and could predict that Girl would get to four given her age and household income. He would simply round up to five and give Girl her prize, earning more loyalty from his largest depositor. Banker Jamin loved Girl's unusual name, which had resulted from Jimmy and Sally forgetting to sign her birth certificate when they took their first baby home for the first time. There had been alcohol and weed involved, but forgetting just sounded better. Whatever, Girl was straight and to the point, just the way he liked to do business.

1

A robber armed with a pistol charged through the doors of the bank, demanding that everyone lay down, shut their eyes, and place their hands on their privates lest they be shot off.

Jimmy had always disobeyed authority, as all Jones were predestined to do, and attacked the robber. The first shot hit Jimmy amidships. The robber shot Jimmy twice before he even could lay a hand on the bastard. The robber demanded every source of cash in the bank and thrust an extra-large yard waste trash bag at the teller. Jimmy moaned while Sally knelt beside him and wailed. The robber pistol-whipped Sally into unconsciousness.

A first time tourist visitor to Donny Brook heard the commotion from just outside the front door and waltzed in with his wife to see the show. He headed straight for the robber to get an autograph, telling wifey that the blood next to the downed body even looked real. The robber shot him dead and smacked his wife with the long pistol.

Jamin pushed Girl behind his desk, grabbed a pistol from his desk drawer, rushed to the bank lobby, and demanded that the robber drop all weapons and demands. The robber shot Jamin twice before he could get off a round, which sailed harmlessly into the ceiling. Jamin lay twitching, blooding the faux Oriental rug on the original hard wood floor.

The robber hissed to the teller to hurry. The teller opened the safe and crammed every stack of bills she could find into the bag. Girl Jones ran out of Jamin's office crying for her mother. When Girl saw her on the ground the toddler jumped on her motionless body screaming in fear. The robber grabbed the stuffed trash bag and Girl Jones as he backed out of the door onto Lettie Jones Road.

One witness said the robber fled on foot into the corner of Mark Twain National Forest bordering Donny Brook, dragging and smacking the screaming child, never looking back. Another swore there was more than one, though she was seventy-eight years old and by all accounts could not tell the difference between a pole cat and a black bear at twenty paces.

Chaos reigned as innocent lives hung in the balance. Doc Karst, who was better at delivering cattle than saving lives, began triage with few good choices as to where or on whom to begin.

As Pierce Arrow headed toward Interstate 70, choosing the faster, colder, concrete route home rather than the one on which he had taken his family westward several weeks earlier, he finally plugged in his cell phone for a recharge. He wondered if he had missed anything. Partner Lettie nodded off to take advantage of napping kids.

Once powered, his message board ignited. "Call me!" begged Billious Bloom six times over the past twenty-four hours. "Call me!" ordered Sheriff Sephus Adonis three times over a similar period. Li'l Shooter, who was watching their older children, had called sobbing.

Pierce called her first, wanting to know if the kids were okay. She confirmed yes but said the village was a wounded, sobbing mess before the connection was lost.

Pierce waited for cell phone bars and called Sheriff Sephus next. The sheriff's report was swift and complete. It started with a "where the hell are you when we need you," and ended with the scorecard: one dead, two critically wounded, one child kidnapped, and all the cash in Donny Brook taken by a brazen bank robber, perhaps two.

Pierce flipped on the speaker phone and asked for details, which Sheriff Sephus provided.

"We need you and Lettie home, Pierce," Sheriff Sephus ordered. "We're dying around here."

3

Pierce Arrow sobbed out loud, which was not his style. He pulled to the side of the road, set the parking brake, reached over to dozing Lettie, and hugged her with all he had. She hugged him back and began a deep kiss until the wetness of his tears awakened her fully to his grief.

Pierce could not speak for several moments, raising her anxiety from zero to sixty in a heartbeat. She broke free of his clutch and slapped him lightly to restore order to place and time.

Pierce repeated Sheriff Sephus's tale of violence and tragedy word for word, assuring Lettie that their other kids were okay, but Hardlyville, Donny Brook, or whatever they called it now, wasn't.

As Lettie lay shaking in Pierce's arms, his mind wandered back to how they got to here from there and then . . .

SOLD

Pierce Arrow, Managing Editor of the *Hardlyville Daily Hellbender*, distinguished former congressional representative, powerful and honorable voice of the community, partner of Lettie Jones, and father/stepfather to her five children just couldn't figure it out.

How can you sell a way of life, pondered Pierce?

Hardlyville's nearly century and a half of existence—, from founding father Thomas Hardly to now, through brutal murders, environmental disasters, presidential visits, yes, as in the United States of America, National Refuge designation, French floozies and Oriental provocateurs, affairs of the heart or mere convenience, holy philandering and evil incarnate in name of same, and most importantly, genuine love of place and neighbors—on the market? Renamed?

Special Skunk Creek, the backbone of it all, life blood to all who lived along her banks, pristine victim of Big Pork greed and avarice, scarred and sullied forever by the Big Pig Flood, nursed back from the depths of destruction by the sheer will of Hardlyvillains, federal money, and periodic injections of anonymous philanthropy. Reclaimed?

Her precious Hellbender, natural barometer for stream and community health, gone forever in the flush of a CAFO toilet, now disowned by syndicated investors.

There's a Hardlyville chapter in each of these snippets, thought Pierce, having editorialized on everything from village jester Dinky Doodle's manhood resurrection to Octavia Rosebeam's grand theft in the interest of scholarly legacy in his fifteen years as a transplant from the east. He was still a "furineer" to some but a proud recipient of their trust and votes to represent them in Congress for a self-declared single term, now served and done.

Hardlyville's history—as meticulously recorded from founder's wife Petunia Hardly's handwritten letters to granddaughter Octavia Rosebeam a century past to recent *Skunk Creek* and *Swine Branch* offerings—is colorful, bold, and unrepentant. Characters come and go but most leave a mark for the good on the Hardlyvillain scorecard. Some have even opined that genuine Hardlyvillain icons like Lucas Jones, Octavia Rosebeam, Sheriff Sephus Adonis, deaf Ol' Dylan Thomas, and little Lettie Jones—Pierce Arrow's partner, not wife—meld into a true hero which is the village itself.

And that was what Pierce Arrow could not get his head around.

Donny Brook? A new name for a new place and time, a new way to sustain an old way of life—so declared by Hardlyvillain civilian leadership in earning the vote for name change—simply shat on Hardlyville's past in search of something else. It was the "something else" that Pierce Arrow could not comprehend.

Sure, there was a new motel under construction at the village edge, with bus tours and casual travelers as target market. None could enter the new life flow without contributing to Hardlyville's financial perpetuation, protected into eternity as generations would come and go.

6

Pierce had assumed that his beloved Hardlyville had dodged this bullshit bullet. First time around, a corrupt investment banking firm—represented by an even more corrupt deal maker—had put forth an private placement prospectus that swayed some of the more progressive elements of Hardlyville's citizen leadership. It promised gads of money to provide financial security to the community and her citizens in exchange for selling the village to investors with an option to repurchase for one dollar after thirty years. The stated objective was to share an idyllic lifestyle with a cynical nation by marketing the hell out of it. Come visit tiny arcadian Hardlyville and restore your faith in America.

The deal was billed as the classic capitalistic win-win, with Hardlyville and her band of heroes as victors plus a fair ROI for investors. Though too good to be true, it took a run of sexual chicanery and mean-spirited violence to burst that bubble and just say NO.

Pierce had led the loyal opposition and prevailed in the end. That was then. This was now.

Money quickly raised her ugly head again as a fresh and more reputable band of venture capitalists got wind of the failed scheme and rushed to fill the void with cash, of which they had plenty. They also sweetened the pot to where civic leaders would have been immoral stewards if they had not offered the community a chance to vote up or down. In that every citizen in Hardlyville, regardless of age, gender, or other abnormality would receive a fat annual royalty check far into the future for doing nothing more than being themselves, support surged. Pierce came across as snooty and academic in his emotional editorials against selling out heritage and history. *He must not need the money or the security,* reasoned most. It was a curious collapse in credibility from those days he served

7

as congressman. He was back on the fringe, where he had started his brief political career.

Even Banker Jamin, who had shared Pierce's early mistrust and discomfort with selling something that wasn't theirs, saw enough cash on the barrel to provide Hardlyville with a well-earned and fully-funded retirement. The village had been through enough over the years, particularly these past few. And, they could always buy it back with all that money flowing to them and into community coffers if they changed their mind. Jamin was a businessman first and a historian further down the list. He voted to support the economic interests of the community after dissecting and deconstructing the deal in search of fatal flaws or risks. He found none.

So, in the end, there were Pierce, Tiny Taylor, and a handful of Agenda 21'ers left behind at the altar. The latter's crazy company convinced Pierce that he was probably wrong, though he couldn't get there on his own. His ultimate "yes" vote was received as a noble gesture of conciliation, served up to bring peace and prosperity to the Hardlyville family. Tiny Taylor, bless her soul, never sold out.

There was even the unprecedented naming of each street in Hardlyville proper and the numbering of each residence.

That hadn't been necessary for a century and a half, most recently due to Postmaster James Bond's single room post office and his faithful personal presentation of each parcel and letter to every residence in the community. His untiring efforts to deliver mail in the face of copperhead bites, ticks and chiggers, tornados and ice storms, feral pig attacks and come-ons from lonely ladies whose husbands were out coon hunting were legend. Pierce had never seen nor heard of anything like it. If he didn't need street names and house numbers to keep track, who did?

J. B., Postmaster and Civic Leader, was as dogged as a black bear in a trash can or a four pound smallmouth on a Zera Spook top water bait. He simply couldn't be stopped.

In actual fact he was, stopped that is, on two consecutive occasions, the day of and the day after the Big Pig Flood. With dead hogs and fetid fecal solids floating all around town, J. B. received no incoming mail, and stacked all received and outgoing as high in his one hundred-year-old post office as he could reach, pinching a clothes pin on his nose to keep from passing out. He slept leaning against a moldy wall and took no sustenance for forty-eight hours. Just another genuine Hardlyville Hero. *There have been so many,* mused Pierce.

And Pierce concluded that maybe it was okay to name streets after these heroes, to perpetuate their memory and inspiration. At least that had an historical grounding to it.

Lucas Jones Boulevard would certainly call to memory the selfless sexual sacrifice made on an altar of hatred and vindictiveness with a Demon Lady which saved several of Hardlyville's youngest from kidnap and corruption as well as spawning the beautiful toddler with the bright-yellow eyes that Pierce and Lettie now called their own.

Then there was **Thomas Hardly Lane**, a dirt road to the creek bank near where the founder's two-story white clapboard residence stood for decades, leaning slightly toward Skunk Creek, before being flushed downstream with hogs and waste in the Big Pig Flood. The house with the upstairs porch where founding father Thomas and wife Petunia always took morning coffee and evening tea gazing creekward. The house where Thomas had been brutally murdered over a crude hand-drawn map for reasons uncertain, and Petunia and daughter Hardlita had grieved his passing until their deaths.

Rosebeam Road was named after the founder's granddaughter Octavia, a classics scholar of all things, trained, then cruelly raped by a yellow-eyed beast in the prime of her Latin studies in NYC, unknowing mother of the Demon Lady herself. Ms. Rosebeam, old-maid Hardlyville High School Latin teacher to her death, toga partier extraordinaire, bank robber, and subsequent endower of the Rosebeam Foundation to forever perpetuate a world class Latin collection and curriculum in the village's conscience and life.

Flo Ho' Highway lovingly recalled the visit of legendary French porn actress Florence Hormele, who spread more love, passion, and international good will around Hardlyville in two weeks than all who had collectively come before her. She had touched Pierce Arrow as deeply emotionally as she had a quarter of the males in the community physically, leaving most the better for her interventions. It was a long and beautiful tale, worth retelling in times of trial and trouble, and a naming serves history well. Pastor Pat had provided the nomination with a strong second from Ol' Dill, an ecumenical and divinely-inspired blessing that confirmed her timeless contribution of passion to community beyond the affections of her nominators.

Finally, there was the only non-posthumous recognition, **Lettie Jones Street,** the principal path through the heart of town, so named in tribute to Pierce's own partner Lettie for service above and beyond the call. No one talked about her secret offer of sacrifice and yet everyone knew. Call it the immaculate mis-consummation. Her willingness to take one for the village to save Skunk Creek, "one" being an amorous president of the United States who lusted over Miss Lettie to the point of trading a post-Big-Pig-Flood-presidentially-decreed-Skunk Creek-National-Watershed-Refuge designation for a simple roll in the hay. Quid pro quo, so to speak, if sex and environmental protection can be linked.

The end game, which spared little Lettie, led not only to a presidential Executive Order in Skunk Creek's favor and multiple presidential visits to tiny Hardlyville for presumed consummations, but more—a legend borne of selfless love and a willingness to sacrifice person, pride, and fidelity for precious Skunk Creek. Pierce Arrow could only chuckle at the duplicitous schemes and double doing that carried the day and shielded Lettie in the end.

Confused? *Swine Branch* tells all. Pierce Arrow's chuckle turned to a belly laugh when he recalled the tale of attempted White House seduction, an undersized presidential perpetrator, and the unprecedented international emergency that spared Lettie her sacrifice and provided a lifetime of guffaws. A buck naked Commander in Chief in semi-erect state, if one looked very closely, marshaling military resources and ordering Generals to war, all cell phone videoed for the record. An image for the ages!

It is a long and glorious story of justice served and innocence spared. He loved and admired his partner Lettie beyond wordily description.

No. No "Main" or "Commercial" Streets in the village of Hardlyville. Only tributes to the pieces of her heroic history that meld together in a statement of valor yet today. Every street now with a name. Each house now numbered. A concession to modernity.

Nor was there a thruway, a bypass, or even an alley named in fear of Demon Ladies or She Devils. All of Hardlyville knew of her, her cruel efforts to intimidate and maim the village, but none admitted it or acknowledged her existence. If she was real, most feared deep down, she would ultimately prevail with her otherworldly sense of anger and meanness. If she didn't, why conjure up bad dreams needlessly? Most just lived with a shadow of superstition lurking behind corners of sun-drenched streets and occasionally-forced smiles.

Ol' Dill Thomas, octogenarian and town curmudgeon, shook exactly three times after each and every urination to ward off the aura of evil. Dinky Doodle—Village Jester, aka The Donald—after capturing the hearts and passions of his neighboring old maid sisters, made a loud clucking sound after bedding either or both, to camouflage their pleasure from her world of fear and pain.

Jimmy Jones began rolling his joints from left to right instead of his natural inclination to start from the right to keep his beloved Sally and daughter Girl safe from her spell. And so it was that most in happy Hardlyville never admitted, never acknowledged, never confronted this evil figment of their imagination, real or otherwise.

Still, Hardlyville—in all of its glorious past and present—now Donny Brook? It all troubled Pierce Arrow deeply.

ROAD TRIP

Pierce told Lettie they were going on a road trip. She didn't ask why or where, but simply nodded in the affirmative. She was more than aware of Pierce's pent up frustrations and emotions about the direction civic leaders were taking Hardlyville.

This previously innocuous, do-nothing-except-play-cards, meet-and-greet doormat to Hardlyville's future had morphed into a full leadership role once Steele, Rifleman's wife, and recently arrived banker Jamin Bennell joined the group. They still played cards, but economic development and financial sustainability entered their lexicon.

Pierce Arrow had at first greeted their broadening footprint with enthusiasm and praise for progressivism, all consistent with his third-generation, New Deal political roots. He consistently provided editorial encouragement and endorsement. The swing to Donny Brook caught him by surprise and shook him to the core. He understood the need to look forward, the need to plan for a sustainable future, even the milking of newly minted Skunk Creek Watershed National Refuge in the interest of promotion. It was the swiftness of transition from

13

comfortable way of life and modest standard of living to selling the one and raising the other that shook him and caused him to take a deep breath. While he trusted new leadership, he began to question it, personally and editorially. Each call for pause and reflection spread an ever-widening gulf of suspicion and mistrust.

Pierce Arrow the journalist and Pierce Arrow the skeptic soon joined at the hip, to the dismay of many who had always known Pierce as a "can do" kind of guy. *We can beat Big Pork, we can convince the president of the United States to back our cause, we can rid the hills of evil religious sects and squealing piglets. We can because we are Hardlyville.* Donny Brook was not part of this timeless formula.

Lettie watched Pierce stew and simmer and knew it was time to get away. Still, she was not aware of the magnitude of his displeasure. When he advised her it might be appropriate to relocate the *Daily Hellbender* to points west, specifically the Red Rock Country of southern Utah, she knew it was serious.

Lettie had left the Ozarks only twice in her life, which was more than most natives. Her trip to Washington, D.C., to save Skunk Creek was the stuff of legend. She had enjoyed the experience, at least most of it, and was elated to have prevailed over immense odds and presidential lust to help secure National Refuge status for her precious creek.

Her second outing to Denver, Colorado, to solve the mystery of naked dead men without gonads floating down Skunk Creek, had carried even more risk and ultimately helped Hardlyville survive another onslaught of pure evil.

No, Lettie was not against occasional travel, though preferably less stressful than before. But to pick up and move? And why on earth Red Rocks?

Pierce assured her he had done his research, was not engaged in a reckless pursuit, and that any decision to relocate would require mutual endorsement.

That said, this Red Rock Country really intrigued him. Had Lettie ever heard of Arches and Canyonland National Parks, of the quaint, eclectic town of Moab, of giant red rocks that stood on end, of sandstone constructs that resembled Roman ruins, of graceful rock arches large enough to drive an eighteen-wheeler through?

No, to all, was Lettie's response.

Pierce shared his sense of their similar roots, this Red Rock Country and the Ozarks. Uniquely beautiful landscapes each, originally populated by resourceful Native Americans, then simple folks wanting to get away. Mormons escaping persecution for their heretical beliefs and multiple wives, Scotch-Irish forever running from someone, both tribes fiercely independent and self sufficient. Both regions self contained in terms of geology and culture. There were even BIG rivers to blame for natural congregation. The Colorado and The Green. The White. Mighty, untamed in those days, drinking water for anyone who dipped a tin cup.

Pierce remembered a conversation with his Dartmouth professorial semi-friend Doctor Felix Feelgoode. It was this same Doctor Feelgoode who had delivered the legendary Flo Hormele to Hardlyville for a couple of weeks of love and good will. If nothing else, Pierce and most of Hardlyville were contingently indebted to the arrogant professor for this act alone.

Doctor Feelgoode, who had stolen Pierce Arrow's first wife while in grad school together only to dump her for another's wife, was a serial scumbag. Pierce had long since forgiven the affair, particularly when Lettie became part of the bargain years later, but back to the point.

Doctor Feelgoode taught a course at Dartmouth on unique American cultures, including the Ozarks. It was, in fact, this course—and in particular the well-written but brutal *Winter's Bone*—that had attracted dear Flo to the good doctor

15

and ultimately Hardlyville. Flo had wanted to meet a real "hillybilly" as she called them and—oh my—did she ever.

Doctor Feelgoode had called on old friend Pierce to host them over one glorious spring break in the Ozarks, to dispel the myth that a single cruel book could capture the essence of a rich culture. Their visit turned tiny Hardlyville on its ear and spread affection and cheer to any corner of her citizenry with half a heart, igniting a reign of passion and purpose that came to carry the village through its darkest days. Though he had chosen not to sip from Flo's cup for a reason he later called Lettie, Pierce Arrow would forever be grateful to the French bombshell for the large footprints of love she left behind.

But back to Red Rocks and the Ozarks. One conversation between Doctor Feelgoode, Pierce, and Flo particularly stuck in his mind. Felix explained to both that the capstone project in his class on unique cultures called for students to select a single brand and prove it "exceptional," or accept it as just a cheap iteration of another.

For instance, Felix had asked Pierce whether the Ozarks was exceptional, or just another version of poverty? Like Appalachia. Like northern Mississippi or rural Oklahoma?

Pierce argued exceptional. And, he knew he was correct. The precious folks he had lived and grown with over these years were not normal. They were exceptional. Different? Yes. Entrepreneurial? Yes. Flawed? Yes. Funny? Yes. Passionate? Yes. Unpretentious? Yes. Grounded? Yes. Exceptional? Yes— undoubtedly—exceptional. This is what intrigued Pierce about Red Rock Country. It too seemed different, self contained, perhaps even exceptional.

Madame Flo had argued exceptional as well. Though she was basing her position on stamina, size, heart, soul, and naiveté, she could argue her case with substantial credibility. Where else could a naked lady take a float trip on a warm spring day and be honored with a village-wide holiday so all could partake of unadorned seasonal beauty from creek bank perches, escort canoes, and john boats? What a day it had been smiled Flo, exceptional in every way.

Pierce Arrow chuckled at the memory, then pondered the link between Red Rocks and the Ozarks.

What he didn't share with Lettie was the recollection of a young lady from his past from tiny Moab itself. He had met her their sophomore year in college and they soon had a thing going. He had stayed with Sadie May and her parents, both artists, the better part of a summer in their quaint Moab digs. He had guided raft trips down the Colorado, hiked rock fins and slick rock domes, and slept with her under oversized moons and uncompromised stars on an unlit desert floor whenever they could slip away. This memory really warmed him, and in a way Lettie could never understand. Sadie May had been a confident, wild, and free thing who soon passed beyond Pierce's reach, but left him enamored of her red rock homeland. Another bridge from past to present to possible future.

"Do we take the kids?" Lettie wondered aloud. Pierce suggested the three young ones as they might be gone a while. Lucas Jr., Vixen, and baby Mona would love a road trip, he believed, and Li'l Shooter and her recently betrothed Booray Abdul could keep tabs on the middle-schoolers.

Lettie asked for a night to sleep on it. Leave Hardlyville? Live in Utah? This was harder than losing your first husband to an evil lady's lust and murder. This was tougher stuff than a U. S. president with a diminutive stiffie. This was more complicated than solving anatomical riddles. This was choice and free will, life changing forever. Lettie was surprised and nonplussed. She loved Pierce Arrow to the moon and back, but giving up on Hardlyville? She had stood up for the village and the creek with all she had to offer. To walk away?

Lettie awoke to an exhilarated Pierce partner, Rand Mc-Nally map spread across kitchen table, red line drawn from the Ozarks to Utah. She could not deny his passion and enthusiasm for the future. She could not believe she might abandon her roots for a strange land that wasn't stained with her sweat, blood, and tears, carry her love for place and time, or didn't have Lucas Jones's gravestone in the neighborhood backyard.

Lettie Jones and Pierce Arrow were deeply in love but now potentially rent asunder by the path to the future. In her mind, Hardlyville was sacrosanct—her home, her life, all she had ever known.

Why not Utah? Why not Red Rocks? Why not arches and mountains and holes in walls of ancient sandstone? Why not wisps of spirits past and beyond? Why not a shot in the dark? Almost sounded a little like the Ozarks, come to think about it.

Their final discussion was brief and to the point. Pierce Arrow needed to follow this strand of rebellion against the Hardlyville establishment to its end or he would simply meld into the accepting flock. He needed Lettie with him or he would melt into nothingness. If she would not go he would stay here. If they went and she couldn't abide the change, he would bring her home. If they found more solid ground than the shifting gravel of their Ozarks soil, they would stay there and begin anew with their precious children. They would bill it as an extended vacation so as to not arouse suspicion or resentment. He would turn daily doings at the *Hellbender* over to Billious Bloom, Librarian and Executive Director of the Ms. Rosebeam Foundation, confident of her ability to provide a steady and objective communicative hand at a time in town history of great divide.

Lettie nodded yes. Pierce handed her a small paperback book entitled *Red,* by Utah native Terry Tempest Williams, and asked her to read it. She did, and was particularly touched by the author's stories and fables grounded in mystery and history, as well as her passion to protect and preserve Red Rock Country.

Her favorite was the tale of Kokopelli, the deformed, flute playing spirit who roamed late spring nights through each Hopi village, planting seeds of corn and life, leaving fields and young women full and plump with the season. It was all so beautiful and poetic, so full of hope.

Lettie immediately commenced preparations for a long journey into a new adventure with the man she loved. There was great hope in this as well. Pierce rented the same RV that had carried them safely to and from the nation's capital and, in a sentimental editorial, subtly bid farewell to the village and its citizens he had come to love. He honestly didn't know if things would ever be the same again. For him? For Hardlyville? For Donny Brook?

WHERE'S THE WATER?

It didn't take long to leave the blues, greens, and early fall golds of the Ozarks behind. Graveled streams and dappled hardwoods quickly gave way to fields and space and browns and grays. Pierce wanted to push the little RV on as fast as possible through the neverlands of Kansas and eastern Colorado and find red rocks as soon as possible. Nothing personal against roadrunners and Jayhawks, but southern Utah lay far beyond. Lettie played with the kids, nursed the baby, read Red several times over, and— as usual— found joy in contemplating what lay ahead with her restless partner. Pierce seemed more driven and focused than usual in this particular pursuit. She sensed he was not sure of course, not confident of objective, more searching and seeking than charting, and that this was not like him. She knew and loved him well.

Their drive through southern Kansas took them across a boring Arkansas River at least twice, and that only and finally caught their attention as they crossed it at the Royal Gorge in southern Colorado and through a quaint rock-encrusted river valley beyond. That this Ozarkian namesake got more beautiful and pristine the further west upstream they followed it was not lost on Pierce. They were headed in the right direction.

Western Colorado returned the voyagers to grand vistas and dry lands. The cross over into Utah exacerbated both conditions, until the left turn south onto Highway 191. Thirty minutes later they were in Moab, UT, and parked in a slot on the north of town at Slick Rock RV park, adjacent to the mighty Colorado River. They were here. It was now or never.

After breakfast at a goofy little place named Erotica or something like that—where you stood in line between works of local artists and herbal uppers to place your order, were given a piece of wooden fruit to help the one wait staff find you on the outdoor patio, and soon received something to eat, ordered or not—Pierce sought to seal the deal early on. He took his tribe directly into Arches National Monument and drove them amongst breathtaking rock cathedrals, ruins, and natural arches. Lettie was speechless.

They loaded baby Mona into Pierce's backpack, and charged with the children up a vast mass of slick rock toward hidden but oft photographed Delicate Arch. They pressed Lucas Jr. and Vixen close to the rock face along a ledge trail that opened to face a standalone rock structure that was anything but delicate. A perfect arch, with sturdy stone legs, leaning slightly in from a sheer drop off, gleaming red within an azure blue sky frame dotted with puff clouds that glowed white was Lettie's first real grasp of Red Rock Country. She gasped as if confronted with an apparition. She had never seen or imagined anything like it in all her life.

Pierce was distracted by the small sheltered rock shelf far right, within a smaller arch, where he and a certain Miss Sadie May had bed-rolled down decades past. He recalled a three quarters moon bathing the red rock arch in ghostly white as the two had squirmed and loved one another with passion befitting the night. He slapped his own cheek to return order to time and place, and dashed after Vixen as she bolted down

21

slick rock toward Delicate Arch and land's end beyond. Lettie's scream slowed the toddler enough for Pierce to catch and scoop her up. Both giggled, but Pierce chastised himself for lapsing into the past and losing track of his little ones in such an unforgiving environment.

They sat for a picnic lunch as tourists, young and old, filed past to have photo memories digitalized beneath the massive curved picture frame, unsuspecting that most faces would not be recognizable in the scale of things. One hundred million years, give or take a few, of upheaval and erosion, and this massive monument was all that still stood on this particular rock pedestal? It boggled the mind and short-circuited the senses. Its timeless beauty rattled the theories of creationists and evolutionists alike.

How could something so perfect be random? Had to be a creator's hand in this sculpture. And yet, who could argue with the hand of time that smoothed edges so finely and wiped away all else beyond the strongest piece of the eternal jigsaw? Pierce babbled all this mumbo jumbo to his unsuspecting audience of two-year-olds as they nibbled at grapes. Lettie nursed baby Mona in silence, awe, even reverence.

They traipsed back down the ledge and slick rock to the waiting RV where Lettie tucked all in for naps in their respective cubbies, then crooked a finger toward Pierce, beckoning him to the penthouse. Their love making was quiet but deep, befitting their sense of place and time. Pierce even felt a touch guilty about sneakily memorializing Sadie May in Lettie's presence but passed beyond into a light and pleasant nap. Lettie lay quietly, pondering the beauty of it all.

Pierce began driving back toward Moab and pointed out to Lettie the famous Balanced Rock sculpture that towered amidst a village of rock ruins. They couldn't agree as to whether it most resembled a red golf ball on a similarly colored inverted tee or a large petrified penis, but laughed at both analogies. Pierce promised Lettie to return next day for more of same, pointing out on the map Devil's Garden with Landscape and Double O Arch, The Windows with Double Arch, and countless other iconic rock formations, more than two thousand arches in all. He explained that an official arch was at minimum three feet wide or tall, and that each was destined to fall over through the millennia only to be replaced by another. "Hand of God or whim of nature," he mused again. Lettie wondered how Pastor Pat, minister to most of Hardlyville through the Skunk Creek Church of Christ, would answer? Pierce assured her it would be "thoughtful, vague, and devoid of controversy, which was why all love the good reverend."

As they pulled back into Moab, the question that had been lurking behind Lettie's eyes burst forth.

"Where is all the water?" she wondered aloud. Amidst all the red rock formations she hadn't seen a drop.

Pierce cringed at the implications of her question, and quickly pointed out the mighty Colorado River below as they crossed it into town.

"But it's dirty and brown," observed Lettie, allowing that she would never permit her kids to swim there and wondering where she could find a simple clear gravel-bottom creek. Silence ensued.

"Where's the water?" Lettie mumbled.

Pierce Arrow knew, then and there, that they would be returning to Hardlyville or Donny Brook or whatever they wanted to call it, though it would take several days to confirm his intuition.

There was a large gathering in town just east of the bridge over the Colorado, with a hand printed sign inviting any and all to join the festivities related to the dedication of a new foot and bike bridge across the pulsing brown water. Pierce pulled in and parked. The sign said free food and entertainment, which was always a draw.

An enthusiastic crowd gathered as a speaker droned on about the beauty of place and moment. A stranger whispered "Governor" to Pierce's inquiry. As platform party dispersed and a country western band set up, Pierce led Lettie and kids forward to the chow line, where he ran smack dab into "Holy Shit! Is that you Pierce Arrow", followed by a big hug and a kiss on the lips. His left eye began blinking wildly, as it did in any personal situation of high stress, causing Lettie to laugh out loud as she always did despite the obvious affections showered on her man.

"Sadie May," Pierce Arrow stammered, turning the color of red rock. "Sadie Susie May, my God," repeated Pierce as Lettie waited quietly to be introduced. Lucas, Jr. wanted to know "who dat was," while friendly Vixen ran up and hugged her leg. "Must be a friend of your Dad's," whispered Lettie.

"These pups yours?" guessed Sadie, adding that the beautiful lady must be as well. Sadie stuck out her hand to Lettie and began the introductory process as Pierce babbled something about how well she had aged offending both Sadie and Lettie. Sadie shared that she and Pierce used to hang out together in college and that he had even spent a summer with her and her folks in Moab. Pierce asked how her folks were, trying to fill the air with something. "Both dead and gone," ended that foray into polite trite.

Lettie was starting to recognize the missing piece of the Red Rock puzzle. Exceptional cultures, cut from the same cloth? Lettie called BS on that as her friendly gaze warmed Sadie then punctured Pierce. There clearly was more to Pierce Arrow's fixation with the Red Rock Country than rock color and culture.

"You must come dine with me tonight," offered Sadie warmly. "Still living in the old place you loved so much Pierce," adding that she bet he could still find it. "Six o'clock sharp, as I have a City Council meeting to chair at seven thirty," she said before turning to a reporter who asked her what the significance of this dedication was to her as Mayor of Moab.

Mayor of Moab? Both Pierce and Lettie shook their heads at this. They would be dining with the Mayor first night out in their new digs.

Lettie suggested coolly that perhaps Pierce should go it alone as he and the Mayor had so much catching up to do.

Pierce begged her to come. He did not want to spend one minute alone with Sadie Susie May at this point, and struggled to reconcile the emotions that flooded his limp carcass. Was he still a little in love with Sadie? What about Lettie and the kids? He knew he loved them more than anything. Why was Sadie so happy to see him? What in the hell was going on here?

They all showed up at Sadie's front door at five fifty-five. Pierce had no trouble retracing the dirt track he had lovingly followed decades past, as Sadie had predicted. It led to a beautiful plot of land set back into a small red canyon, surrounded by trees and a sizable garden. A big blind dog greeted them, knocking both kids down in his urgency to find them, then licking and slobbering heavily on both.

They loved it.

Sadie gently chastised Rufus—hadn't that been her Dad's name, Pierce recalled—and invited all into a place very familiar to Pierce. Lettie's insecurities were quickly enveloped by Sadie's warm embrace and sincere welcome. She poured wine all around as the kids ran around with Rufus outside. Lettie sought and received permission to nurse baby Mona as the three adults began a delicate dance.

"You go first," offered Pierce to Sadie, the first polite thing he had attempted since their fateful encounter.

Yes, Sadie had returned home to Moab after a successful career as a political consultant in Washington, DC. Lettie's eyes rolled slightly knowing what that meant, at least in the context of her brief experience there.

Your serve, smiled Sadie.

Pierce shared his early years in journalism and the joy and purpose he had found in relocating to the Ozarks, the quaint village of Hardlyville, and founding the *Daily Hellbender*, a sporadically published, culturally correct, voice of right and wrong from his editorial perspective that kept his friends and neighbors abreast of local ongoings. Back to you Sadie, Pierce returned serve.

Yes, Sadie was jaded by her years in politics and the national capitol, and in need of grounding as much as her parents were in need of someone to care for them to their end.

Yes, Moab had changed and yet had not. The free spirit that had nurtured her own as a youth was still here. The beauty of Red Rock Country struck her dumb at times. But the threats to sustainability, way of life, and glorious landscapes were real and escalating. Oil and gas leases on government lands to mega-energy companies brought revenue and economic security, but at what cost?

Sadie urged Pierce to carry on as baby Mona nursed away and Lettie studied the exchanges, looking for clues to something of which she was not sure. Her head bobbed back and forth between speakers.

Pierce reported his unhappy first marriage and his vows to avoid future entanglements . . . until he fell for the widow, Lettie Jones. Her first husband was a town hero for sacrificing his life to save village children while being savagely murdered by a wicked priestess of an evil religious coven. Lettie could not leave his name and their shared memories to a second marriage, but agreed to partner with Pierce into a future of love and respect.

Sadie confirmed that she knew a lot about Pierce and Lettie. She had followed with a sense of pride his Pulitzer for rooting out the coven, his rise and fall and rise again in politics, their lobbying the president of the United States for the Skunk Creek Watershed National Refuge, his election as Congressman from one of the baddest, reddest, congressional districts in the country, and his promised and unprecedented retirement after one term. She confessed to wondering how much it cost to secure such an unusual executive order from the president, evidencing her knowledge of Washington ways.

Pierce nodded proudly toward Lettie but she nodded NO vigorously.

Sadie smiled softly at Lettie's gesture hinting at a "been there, done that," sense of mutual understanding.

Sadie confessed to have never married, to both Pierce and Lettie's astonishment. One so fit, shapely, intelligent, beautiful, and important never wed? What's up here?

Must be gay, silently hoped Lettie.

"Many runs up the flagpole, so to speak," Sadie smiled, "but too many half masts."

Pierce started to inquire as to literal or figurative but saw Lettie's look of disapproval and backed down.

"Just saving commitment for the right dude," she concluded.

It was seven o'clock. Pierce was obviously still infatuated. Lettie was jealous. The kids were having a ball playing with blind Rufus, and baby Mona was loving the extended suckling offered up by Lettie as she followed Sadie's and Pierce's back and forth.

Pierce closed with the observation that he and Lettie were considering uprooting their family and the *Daily Hellbender* to Moab because of recent political and cultural events in Hardlyville.

27

"Over my dead body," whispered Lettie to baby Mona. Move to a locale with no clear water, no running creeks, no green hills, and an ex-lover in power and probably in heat? "No way," repeated Lettie to her contented suckler.

Sadie lit up with Pierce's news bulletin. Moab needed an independent voice to help fight big energy and the bribery of promised economic development. Sadie could not do it alone and Red Rock Country needed a crusading editor to arouse suspicions and awaken grass roots emotions. What a team they could form, pen and voice, to draw a line in red dust that could not be crossed.

Sadie May mistrusted the U. S. Bureau of Land Management as much as she mistrusted most men, she announced, unfolding a large multicolored map showing how much BLM land in Grand County—home to Moab and just north of precious Arches N.P. —was currently leased for oil, gas, potash, and tar sands strip mining.

"Almost forty percent of the people's land in Grand County, sold out to highest bidders? How much destructive impact on air quality, limited water resources, and red rock infrastructure?" screamed Sadie with genuine emotion and eyes aflame with passion.

Pierce sat transfixed.

Lettie heard only Sadie's mistrust of "most men" and was certain Pierce was not like most.

Sadie glanced at her watch with an "oh shit," noting that she was late for her meeting but desperately needed to meet with Pierce tomorrow if they could spare the time.

Pierce nodded yes without consultation and Lettie could only fume, stick her breast back in the nursing bra, and burp baby Mona. The roar from her diaper confirmed a need for change as Pierce and Sadie strode out side by side to set a time.

28

"Just close the door behind you," hollered Sadie to Lettie.

Lettie was stunned and crushed. She loved Pierce's call to environmental causes but feared it ran deeper this time.

They rode back to the RV park in silence.

What Next?

Pierce had agreed to meet with Sadie in her office at ten o'clock the following day. He described it as a strategizing session.

Sadie was serious about the need for a *Daily Hellbender* to take on corporate greed and government duplicity. He might have to rename it *The Daily MOUNTAIN BOOMER*, but the parallels to Big Pork, the Skunk Creed tragedy, and need for grass roots leadership were imbedded in the moment.

Pierce promised to be back by lunch to ferry Lettie and the kids to the amazing Windows area of Arches, featuring iconic Double Arch which would again leave Lettie's senses whirring. They would grab a sandwich and spend the afternoon exploring.

When he returned about two thirty, all kids were napping and Lettie was fuming. "Did you screw her just for old times' sake?" were the first words that came out of her mouth.

Pierce didn't get it at first. He was lit up with energy and a game plan. Sex was not a word that computed in that context. Lettie repeated her charge hoping to penetrate the glazed cocoon that had enveloped Pierce.

Pierce sat quietly at the eating table trying to deflect or absorb Lettie's anger, not sure which would calm the storm that brewed in his true love.

He looked up to gaze into her eyes which were ablaze with anger.

"Okay," she roared, "do I have to use the "F" work to get an answer?"

This awoke all the kids who tumbled out of cubbies onto the field of play. Pierce's anger was now rising.

"How could you even consider accusing me of something so crude," he spat. "Of course I didn't. We worked on a comprehensive plan to touch and move the needle of public opinion against Big Energy and its cozy relationship with our own government's BLM."

Pierce carried on with energy and passion. "We also drafted a powerful letter to the editor of the only existing local newspaper, calling friends and neighbors to arms. That particular editor has ties to powerful insiders, so the likelihood of its publication as written is little or none. Which, of course, opens the door for a new written voice of the people."

Pierce apologized for being late and urged Lettie to gather the kids for a shorter but equally stunning hike before dinner, which Sadie had again kindly offered to provide at her home.

But Lettie wasn't finished. She gave the toddlers bowls of dry cheerios and planted them in front of the small TV, attached baby Mona for her afternoon snack, and ordered Pierce to sit down with her in the front of the vehicle.

She acknowledged that, given all they had accomplished, there probably hadn't been much time for hanky-panky, at least this morning. But she wasn't some hayseed idiot. She knew what was coming. She could see it in their eyes, feel it in the pulse of the space they shared.

She compared it to artists collaborating on turning the mundane into a masterpiece. They shared an urge to make the other better, to rise above together. She acknowledged that most great artists were loners, but that on rare occasions—when chemistry was right and shared passions afire—they burned barriers and became as one in pursuit of a dream. She had felt that with Pierce when battling for Skunk Creek and Hardlyville in Washington, D.C. She felt it tangentially this time. She wasn't a part.

Pierce Arrow and Sadie Susie May were aflame with each other, as they had been decades past. Their art was an editorial, a righteous cause, a wrong made right. The spark so unexpectedly and casually lit with the "Holy shit, is that you Pierce Arrow?" was quickly becoming a raging inferno. They were lifting each other up and leaving the others behind.

Lettie informed Pierce she would not be left behind. She loved her man for who he was, not who he might become. She had no need to take him higher in search of shared fulfillment. She loved him more than . . .

Pierce Arrow filled the void with Lucas Jones's name.

Lettie was taken aback and her anger flared again. "That was never part of any deal," she stuttered. "He was my first love, my first lover, the first father to my children, the first who asked me to share his name, the first to stand up to the evil lady with the nasty yellow eyes."

"If that is what you want, me to love you more than some tragic loss in my past, you're reading the wrong tea leaves, searching for the wrong answers, living with the wrong lover. I love you more than anything in my life today and that is what matters, at least to me. If it is not good enough for you, return to your own past to seek answers, old lovers, and stale—if well-written—news."

Lettie advised Pierce Arrow that she intended to return to Hardlyville as fast as the little RV could carry her and the kids.

She was going home to water, to clean creeks where her young ones could frolic as she did growing up, to blues and greens with nary a touch of red, to noble history no matter what you named it, to a village that was the hero—not its individual pieces of glory. Lettie Jones was going home where she belonged. She hoped Pierce would join her as the journey there and beyond would be a long one, but she was not waiting for him to slay another dragon or take on another cause. She was not hanging around for him to find out if the passion that had evidently burned so deep with Sadie Susie long ago was still smoldering. No, Pierce was free to do what he felt compelled to do, but if it was to include her and the kids, it would be in Hardlyville.

Pierce Arrow was stunned. He slumped over the wheel of the unmoving vehicle at the weight of it all. Sure, it had been exciting to see Sadie again, exhilarating to think in terms of working together to save an irreplaceable environmental heaven on earth, invigorating to feel the power of the pen again. Sadie had lifted him up to a higher plane for a moment or two. But Lettie was his rock, his solid ground, his true place in the sun. And she and the kids were his future, wherever that might be.

Pierce dropped all pretense of defense. He tried a bit of humor with a "I did not have a sexual relationship with that lady" response, but Lettie didn't even hint at a grin. He awkwardly knelt to the floor of the RV trying to straddle the gear shift and kneel on the floorboard directly in front of Lettie and his nursing baby. He got his pant leg caught on the parking brake, crashed into the side of the passenger door, conking his head and emitting a groan.

Lettie finally laughed. "Did this move get you laid in high school?" she queried with a slight grin.

Pierce could only look up from his prone position and promise that he had a rubber.

This set them both into fits of laughter, even causing baby Mona to pop off her meal plan to see what was going down. Lucas, Jr. and Vixen heard the commotion and jumped on the pile that was Pierce before he could regain his dignity. Vixen wanted to know what the large lump on Pierce Arrow's forehead was and kissed it well on the spot. Lettie concluded that this must mean that Pierce was going back to the Ozarks with his flock. Pierce smiled and nodded.

They arrived at Sadie's for dinner about six as before. The kids ran off to romp with Rufus and Lettie asked Sadie for permission to nurse the baby.

After wine had been poured, Sadie launched into how grateful she was that Pierce and Lettie had converged with her arc in life at this magical moment. They would make a stand against corporate greed and political hijinks in the name of the almighty dollar. They would force the conspirator's end-game out of the shadows and into the public discourse, where common sense and love of precious land would surely prevail when the full story was exposed. Pierce would write and she would lead, with passion and fury, to preserve and save Red Rock Country from exploitation and destruction. Her high cheeks were tinged with color, large breasts heaving. Lettie particularly took note of the latter, watching Pierce out of the corner of her eye. Lettie's own, even gorged with Mona's life blood, were pretty tiny in comparison. She wondered what would happen next but she had taken Pierce at his word. She only knew she was out of here before high noon tomorrow, with or without the man she loved.

Pierce interrupted Sadie with an apology. Plans had changed due to unforeseen developments on the home front. He had no idea how portentous his statement was, knowing nothing of the tragic circumstance of robbery and murder at Hardlyville National Bank.

He continued that they must leave for the Ozarks the following day and that all plans to transition from the *Daily Hellbender* to *The Daily MOUNTAIN BOOMER* were on hold indefinitely.

What followed surprised Lettie as well as Sadie.

Pierce said Lettie had picked up on the passion and energy Sadie stirred in him and feared it would draw him away from her and the children. Pierce acknowledged the spark Sadie had immediately lit in him, rekindling something inside that transcended causes and bridged time. It frightened him because he could not name it. All Pierce knew was that he loved Lettie more than anything in his life and would do nothing that might risk losing her.

Sadie smiled subtle acknowledgement. Her gaze shifted to Lettie as she began to softly laugh. She complimented Lettie on her instincts and intuition. She had read it all as written, both past and now. Pierce and she, Sadie, had always triggered a bond of magic between themselves. They stirred emotion and passion within the other that built to crescendos quickly and without thought to others. But they always flamed out. Their prior affair was ash in the wind, as would become anything that could materialize now. They both knew this to be true. The respect and inspiration they shared was not love. It had no base, no foundation, only acceleration to a predestined conclusion.

Tears leaked from Lettie's eyes as Sadie moved forward to embrace both her and the baby. Baby Mona took note of a new and somewhat sizable udder in the neighborhood and tried to latch on, bringing laughter from all and punctuating the intensely brief and honest exchange that had just occurred with an earthy reality.

Sadie had only one favor to ask of Lettie. Would she consider allowing her to keep the kids tonight, presuming Lettie could pump a bottle or two for Mona? It would be a light day at the city tomorrow and Sadie wanted Pierce and Lettie to make love on the desert tonight beneath a full moon and within the clasp of red rock turned silver. She had bedrolls and camping equipment. She knew camping was not allowed beyond prepared sites, but she was aware of a special hidden path and place to share with them. She had gone there alone on needy occasions, never with another, soaked up its glory, and run rubbed only in red dirt, screaming to the heavens in ecstasy and adoration. She wanted them to do the same. No one would ever know beyond whatever they believed in above, and they would remember it always, perhaps even leaving a faint touch of themselves on holy ground. Besides she wanted to be a mother, if only for a night.

Pierce and Lettie looked in wonder at Sadie then each other, simultaneously nodding their gratitude and acceptance of her magnanimous offer.

"You must leave immediately," ordered Sadie, sketching a rough route on a napkin.

Pierce wondered aloud if they were engaging in a little environmental hypocrisy by treading on the precious tiny infrastructure of desert support systems.

"We're only human," smiled Sadie. "Imperfect, selfish, and driven to heights of glory and inspiration. We're all forgiven an indiscretion or two or three, or I wouldn't be here," she laughed out loud, tossing a duffel, with sleeping bags and tarp to wrap in, toward Pierce. If they got caught, she certainly didn't know them, but could probably get them out of jail on bond. Just kidding, of course.

Sadie insisted that they take her four-wheel drive jeep and leave for Arches immediately. Lettie finished off Mona and pumped a bottle in reserve, promising that she would return in time for a late morning meal. The kids were delighted to have a new adventure and to get away from their quarreling parents. They wanted to sleep with Rufus anyway. Mona cooed her approval.

Sadie packed a cooler with dinner and a full bottle of wine, twist off top, paper cups included, tossed the keys to Pierce, and pushed them out the door.

"No fires," Sadie hollered, "you can only break so many rules at one time. Besides, body heat trumps desert cold."

The slight dirt track shown on the map was difficult to locate in the dark. As they stared at the napkin definitively marked and ending at an X, both passed a glance that bespoke the memory of the map left for Octavia Rosebeam by her mother Petunia that Hardlyville founder Thomas Hardly had been murdered over. Pierce pronounced that he was homesick. Lettie nodded in agreement, a small tear leaking from the corner of her eye. It was an emotional moment.

Pierce passed the marked map area indicating the turnoff twice, lights dimmed to avoid detection, before settling in on a faint indentation in the desert. It didn't take long to know why no one would ever find them. The track became bolder as they passed behind a short span of rugged red hills, between two rock formations, and around a sharp corner to emerge face to face with a red rock arch, shimmering white in the full moonlight as Sadie had promised.

Pierce reached for the cooler of food and wine in the back but Lettie guided his hand to the tarp as she grabbed the sleeping bags. Her hunger and thirst were of a different bent. She pointed to a spot that centered on the moon's shadow behind the arch. Pierce laid out the tarp there while Lettie unzipped and spread both bedrolls on it, one atop the other, and quickly removed her clothing, crawling between the two. Her teeth chattered in the desert chill until Pierce dove in after her, their bodies generating heat and love.

Later as they lay spent, and still slightly joined, Pierce Arrow suddenly leapt to his feet, screamed an other-worldly cry, and rolled quickly in the red dirt before racing between and around the arch legs. Lettie gasped at the crazed apparition, before doing the exact same thing, pagan ritual in full play, howls and yelps in full voice. It could have been mere seconds, perhaps maybe a minute or two, or even timeless, as they escaped the bounds of known dimensions, red dusted bodies whirling within a ghostly white glimmer, chanting love of life and each other in tongues unknown.

Thankfully they ran smack dab into one another, breaking the trance and blackening Pierce Arrow's eye, though he didn't notice at the time. Lettie's flying elbow had done the trick. Pierce wiped away a rivulet of blood from the cut beneath, lifted tiny shivering Lettie to the sky as best he could, and returned them to blankets for an encore, this time ending in sleep.

As Lettie drifted away she sensed a gentle sound in the distance.

It almost sounded like a flute. She blamed it on the wind, but would learn several weeks later that her first inclination had been correct. Kokopelli had blessed their passion with the seed of life and a tune of hope.

They awoke entwined in one another, sweating and shivering at the same time, moon and stars lost to dawn's light, red returned to the arch. They lay like that for an hour, trying to soak up every remaining blessing their surroundings had to offer. Pierce swore to Lettie that she had become a graceful antelope during the height of their previous night's frenzy. He confessed to lusting after her taut slender body as she danced beneath the moon-encrusted arch. Lettie blushed and wondered if the coyote who had been chasing her was hungry or horny. Both retreated into the magic of a memory that might fade in time but would always live embedded within.

Pierce finally broke the spell by rising slowly and peeing. Lettie followed. After all, Sadie had said it was okay to leave a touch of themselves on holy ground. They laughed as they stared at their red dusted bodies, ground into skin in the places they had fallen. Pierce's eye was swollen and darkening, cut scabbed over.

They reclothed quickly in the chill, wondering what had really happened during the night. Wine was corked so they hadn't been drunk. Or maybe they had simply sipped of a different spirit. A spirit of love and passion that lay beneath the surface of those who knew they loved but could never fully spell it out. A spirit begging to be awakened but generally left dormant and unrequited, despite the love shared. A spirit that could only be touched when aligned with a moment of natural or even supernatural abundance, and shared within the confines of that mythical juncture. Pierce tried to express this obtuse theory of what they had experienced beneath the moon-struck arch as they drove back into town to rescue Sadie. "Better let it lie," cautioned Lettie. To delve too deeply carried risks beyond ecstasy of experience. Hang on to magical memories and settle for less, she concluded, gently touching Pierce on the cheek beneath his purpling lump.

All hands were on deck to greet their return. Mona was screaming for mother's milk as Sadie gently rocked her on a bountiful but unfunded bosom. Mona simply couldn't figure that one out and expressed her profound frustration. So much to choose from, so little to tap.

Lettie latched her on in one swoop and all was sort of peaceful again. Old blind Rufus was running in circles knocking Lucas, Jr. and Vixen flat, to their screams of delight. "Still want to be a mother?" Lettie laughed. Sadie could only shake her head in wonder.

She then noticed Pierce's swollen eye. As Pierce began to explain in great detail Lettie whispered NO, proclaiming it a moment between them.

Sadie knew. She could see the red dirt ground into glowing skin. She could sense the aura that engulfed the two lovers. She knew what had happened, what they had felt, what they had learned about one another beneath the desert moon. It had happened to her. She only wished she had one with whom to share it. Maybe some day before she got too old to shed her clothes and run screaming like a banshee in a red dirt robe beneath passion's eye.

Lettie said little while she nursed Mona. Pierce and Sadie talked strategy and tactics. Pierce wanted to be a visiting editorialist for Sadie if she could find anyone to print his sacrilege.

Lettie apologized to Sadie in private for her mistrust and suspicion. Sadie sloughed her off, confirming that it was well placed as she and Pierce had always fed off of one another to the point of risk beyond reason. She urged Lettie to take care of her man because she had a good one. The women hugged and nodded their mutual respect and understanding.

Lettie asked if Sadie had ever heard a soft flute playing in the desert night? Sadie said unfortunately no, and then smiled her congratulations to Lettie without explanation. Lettie shrugged and gathered the kids for clean-up and readying for departure.

Pierce was brief with his goodbye. It had been exhilarating to see his old friend, briefly tempting to be drawn directly into her circle of causes, exceptional of her to share her desert secret, and inspiring to see her still slugging it out with the bad guys. His only wish for her was love. He pecked her on the cheek, as did each of the children before loading up. As they pulled away from Sadie's family home, Pierce thought he detected a whimper in the far back. He stopped the RV and wandered aimlessly back toward the kids, only to find them curled up with Blind Rufus under a blanket. He turned the RV around and returned Rufus home between sobs and tears, and ultimately laughter.

Pierce and Lettie showered away the remaining red dirt, belatedly placed a little ice on Pierce's eye, bathed the kids, and headed home. He explained his "hurt" as a battle wound incurred while protecting their mother from a giant desert lizard which seemed to satisfy the kids' curiosity and briefly elevate him to hero status. Lettie confirmed his amazing bravery and rescue, omitting how sexy he looked in red.

They pulled the RV out and turned north on 191 away from Moab. Pierce lamented not having had the opportunity to share more of Red Rock Country with Lettie. He spoke of places like Bryce Canyon with her shimmering slender spires and silent rock cities. He didn't know Grand Escalante well but could see Zion's "Weeping Rock" in the rear view mirror. Maybe they could return one day, he wished. Lettie nodded absently. She didn't want to leave her precious water again, eastward or westward bound.

She did have one parting observation to share, wondering if Pierce had seen any African Americans during their stay. He shrugged, looked puzzled and finally shook his head no, not one. Hispanics, yes. African Americans, no. He couldn't explain it either.

"Not unlike the rural Ozarks," he concluded, "another similarity."

41

Lettie pointed out that Hardlyville did have little Otis Hendricks, son of deceased Sabrina, and best friend of Lucas, Jr. and Vixen, which probably made the Ozarks more exceptional than Red Rock Country in the context of Pierce's analytical model.

"Wild duck tamales and bison meatloaf from Buck's Grill may help balance the ledger," Pierce countered. A return smile closed the debate.

They headed home to their Ozarks with an as-yet-undetected twitch in Lettie's womb, Kokopelli's tribute to passion, love, and red rocks.

That was the "before" . . .

BACK TO NOW

"Now" was a world beyond. A single otherworldly conversation had provided the bridge.

The long drive home was muddled and maudlin. Additional cell phone conversations did little to add clarity.

Jimmy Jones was still alive. Barely. Life support kept the breaths coming. Sally had survived her pistol-whipping but was heavily sedated. They had allowed her a moment or two of consciousness, but her shrieks cracked mirrors and broke water glasses before they could needle her down again. Doctors would awaken her when there was something good to share. They weren't sure what to do if there never was.

Banker Jamin had almost bled to death on the bank floor, waiting for the big city ambulance to arrive. His condition was critical, but not worsening. Captain Happy, Jamin's personal advisor and spiritual guru, sat in stunned silence beside Jamin's hospital bed, praying as best the good Captain could, for his friend and mentor's special brain. Captain Happy and Jamin often communicated without speaking. "Brain waving" the Captain called it, and he was devastated that he was receiving only crackling static at this point in time. He held Jamin's wife Mabel's hand in his large uncleaned paw, brushing it lightly with his coarse, cracked lips on occasion.

Both Jimmy and Jamin were administered Last Rites at the crime scene by Pastor Pat, despite his lack of Catholic credentialing.

One tourist was indeed dead, now part of a reality show.

And there was no sign of little Girl Jones. Was her snatching a random act or a carefully planned plot for ransom? If it was the latter, there was no cash in Hardlyville to pay up. The robber(s) got it all, down to the last stack of one-dollar bills.

This was the chaos Pierce and Lettie returned toward after driving straight through two nights. This was carnage and tragedy beyond their capacity to comprehend.

Sheriff Sephus Wilbur Adonis felt a theory forming from his ruminations.

He hadn't slept since the morning of the crime, his mind a blur of evidential calculations. Except there wasn't any . . . evidence that is. Nothing except spent shells, shed blood, and dead, broken, or missing bodies. Not much to glean from there.

His theory centered on no good Aimless Bevel, who had dealt heavy harm to Hardlyville in the recent past. Bevel and his gang of Agenda 21'ers had attempted to lynch Li'l Shooter's Lebanese husband, Booray Abdul because his skin was dark. Sheriff had been wounded in the ensuing firefight which had been bloody and filled with casualties. Aimless and his band of scurvied savages had drifted back into the deep woods, returning once to torch Pierce Arrow's *Daily Hellbender* because of his passionate opposition to selling Hardlyville. "The Deal" died, but not from lack of scurrilous interventions on behalf

44

of the "deal makers." They had roughed up Tiny Taylor in their escape before melting again back into the rugged Ozark Mountains.

There had also been a string of regional bank robberies over the past year. The raiders always included a well built blond wing woman thought by some to be the discredited investment banker that tried to bring ruin to several married Hardlyvillains, including Pierce Arrow, through sexual entrapment while pushing to close the first deal to sell Hardlyville.

She failed and disappeared from the law and public view until Bonny and Clyde copycat antics began to surface.

Aimless was stupid and very mean. Blondie was smart and resourceful. Bevel's other gang members came and went as their pockets filled and emptied of spending money. Bevel and Blondie seemed to do it all for pleasure. It was true that they had never taken hostages before, but they had not hesitated to kill.

Sheriff recalled the first such attack the very eve of the last presidential, yes US of A, to dedicate The National Hellbender Memorial in the wake of the Great Pig Flood. It had been brutal, efficient, and fatal for two innocent small town bank employees. Eyewitness descriptions put Bevel, Blondie, and his gang on everyone's radar, from local law enforcement to the FBI. Subsequent "drop in shoots and kills" left small town banking in the Ozarks in a state of panic and disbelief.

Everyone from bank presidents to tellers to new account reps began to pack heat. That few, particularly of the former, had any idea how to handle a firearm led to several self-inflicted wounds and errant rounds into ceilings and walls. A community bank's role as gathering center for local chatter and gossip ceased. Depositors stopped putting money in local banks for fear of having to go get it, and returned to buried backyard treasure and sub-mattress deposits for safety and security.

Hardlyville had been spared this societal regression. Banker Jamin truly believed that his community bank should be a catalyst for change and community progress, and he had opened his doors and meeting space to anyone with an idea to share. Until now.

As Banker Jamin lay on his deathbed struggling for survival, The First National Bank of Hardlyville closed and locked its doors for the first time since he had opened the previously-failed bank years before. An entire community mourned his, and its, condition.

Sheriff Sephus was most anxious to try out his theory on Pierce Arrow, his personal confidante in such matters and closest friend.

At least until high school sweetheart Airreal Flambeau had showed up the year past. That they wed within two weeks of her arrival clearly moved her to the top of Sheriff's pecking order, and doubled the African American population in Hardlyville overnight. Sheriff still looked to Pierce for strategic advice and was desperate for it just now. In fact he and one of his occasional deputies, as he called them, had met Pierce's RV at the Kansas line to hasten a discussion. An occasional deputy drove Lettie and the RV home while Sheriff loaded Pierce into the car, siren blaring for the last hundred miles or so. Pierce was so tired not even the siren could keep him awake, so Sheriff Sephus settled on waiting until the next day.

Jimmy Jones lay in a deep fog. An occasional thought would cross his mind, but nothing clear enough to act on. That was,

46

until a strong hand on his shoulder shook him to attention. It was an otherworldly kind of communication.

The hand belonged to Cousin Lucas Jones, who had been murdered in cold blood by the evil lady with the burning yellow eyes.

Jimmy had run into Lucas, or whatever he had transitioned into, in a great natural Ozarkian subterranean Garden of Eden discovered by Jimmy from a map descended from Hardlyville's founding patriarch Thomas Hardly shortly after Lucas's death. At Pierce Arrow's urging, Jimmy Jones shared his paradise only with wife Sally over the years, including several fruitful love trysts that had created Girl Jones and whoever lay in Sally's womb at the moment. Pierce had feared paradise lost if opened to public intrusion and Jimmy had honored his concerns.

Ironically, his last secret soiree had reconnected him with Lucas Jones in a spiritual if not actual sense, and Lucas had promised Jimmy his eternal vigilance. Jimmy really needed that just now.

The hand that shook Jimmy cauterized internal bleeding and quickened his flagging pulse. Jimmy reacted by opening his eyes for the first time since the second bullet had passed through his gut leaving a trail of torn tissue and ruptured arteries. He gasped Lucas's name through clenched teeth, stunning those who dozed nearby. Nurses raced to retrieve a physician who wondered aloud if this was Jimmy's last gasp or a rush of lifesaving energy. Jimmy's unfurling smile bespoke the latter.

Sally was quickly shaken awake from her narcotic-induced nightmares and led bedside. Jimmy's smile broadened into a full grin when he saw her. Sally's sobs shook her and the baby within. Jimmy unscrolled the fingers of his left hand, then his right, attending physician nodding enthusiastically with each subtle movement. He had worried that the first bullet had passed close enough to his spinal cord to paralyze, which was clearly not the case. The second bullet had done more internal damage, but Jimmy Jones was gonna make it.

It was then that Sally burst forth with the news about Girl Jones. Whoever shot Jimmy had clubbed Sally and grabbed their daughter, dragging her into the woods with a waiting accomplice according to one blind old bat. This was too much for Jimmy who slipped into unconsciousness once again, activating Sally's full shriek response system. The doctor shot her up immediately and put her back to bed. At least all those present were going to live.

That was also the latest prognosis for Banker Jamin. Lost blood had been replaced and though not yet conscious, pulse and other vital signs were stable. He was not out of the woods yet, but nearing the fringe.

FROM THEORY TO PRACTICE

Pierce gathered with Sheriff Sephus the next morning, groggy but engaged. The Aimless Bevel theory was certainly plausible, but Pierce could only cringe when Sheriff threw in Blondie, the former investment "bankress" as his accomplice.

It was this Blondie bombshell who had stripped naked in Pierce's office with an offer to trade her love for a vote to sell out Hardlyville to her investment banking firm's syndicated investors. Thank God Lettie had believed him when he claimed innocence. This represented a significant leap of faith in that Blondie had indeed leapt into Pierce's lap in all of her natural finery, snapping an incriminating selfie just as Lettie had quietly entered his office on an unannounced errand. Thank you, Lettie.

Pierce had heard that she was into Bevel and banks now, but the thought still prompted a blush and surge of anger. The thought of her still rankled. And that damn Bevel had tried—and nearly succeeded—in burning down the *Daily Hellbender* in retaliation for Pierce's principled stand that ultimately carried the day in Hardlyville, at least back then.

The sheriff's corollary conclusion to the Aimless Bevel theory was that the bastard and his gang were holding young Girl Jones in their hideout. If they hadn't killed the child they would surely want to ransom her. Time was precious if Sheriff's theory was spot on.

Sheriff wondered to Pierce if he might gather a small posse of Hardlyville's finest trackers and hunters to undertake a clandestine search for Bevel and his gang in the rough, almost impenetrable, briars and brambles of deepest Ozark mountain country. Official searches were stirring up nothing, but guys like Angle Autrey and Whipple Night could find a morel mushroom in an acreage of thorny undergrowth, a seed tick in a sheep dog's groin. Pierce liked that idea and volunteered to join, though he generally couldn't even locate his reading glasses on most occasions. His last search mission with the Sheriff had led to Lucas Jones's capture and ultimate demise, so he didn't make the offer lightly. Sheriff accepted with the proviso that Pierce simply stay out of the way and serve as a freelance recorder of the process.

The next step was trying to find these grand trackers, as they were almost always out trying to find something. Few in Hardlyville knew them, though most knew of them. A sneaky, clandestine bunch indeed.

Pierce suggested that he and Sheriff walk as far out into the woods as they could go and Facebook post asking for help. Given Sheriff Sephus's bulk that would not be far, nor should discovery be difficult. If they left right then, they would likely attract one of the tracker's focus before it got cold and dark. If not, they would simply retrace their steps and re-lose themselves the next morning. Sooner or later they would surely get tracked down by one of the guys, who could then gather the others for Sheriff to enlist in his scheme.

Pierce's plan worked to perfection, except no one came looking. Maybe Facebook had failed or perhaps they had just expected too much of this newfangled social media stuff.

Things got worse when they discovered they could not find their way back. The old saw of going in circles when lost came true. They wandered about for a while before getting logical and sending one forth, then the other, to find their well-marked return trail. Voice contact confirmed circular motion on both in turn, each returning empty-handed and clueless. Cold, dark, then light rain fouled their plan further. They had no flashlight, no matches, no water, no shelter, no idea where they were.

Sheriff suggested that maybe they sit under a tree and hug each other for warmth. Sheriff had substantially more to contribute to this deal than Pierce. They quickly embraced. Sleep came haltingly.

About midnight, Angle Autrey, who was out practicing for the coming month's Needle in a Haystack national tracking competition, finally found them. His wife Angel, who had seen Pierce's Facebook plea, got word to Angle as she always did through a curious combination of telepathic reach and high pitched warbling. Angle soon sensed a pedestrian presence in the general forest neighborhood and homed in quickly on the lost boys.

Angle wondered why they was cuddling, two grown men and all, but he reckoned it was up to them. He cleared his throat loudly so as to give them a heads up. Nothing. So he fired off a round into the sky, setting them jumping and screaming. At least they had their clothes on.

Angle led them on home with a promise to return with his tracking buddies to the Sheriff's Office early next morning for a critical community service project.

Angle Autrey qualified as a Hardlyvillain old soul, though no one knew how old or from whence he had come. Some credited his Native American roots going all the way back before founder Thomas Hardly's arrival. One rumor had him as bastard son of the founder himself through a brief liaison with a local chief's beautiful daughter. No historical markers pointed to that conclusion. All knew he could find anything, anywhere, any time if given a scent or a trail.

His exclusive club of fellow trackers were one and the same, a unique band of brothers, with one exception.

Sarcoxie Combs was a woman. She lived alone in a tree house outside of Hardlyville and had little contact with humanity beyond her fellow trackers. She was older than them, and most thought wiser. She had a lean, boyish build, and was athletic beyond belief. Some even claimed she could swing on grape vines from tree to tree when in hot pursuit of a target.

Yet, she was a real woman, who once loved a real man. Unfortunately, during one of their dating games, they tried to lose each other so deep in the hills that one couldn't find the other.

It worked so well that her true love was finally discovered nearly a year later by a bear hunter, skeletal remains intact, Sarcoxie's friendship ring still clinging to a bleached pinkie bone. She had never loved again, but enjoyed the company of the others who had elevated her to icon status.

Angle reached out to his fellow trackers, including Sarcoxie, with the invitation to track down a lost toddler and a vicious bank robbing gang for authorities to bring to justice. Not one declined to tackle such a challenge and five stealthy souls snuck into Sheriff Sephus Adonis's office early the next morning. That he didn't know that they were there until Angle tied his shoe laces together under his desk, then growled loudly causing sheriff Sephus to jump to his feet and tumble to the ground in one motion spoke to their skill set. It also brought a good chuckle to a tense situation.

Sheriff Sephus was clearly out of his league when it came to organizing a top secret, full scale, all-out combing of at least a hundred square miles of deepest, darkest Ozarks terrain. Angle looked to Sarcoxie for guidance. The wise woman studied Sheriff's map of the Missouri and Arkansas Ozarks and divided it into quadrants, first spitting her Red Man into the dust, rubbing her forefinger in the darkened mess, and then marking the map into four distinct sections. Each tracker would tackle one section, and Sarcoxie Combs would flit and fly amongst them all offering logistical and moral support. If anyone got a hit, they would relay coordinates to Sarcoxie immediately as only expert trackers knew how. She in turn would alert Sheriff Sephus so the logistics and execution of a formal attack could be formulated. At the very least, the trackers would convene at Sheriff Sephus's office within seven days to debrief.

Sheriff Sephus nodded his admiring approval until the end. He cautioned that the potential hostage situation was time critical. Sarcoxie amended debrief to five days. Sheriff offered food and supplies which brought forth a snicker from Sarcoxie. She informed the Sheriff and Pierce that they lived quite nicely off the land, thank you, and began final preparations . . .

Sheriff and Pierce went immediately to see Jimmy Jones with the news that an informal search party of Hardlyville's finest trackers was fully deployed. Jimmy had regained consciousness after the news of Girl's kidnapping had so floored him, and was alert and grateful. He knew two of the crack trackers as weed customers, and offered on the spot a lifetime supply of his best stuff to whichever one could find his missing daughter. Sheriff allowed that this was a kind but illegal gesture, and yet promised to look the other way. Sally was still sedated.

Sheriff and Pierce also stopped by to pay their respects to banker Jamin while at the hospital. His weak nod bespoke his gratitude. Captain Happy and wife Mabel still stood vigil, but were obviously basking in the relief of his full recovery prognosis.

Pierce confessed to the Sheriff, as they drove back to Hardlyville, his prior intentions to relocate from Hardlyville to the Red Rock Country of Utah, and Lettie's insistence that they return home, as she put it. Sheriff had sensed Pierce's great discomfort with the sale of and subsequent name change to Donny Brook, but was shocked to learn that his friend had considered leaving. Pierce confided that under no conditions would he ever refer to Hardlyville as Donny Brook in spoken word or in print. Sheriff advised that he would have to arrest Pierce on charges of perjury and intent to incite a riot, but would front his bail.

Sheriff didn't much like the sellout either, and noted that nothing, not one thing good, had happened as a result. Most had already frittered away their first royalty checks and had little to show for their financial security. Pierce told Sheriff he wanted the deal undone and would spend the rest of his Hardlyville days trying to figure out how to effect that outcome.

Their brief but to the point exchange delineated the new boundaries of their relationship.

A New Face in Town

Billious Bloom's new three-month-old baby was the talk of the town. First of all, Billious wasn't married. Not that most cared about that. It happened every now and again and just gave eighty-five-year-old Dylan Thomas another excuse to claim paternity. He had generally given up such nonsense because of his affection for, and love of, Tiny Taylor, who, at half his age, had restored Ol' Dill's sense of worth and purpose as a legitimate old stud with her monthly fourth-Thursday-night visits. They might have gathered more frequently, but Doc Karst was protective of Ol' Dill's health. And Tiny was wary of the worst-kept secret liaison in town earning credibility amongst town folk and hurting business.

Tiny owned Greasy Spoons Grill and Bar and Ol' Dill was a third generation moonshiner, so their compatibility surprised none. In actual fact, folks flocked to Greasy Spoons to sigh and smile over the gentle pats and touches the two exchanged between the courses of the exquisite fried food she served him, and them.

Some even tried to spy on their monthly trysts, but Ol' Dill's dog Muffle patrolled his yard with ferocity and heightened

55

attentiveness those nights. Two Hardlyville High School seniors claimed to have broken through the protective barrier and observed strange and unnatural acts of lust which they immediately reported to Sheriff Sephus Adonis, waking him and his wife Airreal from deep middle-of-the-night sleep. A seriously PO'd Sheriff sent them to Doc Karst for treatment of their dog bites and admonished them to get more experience of their own before using words like strange and unnatural.

It was just that Billious Bloom was so eligible, so sexy, and so wanton Ol' Dill confessed to Tiny before receiving her permission to boast in public about his most recent siring. She knew it would be good for Ol' Dill to crow out loud, just one more time, and might even help business at the grill.

Billious just laughed.

She hadn't been looking to get pregnant, but boy had she ever. Billious had lived the life of an old maid until Pastor Pat, Skunk Creek Church of Christ officiating minister, had divinely defrocked her well into her middle age. Both had viewed it as an act of faith and for Billious it was truly a life-changing experience. She came to enjoy sex for what it was, power and pleasure, and had applied its virtues to enhance the reputation and ancient Latin text collections of the Rosebeam Foundation, for which she served as Executive Director, as well as for fun.

Billious was taken aback when first one period and then another slipped the calendar. She was so busy traveling the world to secure Latin text treasures she forgot about the first miss. Her passion and laser focus were on bringing tiny Hardlyville an international reputation as a center for Latin studies, in line with deceased founder Octavia Rosebeam's vision, not boring bodily functions. The second carried with it waves of nausea and massive heartburn, which caught her attention.

Having never been pregnant before, despite her advanced years, Billious Bloom hadn't a clue what was going on. When her closest friend Steele, Rifleman's betrothed and mother of Li'l Shooter, whispered the "P" word to her she had laughed out loud.

She was on daily birth control and insisted that her lovers wear condoms for extra security. In addition, she hadn't had many of them recently.

Along the way, she had fallen face-first in love. Chuck Hendricks, Hardlyville native son and now a big city CPA, had helped civic leaders analyze the first investment banking proposal to buy Hardlyville. Their romance was one of the few good things that came out of a sordid period in Hardlyville history, marked with bribery, sexual entrapment, and—ultimately—a community divided. As their relationship blossomed and "The Deal"—as it became known—crashed, tongues began to wag and gossipers grinned. The village of Hardlyville loved a good romance.

Their affair began with smiles and flirtations in important committee-meeting discussions, the substance of which neither could have cared less about. It quickly descended into the sex both were in dire need of. Chuck was a recently divorced father who had embraced abstinence in the interest of obtaining child custody. Billious was simply needy after her strict Catholic upbringing and years of hollow adherence to doctrine. She had bought into the notion of no pre-marital sex for so long that no one would ask such a matronly lady to marry them, a closed circle of deprivation and frustration.

At least until Pastor Pat had ridden in to the rescue. As an ecumenical dispenser of the word, he was able to reconcile Catholic doctrine with worldly pleasure in the context of Christian forgiveness and Old Testament practice, with him as the lead—and only administrator—of this convenient branch of The Word.

Pastor Pat was a decent, if flawed, Holy Man, whose principal interests were those of his flock. He also had an underground reputation as a gentle and giving lover, which occasionally brought several of his congregants' interests into direct conflict with his personal principles. He was a master of compromise and seeing all sides of a story, from lost to lust, and generally found a middle ground broad enough to satisfy all concerned. That had certainly been the case in his saving Ms. Bloom, as he called her, from eternal virginity.

Billious and Chuck had a white-hot, no-holds-barred love-in for several weeks before Chuck's paid engagement ended and he begged Billious to return to the big city and be his bride. Marriage would only cement his qualifications for child custody, and Billious wouldn't have to undergo the pain and inconvenience of child birth since she could help Chuck raise his.

Moving, marriage, and child rearing were the three furthest things from Billious's mind, despite her genuine love for Chuck. She was a professional woman and internationally admired expert on most things Latin—hard earned status in both cases that she was loath to give up. They agreed to part as friends and lovers, with frequent reconnections for nurturing both aspects of their relationship.

And Billious had remained loyal to Chuck, with but one notable exception. "The freakin' president of the United States of America," Billious had blurted out to village physician Doc Karst when she sought his counsel on her sudden affliction. It took the good Doctor thirty minutes to stop hooting. Every time he would slow to take a deep breath and regain his composure, another wave of laughter would engulf him and send him seeking another deep breath.

He was finally able to ask Billious if she used birth control. She assured him that she did, always two strategies worth. He asked if there were any exceptions over the recent past and she responded "NO."

Doc Karst leaned in to hear more about the scandal of the century in tiny Hardlyville. From the beginning he begged. You don't have enough time, Billious had responded, before ticking off stops along the highlight reel:

A presidential deal to trade National Refuge status for Skunk Creek in exchange for a roll in the hay with Lettie Jones during their family lobbying trip to Washington, DC.

Lettie Jones's reluctant concurrence, in the interest of re-claiming and restoring to health and pristine condition the community's precious creek after The Big Pig Flood, and pro-tecting it into the far future.

Non-consummation in the Oval Office at moment of clo-sure due to a national security emergency, sparing Lettie of indignity and infidelity despite the previously committed pres-idential declaration. Had to be there or at least see Lettie's cell phone video, Billious laughed.

Lettie's promise of a "debt repaid" if the president of the United States would personally attend the National Refuge status celebration in tiny Hardlyville.

Billious Bloom secretly stepping in to serve as Lettie in the pitch dark community root cellar and save her from cheating on Pierce Arrow, the ultimate charade and a most historical moment from Billious's perspective.

Successful consummation and a presidential request for more loving if he would consider a return visit to tiny Hard-lyville.

Billious's okay of a rerun with the delighted president, again as stand in for Lettie, all in the interest of history, Billious en-thusiastically explains.

Missed periods, stomach cramps, and heartburn.

Billious Bloom professed to having been loyal to Chuck beyond her presidential indiscretion, and that exception again only in the interest of Hardlyville, Lettie, and history.

Doc Karst declared Billious Bloom pregnant with either Chuck Hendrick's or the president of the United State's spawn.

"How can that be?" wailed Billious in confusion. Doc Karst sought to reconfirm the use of multiple layers of conception prevention. It didn't make sense to him either.

Whoops Billious allowed, confessing that she couldn't find a condom small enough to stay on the presidential stallion during their most recent intercourse. This brought another round of raucous laughter from Doc. "The most powerful man in the world has a tiny one?" he coughed out between gasps. Billious nodded shyly, taking some pride in being one of the few ladies in the country to be able to confirm this anomaly personally.

Again, Billious argued "why," reconfirming her daily use of birth control pills, as a last line of defense against pregnancy. Doc asked if Billious had been on an antibiotic and seen both partners during the time frame in question. After hesitation, she answered to the affirmative. Doc reiterated that Billious was sure as shooting pregnant.

"What next?" a deflated Billious Bloom questioned.

Doc wasn't sure, given the national security implications of at least one outcome. He suggested that Billious try to determine paternity as soon as possible, and start taking good care of this new life inside her.

Billious began with Chuck. He arrived on his monthly visit just days after Doc Karst's consultation. He and Billious picked up where they usually left off, in bed. When she vomited immediately after intercourse, Chuck wondered why. When Billious explained, including the entire highlight reel plus a few more personal insights, she had expected at least a laugh or two. Or maybe an amused smile of understanding. This had indeed been history in the making, and what lay in her belly tonight was either Chuck's or the president of the United States's.

"You slept with the president of the United States in the Hardlyville community root cellar?" bellowed Chuck in disbelief. "You are nothing but a sorry slut," he concluded with an air of certainty that only a CPA can bestow.

Billious was speechless. Sure she had sworn fidelity to Chuck as a friend and a lover. But this was a slip up of such rich historical proportions. Didn't he get that? Wasn't he even concerned that the baby might be, and probably was, his?

"Not good enough company for you to keep?" Billious finally muttered?

"Not in bed," responded Chuck.

They went back and forth for a minute or two about whose fault was what. Billious for not moving to the big city with Chuck? Chuck for not moving back home to Billious? Billious for screwing the president of the United States? Chuck for what he quickly confessed was a one and done with his ex-wife, who had shown more spirit and sexuality in one night than in five previous years of marriage? Hell, he might even try it again, he concluded.

Billious was fuming at this point as she pondered the baby in her belly. Chuck suggested an immediate DNA confirmation of paternity to which Billious agreed. Of course Doc Karst could only send Billious to the big city for such advanced analytics and it might take a while. Chuck provided a skin scraping and went home to the big city and ex-wife, with only a comment about sending a check if it was his. This hot romance was clearly over, regardless of test outcome. And Billious was going to have a baby, presidential or not.

As luck would have it, Hardlyville, aka Donny Brook, though most no one called it that much anymore, despite investment banker covenants, became home to the first child of the sitting president of the United States. Not sure many would have called it luck either. A full range of descriptives could apply.

Neither the president nor any of his men, National Security Advisor, CIA, FBI, Homeland Security, would know anything about it. Not many did. Mother Billious. Doc Karst. Chuck Hendricks. Pierce and Lettie from whom Billious sought advice and counsel. They had none, beyond be quiet. Same reaction from Chuck, relieved to avoid a check, and wanting to leave it all, including his home town, behind.

Doc Karst hadn't a clue what the Hippocratic Oath required him to do in this instance. He consulted Pastor Pat using a hypothetical example:

What would he advise Doc to do if a young damsel showed up pregnant and shared that Pastor Pat was the only male she had ever lain with in her life? A panicked Pastor Pat asked Doc for names, places, and dates . . . whoa, responded Doc, it was all hypothetical, much to the good reverend's relief. He quickly pondered the implications beyond the personal and suggested that Doc forget every such situation he had ever or will encounter in his life of a similar nature. Doc dropped the whole subject.

Billious's pregnancy proceeded without complications despite her advanced age. Nausea gave way to healthy sheen and bulging belly after three months. Doc knew gender but Billious declined his input, preferring the rush of discovery at journey's end.

As the due date approached, Billious sought out Ol' Dill and Tiny Taylor to negotiate a deal. Wagging Hardlyvillain tongues placed everyone from Sheriff Sephus to Rifleman to Pierce Arrow as father, which was doing little good for any of their marriages, or in Pierce's case, partnership.

Ol' Dill wanted to know who was guilty. Billious declined to reveal but asked if Ol' Dill's offer of paternity still stood, subject of course to Tiny's concurrence. The baby needed a dad, and Ol' Dill would be long gone before the baby boy or girl could ask penetrating questions. Ol' Dill took great offense to the predictions of his demise, particularly if he was still siring children. Both Tiny and Billious found his feistiness humorous. "No child support nor any repeat performances either," added Billious to close the deal.

So the official unofficial gossip around town became gospel. Ol' Dill and Ms. Bloom had gotten drunked up one evening on Ol' Dill's finest. Ol' Dill had gotten lucky. He took full responsibility for his mischievous behavior, confessed it to Pastor Pat, begged and received pardons from both Tiny and Billious, and had one hell of a good time along the way. He would of course provide financial support to the youth and Ms. Bloom and refrain from further cattin' around for his remaining days on earth. Signed, sealed, and delivered.

The day of birth revealed a screaming baby boy who bore no immediate resemblance to either Ol' Dill or Billious. Billious looked between the young lad's legs for the tell tale sign of presidential gene pool, but Doc assured her it was far to early to extrapolate or project.

Serious national security implications remained to those who were aware of the truth. Tiny Hardlyville was hometown to the bastard son of a sitting president of the United States. Maybe Donny Brook did fit better in this context.

INTO THE WOODS . . .

They gathered around their spiritual leader Sarcoxie Combs for final instructions. All were clad in camo, each of their own unique design. These trackers embodied their forefathers' ties to time and the land through generations. They were one and the same in that sense.

Angle Autrey, Whipple Night, Normal Ned, and a man with no name, knew their way around the deepest, darkest corners and shadows of the Ozarks mountains as none other. They carried only the clothes on their backs, a knife, and a firearm of choice.

Food and drink would resolve themselves. They could hear a twig break at one hundred steps, distinguish between animal tread down to species, gender, and size, see clearly into the night, and distinguish scat in the neighborhood by scent alone. They lived solely by their wits and instincts.

Only Angle was married. He had found himself one fine woman by, big surprise, tracking her down. He had seen her at a McDonald's on his first visit to the big city and was immediately smitten. Her scent and natural beauty had attracted his

64

attention beyond the Big Mac he was devouring, also his first. She was with a snotty-looking rich kid who drove a big car, and as they pulled away he swore to find her. Her rich and exotic scent, like the breath of a young cougar, lingered in his senses.

Angle spent the next week and a half wandering the big city streets, seeking that scent. When he finally whiffed it late one evening in a park where he was fixing to bed down for the night, he also sensed alarm. It didn't take him long to track down the rich kid's big car which was pulled off the pavement behind a large elm tree. His keen ear picked up enough to know the girl was in trouble.

The rich kid was whining about being nice and spending money on her for several weeks. She was gonna give it up to him this very night.

She scolded him for his arrogance, adding that there was nothing to give up in that she had already done that with his best friend several months past.

Angle liked the authority in her voice, but he didn't like the sound of ripping clothes and hurled himself through the open back door window of the fancy car right in the middle of whatever was going down. It happened to be her jeans, right at that very moment, despite her strenuous objections. He landed face first on her naked chest, and after briefly apologizing for the intrusion, turned to face her attacker. The rich kid had pulled his pants back up and was withdrawing a pocket knife from them which he calmly opened.

Angle warned him that this was probably not a very good idea.

Nonetheless, the kid swung the blade at Angle who disarmed him quickly, snapping his arm at the elbow, removing the knife from his hand, and inserting it into one flabby buttock, all in one swift, smooth motion.

Reckoning aloud over the squeals and howls of pain that they had probably better move on, Angle grabbed the young victim, her blouse and bra, and carried her into the adjoining woods. He pushed them deeper and deeper into anonymity before setting her gently down, covering his eyes, and handing her clothes to her.

When she was properly re-clad, brushing her thick blonde mane behind her ears, and sitting nervously on her haunches, he sought her name.

Angel, she said.

Indeed you are, Angle responded.

She thanked him for the rescue and asked if he intended to rape her now.

No, he answered, adding only that he thought he was in love with her and wondered if she would allow him time to prove it.

Her nodding head confirmed the obvious, and after he led her to a spot with cell phone coverage so she could assure parents of the daring rescue and her safety, Angle carried her, arms around his neck, legs around his waist, back to Hardlyville over the next several days.

And thus began the strange courtship and ultimate wedding and bedding of the only woman Angle Autrey would ever acknowledge or love in his own unique way. Angle and Angel Autrey, another unique Hardlyvillain love story.

Pierce Arrow had heard this fairy tale time and time again over the years and it still brought joy and inspiration to him. He could never write about it in the *Hellbender* for fear someone would get arrested even after all these years, but it was always there, a part of the passion and abiding affection that was the fabric of Hardlyville. Surely a statute of limitations would allow him to go to print one day.

Back to Sarcoxie and her band of trackers.

Sheriff Sephus and Pierce Arrow were allowed to sit idly by, but were not part of the conversation, other than to emphasize that young Girl Jones, daughter of Jimmy and Sally, was at grave risk and time was the key variable.

Sarcoxie again reviewed strategy for this potentially life-and-death assignment.

Pierce marveled at the lack of words in their lives or the profound depth of the few they used.

"Just because you ain't on a trail don't mean you're lost," Angle Autrey had once told him. *Definitely words to live by,* thought Pierce. And on a more personal level, he leaned on that philosophy when stuck on a lead editorial for the *Daily Hellbender* or trying to explain his way out of an incendiary comment to Miss Lettie. Words to live by indeed.

Sarcoxie dismissed the trackers with a challenge to use every skill at their means to find and snatch young Girl, if opportunity presented. Otherwise, report back quickly and precisely on a location so Sheriff Sephus can do what he does best. Bust the bad guys.

Angle folded off south by southeast into the deepest cover of woods. Whipple and Normal Ned headed due south and south by southwest respectively. The man with no name went due west.

Sarcoxie Combs dematerialized in a blink of Sheriff Sephus's and Pierce Arrow's eyes. Where did she go, they asked each other in wonder?

VORTEX

In the beginning . . . were lots of things . . . depending on which religious text one consults. At least that was the conclusion that Pierce Arrow had reached long ago.

And some of those things may have been vortexes. Again, that is what Pierce thought.

When researching where to move Lettie and the kids in the wake of selling out Hardlyville, he had looked at several options. The Red Rock Country of southern Utah carried the day and the decision because of Pierce's sense of shared exceptionality with the Ozarks. And, of course, the memories of his old girlfriend, Sadie Sally May.

A close second was Sedona, Arizona, also a red rock destination, with the added seduction of purported vortexes, fields of spiritual energy swirling from and about landscapes of peculiar beauty.

"More shared exceptionality with the Ozarks," Pierce mumbled to no one in particular.

His mind wandered there this day because he was in the midst of guest editorializing for Sadie in the Moab newspaper, as promised. He was halfway through railing about the evils of the Federal Bureau of Land Management and their obscenely good-old-boy deals with Big Energy in and around Moab and Arches National Park when he felt one of those jolts of energy serpentine up his spine.

He was sitting on a favored rock perch, overlooking a now-protected and recovering Skunk Creek, writing in longhand before committing to print. It was important to get this right as Sadie could only promise one guest editorial shot, given the newspaper owners' shared bed with the bad guys. Sadie still wanted to buy the paper for Pierce, rename it *The Daily Gila Monster*, and move Pierce, Lettie, and the family to Moab, but understood their reticence.

Pierce had felt and acted on these surges and jolts when fighting Big Pork and pig CAFOs in the Skunk Creek watershed. He had been right, but Skunk Creek Ranch prevailed through back door deals, cash, and sex—human, not porker. The Ranch's ultimate demise from the Big Pig Flood was a near death-knell for pristine Skunk Creek, but federal protection and local awareness had allowed her to regain her clarity and natural color, if not all of her species.

He loved this bluff protrusion, legs dangling casually in the wind, communing with energy all about, empowered and alive. He wasn't so sure that if he set his spirit to it he couldn't spiral above his physical confines to a higher level of consciousness looking down on all below. He was simply too busy to try now. Maybe another day. All he knew was that this and several other Ozarks rock formations set him off on paths he had never followed to journey's end.

Pierce laughed to himself about native mushrooms and their hallucinogenic proclivities, and Jimmy Jones weed, neither of which he had partaken of this magical spring day. Vortex energy was most certainly part of the Ozarks aura.

He finished his piece with a fully loaded rhetorical flourish, challenging the community of Moab to step up and call out the co-conspirators—Big Oil, Big Government, Big Money.

"Stand up and save your precious heritage of sand stone arches and fragile hoodoos," he pled in writing.

Substitute Hardlyville and water and he had written the same several years earlier in the *Daily Hellbender*, all to no avail. It seemed that no matter where one lived, if there was other-worldly God-made beauty and splendor, there was a man trying to make money off of it. He really had is kundalini up again, that vivid Sanskrit descriptive of dormant bodily energy, coiled like a snake, and itching to spiral out.

While he was in this state of mind, his elevated level of thinking began to grasp the predicament Billious Bloom's baby had placed Hardlyville in.

No one except Lettie knew of the presidential pressure that was being periodically applied on her for a return visit to Hardlyville.

Everyone from the president to his principal aide to Pierce, Lettie, and Billious knew that he had been duped on both previous visits.

He didn't know by whom or how but a couple of photos of a smiling Lettie snapped when he was purportedly bedding her in the community root cellar killed the beating in his heart that had passed briefly for love. That accepted, he had greatly enjoyed the two liaisons and was intrigued with his mystery lover. He was also convinced that he could eventually talk his way into Lettie's bed. So he wanted to return for a rematch. He was sly about with whom.

Lettie stalled as best she could, through Billious's pregnancy and delivery, and beyond, but she knew she couldn't hold out forever without serving up the truth, the whole truth. The president's lover was a sexy single lady with an unusual sense of history and was now the parent of his newborn son. And Lettie was simply not for sale.

Pierce had noticed several strange visitors staying at the Donny Brook Inn, paying their ten dollar entry fee day after day, and spending an inordinate amount of time circulating about, raising questions among a broad spectrum of Hardly-villain citizens. Did anyone want the president of the United States to honor newly-named Donny Brook with a third official visit? Is anyone aware of a local lady whose professed love for the president led her to stalk him seeking sex? Who had keys to the community root cellar? *This line of questioning has CIA or FBI written all over it*, thought Pierce.

He was heartily amused by one interaction between Ol' Dill, The Donald, and one of the questioners, as overheard at Greasy Spoons, and where it led. *Only in Hardlyville*, he mused.

It was kind of a double date, with Tiny Taylor serving up fried squirrel and black jack gravy to her secret beau Ol' Dill, the Donald, and the twin old maids who called the Donald their own. Once known as Donald "Dinky" Doodle, the official Hardlyville town jester, The Donald had emerged from his self deprecating comedic shell to serve as live-in lover and friend to the Sisters Sledge with a boost from the aphrodisiac Absinth provided him by Ol' Dill. Another long story from Hardlyville's colorful past that no sentence, no matter how long, could begin to capture.

Point being, the Donald would return to his Dinky Doodle roots when called for. The current situation was one such occasion.

As the government agent of whatever offending branch asked if he could join the foursome for lunch, they readily agreed. By now most of Hardlyville was aware of the spies in their midst, if not their purpose.

One of the sisters even thought him cute and began to flirt a bit. At least, that is what agent man thought.

As he pursued his standard line of questioning about Hardlyville, sex, and root cellars the sister placed one of her over-sized paws on his leg, causing the agent man to jump and spill his coffee all over The Donald, who quickly excused himself to change clothes with a wink at the amorous sister.

One thing led to another, and then another. Soon Ol' Dill was bragging about having a key to the community root cellar if the agent man wanted to borrow it. Ol' Dill claimed there was no better place to get a true sense of Hardlyville than within its dark and private confines.

The agent man knew all this from his presidential briefings and thought maybe he was on to something. If he could bring a positive ID back to his superior and then to the president, he might be up for a presidential citation and promotion.

The Sisters Sledge offered to provide him with a private tour of the root cellar if he had the time. While they were neither pretty or not, sexy or not, or nattily attired or not, the agent man thought, why not, and nodded yes.

Each took him by a hand and led him slowly down Lettie Jones Street to the dirt path cutoff to the community root cellar. It was precisely the same path Lettie Jones had led the unsuspecting but ravenous president of the United States down a year or so earlier to a waiting Billious Bloom. This time it was Dinky Doodle who was waiting.

One of Dinky's favorite costumes was that of a Hardlyville cheerleader. He would don a wig, stuff socks in a bra, and lipstick-up before entertaining at high school basketball games on occasion, to the joy of hometown fans. And it was cheer captain Dinky who sat on a blanket in the pitch dark where even he couldn't see a hand in front of his face. Damn roots sure needed black dark to thrive, he laughed, the first of several over the coming minutes.

This might be fun, the agent man smiled to himself, preparing to tread where presidents go—big footsteps indeed! And two for the price of one. Not even the president went there according to the briefing book the agent man had reviewed.

One sister cracked the root cellar door and admonished the agent man to shut his eyes in that she only undressed in the dark. "Sure," he smiled as she led him in, second sister quickly shutting the heavy wooden door behind them. She whispered for the agent man to get birth naked and prepare for the lovin' of his life.

One thing about being a government agent, you followed orders or you were soon without a job. The agent man did precisely as told. Soon he felt a hand on his thigh and responded with a like gesture, quickly moving upstream to a large pair of breasts.

He began to fondle them, marveling at their size and softness and eliciting a deep moan from the object of his affection. He reached quickly behind, unsnapping bra and freeing what lay within, which promptly fell into his lap.

It was at this precise moment that both sisters shined flashlights on Dinky and his obscene red lipsticked smile while the agent man grappled with the fallen socks.

Pierce laughed out loud every time he envisioned the scene and its aftermath.

Evidently the agent man shrieked and ran birth naked out the root cellar door, streaking for Lettie Jones Street and the Donny Brook Inn, bloodcurdling scream trailing behind. Hardlyvillain residents and the tourists milling about applauded loudly at the show, planned for their entertainment they assumed. A bare-chested Dinky Doodle, still adorned in wig and cheerleading outfit was gaining on the agent man. Hardlyvillains

73

had seen this one before, but several tourists opined that the entertainment had gotten a little risqué for their tastes. One even demanded his ten dollar entry fee be refunded, which a gasping-for-air Pierce Arrow did on the spot.

While government agent traffic slowed appreciably over the next several months, the national security implications of secretly housing and raising the bastard son of the president of the United States remained.

Amidst the tragedy, humor, scandal, and unexpected that seemed always a part of the Ozarkian landscape, a slight stirring in an unsuspecting nest began to garner attention.

Lettie Jones blamed her increase in appetite on the long journey to and from Red Rock Country. She was surely glad to be home, grateful that Pierce had willingly followed her here, and anxious for a return to normalcy, if such was possible in the wake of murder, kidnap, and the robbing of banks.

Lettie felt closer to Pierce than ever before, despite his voyage back in time with Sadie Sally May, their lightning-rod intellectual attraction, and his subsequent re-grounding in Lettie. She would never be as smart and sassy as Sadie, but she could sure find her way around a glowing moonlit rock arch, stirring up red dust, prancing like a stark naked antelope with the best of them.

She laughed at the memory, squeezed it into her heart with a self-hug across her breasts, and ordered a side of Tiny's carrot fries.

For the first time in her Hardlyville life, she was drawn to daily lunch at Tiny Taylor's. Tiny's jalapeno-fried cheeseburgers were her feast of choice. She hadn't eaten cheeseburgers since she was a senior in high school. Though she weighed about the same, that was two husbands, four kids, one yellow-eyed wonder, and years of tears and laughter past.

Pierce loved the color that returned to her face and the slight softness, imagined or not, that nudged her frame.

It wasn't until the first period passed that color receded and panic ensued. She told Pierce that she might be pregnant. How, he wondered aloud. Their overactive sex life had been stored on the shelf during their grand tour of the west due to confined quarters, child cohabiters, and bouts of jealousy. And there had been neither time nor energy since returning.

But there had been that night, that one glorious night beneath a full moon on red dust. Almost extramarital in its madness, animalistic fervor, and spontaneity. One night alone with only the intermittent hum of a flute amidst multiple consummations. Both blushed at the memory. They were too old to believe in magic, or raise another child. Or were they too lucky not to?

Doc Karst confirmed what had become obvious. Lettie would birth with the does and the rabbits and the ewes next spring.

It would be a son, Pierce's first. All of Hardlyville smiled at the news, above and beyond the tragedy that bowed most shoulders.

Woods were a heavy part of Ozarks aura, though more in an energy-sapping kind of way. Tall oaks and sycamores provided a canopy for the next layer of pawpaws, dogwoods, and redbuds, and then ground level thorns, briars, and sumac in alarming abundance. Tiny Taylor's milkshakes, squirrel gravy and crawdad gumbo were thick. Ozarks underbrush was thicker. A novice would attempt to plow through the tangled mess. Trackers somehow moved slightly above it.

Whipple Night was doing just that about midnight of day one when he sensed a slight movement to his left. He thought he smelled cougar, but it was muddied by another sense. Cougars could be troublesome but he always managed to avoid confronting them, which is what he attempted to do at the moment. Still something didn't seem quite right as he halted beneath a large pin oak to stretch his senses.

The swipe across his throat had him gurgling blood before he could even grab his antique Bowie knife. Something told him it had come out of the tree above, but he was gone before he could close the thought.

Whipple Night lay stone dead in a warm pool of blood, claw mark indentations deep into his windpipe. The large cat had struck swiftly and surely.

Catch and Release

The man with no name had followed his westward course with amazing rapidity. His path was not as constrained as those of his brethren and he took advantage of several stretches of relatively open ground to hasten toward the setting sun his first night out.

It was about noon of day two when he spied a tiny glint peeking through a tuft of dying grass in a stand of red-hued sumac cornering a small, open field. He initially took it for a chewing gum wrapper, but on closer inspection determined it to be the back of an earring. This threw him initially. Then he recalled that a woman was part of the gang. He was definitely on the trail and squatted on his haunches, looking for additional signs of human activity. Beyond the sumac patch, he found it.

Someone, maybe more, had strayed from the cover of the woods and had ruffled dead grass along the field edge. Since a creek lay just beyond, he deemed that to be an object of attention.

The man with no name tread lightly through the remainder of the field to the cover of the woods, followed the tree line to the edge of the riparian corridor, and slipped slightly downstream where he came upon a camouflaged tent tied neatly between two large sycamores. He sat immobile for five minutes to assure no presence about and then unzipped the tent flap to find a single sheet and blanket. The sheet smelled of sex and the blanket featured several long blonde hairs. Several used condoms littered the premises. He had clearly stumbled onto someone's love nest. A dead campfire fronted the creek. He admonished himself for missing the subtle odor of ash, wondering quickly if he was getting old and careless. Neither was considered acceptable in the tracking community.

He had a critical decision to make. Should he secret himself in the bushes on the opposite creek bank and await the lovers' return, allowing them to complete their frolic before following them back to base camp? Or, should he fan out about the premises, seeking more clues and risking discovery?

The giggle he heard in the far but nearing distance determined his course of action. He waded quickly but silently across the creek, sinking chest deep before emerging into a thicket of bramble. The late fall water and air were bracing. He settled into a bed of thorns to dry out and await the next move.

The man with no name couldn't see much, but it was not hard to follow the action. A female voice challenged another to get wet, followed by a series of splashes and squeals of shock as cold water slapped them hard. He peeked through a tiny slot between bushes to catch a glimpse of a large hairy man hoisting a well endowed naked blonde lady from the water and retreating quickly toward the tent. A loud zipping noise confirmed entry. More noises followed, but these were almost animalistic as the lovers tore into each other with lust and a sense of urgency.

As they soon lay quietly he could pick up that she was so pleasured and pleased to have a real lover beyond that prick,

Bevel, who was stupid and tiresome. She was wary of being caught by him or one of his henchmen, but the hairy one assured her they were safe in this secret spot before initiating act two. They ravaged each other for at least another hour, the man with no name estimated, before emerging to reclothe he guessed and backtrack through the thick woods. They did not repeat their previous mistake of setting even a single foot in the field's edge.

He let them go ahead, confident of his ability to follow their trail to what he hoped would be the big bulls-eye he was seeking.

Sarcoxie Combs' senses were ablaze. Something was wrong to the south. She didn't know what, but she was certain of it. At the same time she felt a surge of adrenalin emanating from the far western quadrant. She determined to follow that instinct first and was off through the tall trees. She soon joined the man with no name who wordlessly communicated his findings. He would track on to Aimless Bevel's hideout and she would alert Sheriff Sephus to the vicinity of their discovery so he could marshal resources for a rescue mission.

By early evening Sheriff had his posse deputized and heavily armed for the firefight he knew lay ahead. He had borrowed men and weaponry from several adjoining communities, hesitating to bring the Feds into something he and his men could handle. Sheriff would keep both State Highway Patrols aware of his activities without revealing Bevel's gang as target, which would probably bring in the FBI because of suspected bank robberies and slow the process days or even weeks. Girl Jones could not wait that long.

It didn't take the man with no name long to discover Bevel's cleverly concealed hideout in the side of a mountain. A large cave indention carefully camouflaged with a thick screen of underbrush served as cover for vehicles. He noticed several men coming and going from within which implied passages and caverns behind the large hidden opening. He was also able to discern a dim dirt track which he followed several miles to concrete and eventually a tiny town he had never heard of. He was ultimately able to communicate coordinates to Sarcoxie who quickly helped Sheriff Sephus zero in. She messaged the other trackers to return to home base immediately, their initial job complete. Sheriff Sephus would await their support in finalizing the plan of attack. Their return would also help sort out the uneasiness that lingered within Sarcoxie Combs.

By early morning of day three, all trackers were accounted for but Whipple Night. Sarcoxie knew they would have to proceed without him but worried deeply about his safety and whereabouts.

The trackers would help Sheriff Sephus and his men surround Aimless Bevel's hideout. The sheriff would issue a surrender ultimatum. He guessed they might use Girl Jones as a shield to escape, but he and his men would be positioned to follow them to hell and back. Having them on the run was better than allowing them safe sanctuary, he reasoned. Under no circumstance would Sheriff and his men open fire until Girl Jones was safe. Pierce Arrow concurred and tagged along to record the daring rescue attempt.

Anti-climatic was the only word that came to mind, thought Pierce Arrow. The carefully planned and executed raid of the Aimless Bevel gang's hideout produced only confusion.

When Sheriff Sephus issued his surrender ultimatum, Aimless, his men, and their women slowly walked out with hands raised, a look of dazed and stoned confusion on most faces, and nary a weapon in sight. When Sheriff demanded the release of kidnapped Girl Jones, Aimless could only shrug in ignorance. Who, why, where? he had sputtered. When Sheriff described the toddler, more shrugs and headshakes.

Aimless Bevel claimed that his clan was peaceful by nature, just wary of others, reclusive not violent. He denied robbing banks, killing innocent victims, and above all kidnapping children. Nothing against kids, but them was the last thing that fit in around here he mumbled, adding that's why they have all the condoms. House rules required it. In fact, that was the only house rule. No protection, no sex. No exceptions.

Bevel continued that all he and his friends wanted was to live in peace and love and the good sheriff was disrupting that vibe right at the moment. Aimless delivered this message with his hands up, finally asking Sheriff Sephus if he could drop them.

After nodding concurrence, Sheriff was at a loss as to what next.

"Search the hideout for Girl Jones," Pierce suggested.

When that turned up nothing but food, water, beer, weed, a few sidearms, a pet raccoon, and—as Bevel had promised—boxes and boxes of condoms, frustration deepened.

Sheriff Sephus knew he was dealing with a bad guy. He had heard stories of the brutal bank robbers who looked and acted like Bevel and his blonde bombshell accomplice, killing indiscriminately, marauding and plundering in the tradition of centuries past. Tiny Taylor had even ID'd Bevel as being behind a past attempt to burn down the *Daily Hellbender*, and she had the scars to prove it. But come to think of it, Sheriff had never seen Bevel do anything, except act stupid. He couldn't ring him up for that.

Sheriff Sephus mulled all of this over in his mind while everyone just stood around, yep, acting stupid. Pierce Arrow finally prodded the good Sheriff to do something, anything.

Sheriff bought time by slowly waddling over to some bushes to relieve himself. He concluded upon return, and against his better instincts, that he was dealing with more of a hippy commune that a dangerous gang of bank robbers. He also knew that surrounding communities didn't have enough jail cells to house even a quarter of the group gathered in front of him.

So, he ordered the arrest of Aimless Bevel and his supposed blonde girlfriend on suspicion of something as yet to be determined. Sheriff suggested that the others just hang loose around the campfire, so to speak, for the next several weeks while he tried to bring order to a confounding situation. Blondie winked at Pierce Arrow with a familiarity that stirred nothing but disgust. That she was fully clothed this time could not lessen his sense of embarrassment that she hadn't a stitch on the last time they met.

No Girl Jones. No hidden weapons cache. No firefight. No dead or wounded. Just Peace, Love, Dove.

"Shit, brothers," was about all the good Sheriff could muster.

That determined, questions still begged answers. Who had conducted the violent and brutal robbery of the Bank of Hardlyville several days past? Who had gunned down Jimmy Jones and Jamin Bennell, and murdered an innocent tourist bystander in cold blood? Who had kidnapped Girl Jones? Where was Girl Jones? Where was Whipple Night for that matter?

Sheriff Sephus Adonis was stumped.

Comings and Goings

Sarcoxie Combs discovered Whipple Night's remains the following morning. She had departed for his quadrant immediately after the Bevel surrender and searched all night.

She was devastated to have lost one of their own, particularly given the lack of serious purpose in the trackers' undertaking.

No hostage recovered, no shoot outs, no mass apprehension of really bad people, just a tracker down. Forever.

Several animals had feasted on various body parts and pieces overnight but claw marks across his throat were the obvious lethal infractions. She reasoned cougar but that made no sense at all. Whipple Night would never put himself in a situation where a big cat attack could catch him off guard. He never had nor ever would. She couldn't find tracks either. Anywhere. There was something more sinister at work here. Sarcoxie Combs sensed evil deep in her bones.

Sarcoxie hoisted what was left of Whipple over her lean body and carried him back to Undertaker Bob. It took a while in that he outweighed her, even in his eviscerated state, at least two to one.

Her oversized strength and sense of purpose more than compensated. Fellow trackers were waiting as she approached the village, each anxious to place a hand on their fallen comrade, and assist with his journey home. It was a strange and mournful procession of brothers and sister.

Girl Jones sat in the dark corner chewing on a bone. It tasted good. The fire simmered slowly. She was warm. She was full. She missed her mommy and her daddy. But the lady seemed nice.

Girl Jones didn't remember much about how and when she got here. She was only three years old or so. So how could she?

She asked the lady when she could go home. Soon, she was assured, very soon, adding that she was safe here. They resumed playing a version of "pick-up sticks" using twigs they had gathered outside the cave.

"It's the president on the phone," Pierce whispered to Lettie.

"Not again," she moaned, along with what could she possibly do? Stall was all that either could come up with. If she could wait long enough, maybe her baby bump would become a bulge and turn the wanton warrior away.

Aimless Bevel and his blonde friend were put in a cell together as the other cell contained Hilgrid Hipple, the new village drunk. Hilgrid had shown up on Doc Karst's front porch late one afternoon and seduced him on the spot. Just say Doc had been a pretty easy mark. Wife Miriam knew nothing about it and offered temporary lodging to Hilgrid who appeared to be nice but homeless. This pleased all concerned. At least for a couple of days until Hilgrid got so drunk she crawled into bed with Doc and Miriam stark naked late one night. This had earned her a drunk and disorderly sentence of three days. She was happy to have some company.

Abdul Booray beamed as wife Li'l Shooter nursed their newly born, a beautiful little girl with Li'l Shooter's deep blue eyes and Abdul's rich brown skin. An Arab Patti Page, Ol' Dill proclaimed when he first saw her to the knowledge of none and confusion of all. They named her Abdullah Abdullah Abdul instead, and in honor of Abdul's father, Abdul Abdul. Yet even more diversity in tiny Hardlyville as Booray still called it. The young one would soon answer to Abi.

Jimmy Jones and banker Jamin continued to strengthen and recover. Both had been close to death at various points in their journey. Sally Jones mourned her missing daughter Girl, and was so hysterical that she spent most days and nights sedated. Her infant could only nurse sporadically and soon shared her mother's drug-induced sleep. It was critical that Jimmy get home as soon as possible so he could help the Sheriff find daughter Girl and add some semblance of order to all of their lives.

They cremated Whipple Night on Ol' Dill's pit BBQ grill. It took a day for his ashes to settle but, once complete, Sarcoxie Combs gathered and scattered them across the Ozarks as only she knew how to do.

Life carried on in Donny Brook, or Hardlyville, or whatever one called it, as winter moved in. Sheriff Sephus remained baffled and confused, which was not his way. Even wife Airreal had never seen him like this.

THE NEW SCIENCE

Pierce Arrow wrestled with where to go next with a *Daily Hellbender* editorial. Hardlyville, aka Donny Brook, had been hammered with a run of horrid events. While Pierce blamed it all on the sell-out and new name, he couldn't prove that the move to Donny Brook had led to the ghastly shootings of Jimmy Jones and banker Jamin Bennell, the kidnapping of little Girl Jones, the death of tracker Whipple Night, and the loss of all of Hardlyville's cash with no one to blame, not even the scurrilous Aimless Bevel. The one direct link to the name change was the poor tourist who was murdered in the bank robbery. He likely wouldn't have been there without it. Hardlyville had, in fact, been spared tourists throughout its long history. Until now.

Sure, Jimmy and banker Jamin were recovering and the FDIC or FED or some such cluster of government acronyms would cover part of the cash loss, but Girl Jones was gone without a trace or hint of why.

Fact is, none of this made sense with or without the name change. It was as if there was something more sinister at work in Hardlyville right here and now.

So Pierce Arrow decided to shift gears. The village deserves a break from bad news he determined, and he would go down a totally different path for one lead editorial only.

A new science teacher at Hardlyville High School had caught his ear and his eye. Abraham Isaac Joseph Smith had moved to Hardlyville at the beginning of Fall semester, before all this bad stuff began, to teach Science 101. Ironically this was the only science course most Hardlyville High schoolers would ever have. There was no one to teach advanced science except Doctor Smith and his simple approach did not require much further elaboration. Billious Bloom's classes on Sex Education, Diversity, and Latin filled holes in the curriculum and Hardlyville didn't have to worry about national standards because they weren't accredited anyway. Not that anyone worried much about that. Hardlyville High School graduates generally hung around after commencement, contributing richly to everyday life in the village. It was a closed loop system that seemed to work pretty well, mused Pierce Arrow.

Anyway it hadn't taken Doctor Abraham Isaac Joseph Smith long to stir things up. His principal scientific text was the good book, yes, the Bible. He supplemented required readings from therein with a vast array of unusual literature including "From Creation to Truth," "From Truth to Creation," "The Hoax of Evolution," "The Evolution of Hoax," all researched and written by his dissertation advisor at Good God University, Doctor Wretchel Right, a noted dissident of sub-Asian descent. Doctor Right had been persecuted for his religious beliefs in his own country and fled to establish GGU on the Rock of Gibraltar, a protectorate so loosely governed by Britain that literally anything went.

Gibraltar was a whole other story in itself, as Pierce had discovered when researching a paper in college. Britain claimed it, a Moorish castle guarded it, Spain wanted it but not badly enough to go to war over it for the past several centuries, and John married Yoko there in 1969. What more could a big rock ask for? But Pierce digressed. Back to Doctor Smith and the Science 101 course he simply referred to as "The New Science."

Pierce remembered reading about the new math, created and taught in a rush after the Soviets beat the US of A into space with Sputnik. He was too young to have been tortured with it but knew it to have been heavy on theory and abstraction and light on the basics. He had read once of a brilliant theoretician who could work Boolean Algebraic equations keyed to truths and values not numbers, but couldn't divide sixty-four by two-and-a-half. That this PhD's work contributed mightily to the digital designing and programming so important to our modern world of micro chips and consumer electronics was shadowed by his inability to calculate a fifteen-percent tip.

At least that was the point of the article.

The new math evidently never reached the Hardlyville school district. Students learned math now as they did then, closing each class period, regardless of grade level, with a lesson in mental mathematical acuity, no pencil or paper allowed. For instance an eighth-grade class might solve:

2 plus 2, times 3, divided by 4, plus 2, times 20, minus 10, divided by 3 equals?

Nearly every Hardlyvillain eighth-grader could arrive at the correct answer of thirty in a matter of seconds. Complexity ranged up and down by grade, but Hardlyvillain students knew how to do it all in their head each step of the way. This seemed adequate for daily toil, and was in fact preferred by the citizenry. In many ways that seemed to be how great Hardlyvillain minds like Banker Jamin and Jimmy Jones conducted business. It worked for them and therefore should be enough for others, the reasoning went.

New math or not, there was definitely a "New Science" in town.

Pierce Arrow caught Doctor Smith after class one day to discuss his theories. Doctor Smith assured him right up front that he didn't fear the press because he was dad-gummed correct about everything Science had to offer. The Bible told him so.

First of all, the earth and its inhabitants are about eight thousand years old. Check it out in Genesis, he advised Pierce. And while Pierce Arrow and other non-new-scientists might be related to apes, he Abraham Isaac Joseph Smith was not. Ol' Adam spawned his line of ancestors, all of whom had fought their way through evil to the here-and-now. Further, the earth was getting warmer because hell was getting closer for the non-believers, not because of cow shit leaking methane gas into the air. And God protected the good and the righteous from things like polio and tooth rot, not a shot of placebo or chemicals in drinking water.

Pierce Arrow could not believe what he was hearing. He considered himself a religious man, of sorts. He had actually wrestled with religion over the years, finding great wisdom in certain Biblical edicts, questioning the righteousness of others, and often doubting his ability to accurately make such judgments. In the end he accepted the fallibility of his existence, the potential of what lay beyond his understanding. He didn't consider such abdication a cop out, and actually knew many who shared his imperfections.

But this Doctor Smith, he knew everything. Pierce thought it laughable at first. But it wasn't. This was what young Hardly-villains, the next generation of civic leaders, were being taught in high school. The one and only science teacher was anti-science.

He zoned back into Doctor Smith's expose on truth just in time to learn that astronaut Neil Armstrong's giant step for mankind occurred on a movie set in Hollywood, not the barren surface of the moon, which in fact hung stationary in the sky as an adornment celebrating God's greatness.

Pierce thanked the good doctor for his time and wisdom and returned to his *Hellbender* office in a daze. Fortunately, Lettie was there working on a project and was feeling a touch amorous, pregnancy and all. After a good solid round of old-fashioned fornication, Pierce was finally able to laugh out loud about his interview with Doctor Smith. Lettie laughed too when he shared it, but agreed with Pierce that it was hardly laughable in the context of educating our youth. She sure as hell didn't want Lucas Jr., Vixen, and Baby Mona, or especially her two older children by way of Lucas Jones, exposed to it.

Pierce could not believe this claptrap had gone unnoticed for nearly a semester but thought back to his own high school days.

Maybe they are just sleeping through it all he mused. That was still no excuse for letting it ride, so Pierce cut loose with both barrels in his lead editorial the next week. Even Pastor Pat, in all of his ecumenical finery, was appalled by what he learned.

Doctor Abraham Isaac Joseph Smith was sent packing at semester's end by civic leaders who doubled as superintendent and principal for Hardlyville schools. The city couldn't afford either of the latter.

Nor could Hardlyville School District accommodate "The New Science." Surely they could find an old science teacher to teach the old sciences the old-fashioned way. Just like math.

Doctor Smith's last class in "The New Science" predicted the cataclysmic end of time for Hardlyville not far into the future, with devils and goblins seeping up from Hell to administer last rites. The way things were going, Pierce wondered if the good doc might finally be on to something.

Sheriff Sephus Adonis interrogated Aimless Bevel night and day. He prodded gently, then even whacked him on occasion. He learned nothing of substance. He had been able to move Blondie into her own cell after Hilgrid Hipple's release which gave him a little more leeway on the physical side with Bevel. Still nothing.

Every time he tried to pry information from Blondie she simply disrobed, sending him running back to his office and home to Airreal.

After a week of incarceration, Sheriff Sephus had no choice but to release Bevel and Blondie. He could find nothing with which to incriminate them, either past or present, that would stand the test of a judge. He sent them packing, back to their commune in the deepest Ozarks, with an admonition to stay clear of trouble and Hardlyville. Both were more than happy to oblige. Blondie tried to entrap the sheriff to the very end, having heard whispers of his skills and capabilities as a lover. But the sheriff stood tall, eventually keeping Airreal on the premises to shield him from her advances. Sheriff knew Bevel and his running mate were guilty of something. He just couldn't prove it. So he let them go and pondered what to do next.

As always, he leaned heavily on Pierce Arrow for advice. Both agreed that surely someday, hopefully sooner than later, ransom would be sought for Girl Jones. If she was still alive.

She's Back

The ransom note was written in blood. Oddly enough, it made no mention of money. Maybe it wasn't that odd since the kidnapper already had all the cash Hardlyville could cough up.

The note had been left on the doorstep of Jimmy Jones's house. He had returned there to convalesce and care for the baby. His wife Sally was still sedated.

The message was chilling in its simplicity. The kidnapper proposed a deal. It would return the little girl if her parents would arrange for the kidnapper to receive a young child named Vixen who currently resided with Lettie Jones. They would have forty-eight hours to effect this transfer. Otherwise, the little girl would be delivered stone cold dead with attendant mutilation. Instructions on how to proceed would be provided soon.

Jimmy ran as fast as his recovering body would carry him to Sheriff Sephus's office. They both shivered as Jimmy reread the demand. Sheriff called it the most devious, evil, demonic proposal he had ever heard of. Pitting neighbor against neighbor, friend against friend, one child's welfare against another's.

He cringed at the thought of even sharing it with Pierce and pregnant Lettie, but the clock was ticking on one or both young lives. He also knew in a flash who had to be behind the whole thing. It wasn't Aimless Bevel or Blondie. It was the evil one, the She Devil, the Demon Lady. It had been more than a year since she had raised her malignant head and breathed her fetid breath on Hardlyville. But, she was back.

Girl Jones was a name bestowed in love and laughter. When Jimmy and Sally forgot to put a formal name on the birth certificate of their first daughter, caught up in the joy of it all, the delivering doctor had plugged in "Girl" as filler. When they had read that on the day they brought their daughter home, they had smiled out loud. They felt it caught the spirit of their marriage and parenthood. Informal. Different. To the point. So, Girl Jones stuck, applied with deepest affection and reverence to this special and unique bundle of joy bestowed on them.

The She Devil had haunted and hurt Hardlyville for the better part of the past decade. Maybe even ages before, given her apparent timelessness, but no one dared go there.

From her murderous religious sect, finally broken by Lucas Jones's heroic act of bravery, to the life she took from him, to naked dead men floating down Skunk Creek, to poison in the town's water supply and partial beheadings of those who guarded it, to this brutal bank robbery and kidnapping, she had terrorized an entire community, coming and going with impudence and impunity.

Come to think of it, she probably had something to do with Whipple Friday's death as well. She loved to cut throats, whether with long, rusty knives or animal claws. Sarcoxie Combs had shared with sheriff her gut feeling that Whipple had been murdered, not ravaged by a cougar. Sheriff was now certain Sarcoxie was right.

And now she had returned to claim her blood daughter, conceived with Lucas Jones's last breath, adopted and raised by Lucas's widow Lettie Jones and her live-in partner Pierce Arrow.

This was a deal straight out of hell, with no happy ending in sight. This was an eye for an eye, a child for a child, a zero sum game of the crassest creation.

Sheriff Sephus Adonis reluctantly summoned Pierce and Lettie to his office, asking Jimmy to give him a moment with them alone first.

Lettie burst into tears. Pierce hugged her in stunned silence, his anger building into a boil fueled by fear. "Why can't she just leave us alone?" he spat out to no one in particular. Sheriff asked Jimmy to join them.

"Well, at least now we know who, why, and how," he observed with a studied calmness. He urged them to think about the "where" with all the intuition and strength they could muster. Two children's lives were in the balance and it was only if they could outwit the Evil Lady that both would be spared. This could not be turned into an either-or. It had to be both or she will have won.

They discussed whether to bring in outside help. It was clearly a kidnapping, which possibly involved crossing interstate lines. That spelled FBI. Big city police might have more tools or experience. Both would take time. And neither could understand the depravity with which they were dealing. All present believed they could trust each other more than outsiders, regardless of what expertise they might add.

"Regardless of the outcome?" Sheriff asked with gravity.

Regardless of the outcome, all agreed.

Sheriff Sephus suggested that they play her game. This involved investing precious time in awaiting her next orders. He would place two of his occasional deputies in the bushes outside Jimmy's front and back doors with instructions to shoot and then ask questions.

Jimmy wondered if she was holed up at the old rock fortress out east of town where she had hung out before. It was catacombed with passages and caves which she knew like the entrails of a deer. It had been her evil queendom once, home to the crazies who paid homage to The Sacred Mother and lived a life of servitude grounded in sex and murder. It had also been next door to Skunk Creek Ranch, the ill-conceived industrial piggery which had employed sect members and fueled the Big Pig Flood that literally destroyed precious Skunk Creek and scarred Hardlyville forever. And she had returned there to carry out her most recent acts of terror on the unsuspecting village of Hardlyville.

"Good possibility," responded Sheriff Sephus, calling it the most evil corner of the Ozarks. Pierce Arrow immediately thought vortex, of which there were several he was aware of in the adjoining vicinity, pondering whether such mystical sources of energy and power could breed evil as well as good.

Jimmy could agree with neither about the evil, in that he knew of the magical and mysterious Garden of Eden which lay beneath both ruins, that of her sect and that of the pig CAFO. He and Sally had discovered the garden, a subterranean and untouched natural paradise, with the help of a crude hand-drawn map left behind by town founder Thomas Hardly who was likely murdered by some seeking it.

Jimmy and Sally were likely the first ones in modern times to descend into this Ozarks landscape, long lost above ground to settlers and progress. The pristine spring which served as host to now-extinct Ozarks species ran counter to and deeper than other water table elements, which had spared it the devastation of the Big Pig Flood. He and Sally had shared their discovery with only Pierce and Lettie, who had wisely counseled to them to forget about it if they wanted to preserve it.

Sally and Jimmy had followed that advice except for the several times they had returned there for special handling in a world half crazy.

Their visits to the garden had netted them two conceptions, and immaculate or not, Jimmy knew there was not a more fertile and accommodating love nest in the world. Girl Jones was rooted in that first voyage of discovery and baby boy Lucas Jones, Jr., II resulted from the after play of their christening of baby Girl in the cool but calming waters of the spring.

What only Jimmy knew, and had shared with no one, was his pleasant and profound encounter with the presence of his cousin and spiritual mentor, the deceased Lucas Jones on his most recent visit. He wasn't smart enough to figure out any of the whys or wherefores but he sensed it was Lucas's strong hand that shook his shoulder and his heart back to regular as he lay struggling for life in a cold hospital room several weeks past.

No, Jimmy didn't know shit about vortexes or heavens or hells, but he and he alone knew the neighborhood to be a corner of greater good than evil.

And, he bet the Demon Lady was holed up somewhere in the dark underbelly of the rock fortress with his precious daughter.

Sheriff wondered aloud whether a raid might net Girl Jones. He then followed with the facts as he saw them. The Evil Lady knew that was the first place they would look. She would find places to hide in the labyrinths and catacombs which none could know of. She would likely kill Girl Jones if she got a sense of non-compliance from anyone, and simply kidnap another young one to offer in trade.

Pierce Arrow threw out a novel take that raised eyebrows all around the room. Could this Evil One really be as bad as they thought she was?

Lettie knew where he was coming from. As best as could be determined from Octavia Rosebeam's historical records, the Demon Lady was descended from her gene pool.

Ms. Rosebeam, eternal town Matron and granddaughter of Hardlyville founder Thomas Hardly had been brutally raped and impregnated as a young student in NYC by a beast of sorts with yellow eyes. The baby had been given up for adoption at birth and without view by Ms. Rosebeam in her shame. She never admitted it, never discussed it, never even acknowledged the possibility of such a horrid act or outcome. But letters she had saved, and the life she had lived as an old maid in Hardly-ville to age eighty-five, filled in many blanks. That the Demon Lady had even hinted of Hardlyvillain roots in a pre-violence and long past conversation with Sheriff Sephus Adonis added substance to rumors.

And, added Pierce, if only half her gene pool was evil could she not have "better angels" as Abraham Lincoln had once called them? Where might those be now, Pierce Arrow mused? Nowhere near a soul so evil, Jimmy responded. All, including Pierce, albeit reluctantly, nodded in agreement.

"Best play her game," the Sheriff again concluded. There were no good options, including that one.

⌒⌒

She sat watching the young girl sleep next to a simmering fire, wrapped in doeskin for warmth. Something stirred a memory deep within of a similar scene played out in her youth. While she could name neither time nor place, her mind wandered back to then.

She remembered her head in a warm comfortable lap, slight fingers gently running through her hair.

And then the thought was gone. An icy chill filled the void it left.

She glared at Girl Jones with furrowed beams of pinched yellow light, staring through her to her own Vixen, who would soon know the power of her ways.

THE LITTLE GIRL WITH THE BIG YELLOW EYES

The other actress in this unfolding drama was the bridge between past and present, then and now. The little girl with the big yellow eyes was Lettie's sweetheart.

She loved her two older children with all her heart, the ones she raised with Lucas through their ups and downs of marriage, getting stronger along the way. Lucas Jones had been her childhood sweetheart, first and only lover, the one who could make her laugh or cry with a simple look.

That she became pregnant on her introductory adventure into the world of sex didn't dampen her enthusiasm for it or Lucas. That he married her before their graduation from high school spoke to a sense of responsibility and honor that was the yin of his wild and crazy yang.

Lucas Jones loved the creek, the woods, the natural more than anything, except perhaps Bud Lite and weed, and eventually Lettie and the kids. His fondness for life overshadowed his distaste for work, but provide for his family he did, with painstakingly sporadic and uninspired labor. Set him on Skunk Creek with a full cooler, alone or with his younger cousin

Jimmy Jones, and Lucas found hope and inspiration which he shared with all who touched him.

Lucas Jones's premature demise at the hands of the Demon Lady was a story for the ages. It included pain, sacrifice, logic, and sex, and though many in Hardlyville claimed to know little, most knew every detail:

Lucas had been captured by the evil sect as he, Sheriff Sephus, and Pierce Arrow spied on their rituals in preparation for a raid to shut them down.

Lucas had been tortured, brutally beaten, and ridiculed before being served up to the Evil One herself for sacrifice.

In front of the gathered clan, she set out to use Lucas for gratification before murdering him in retribution for the three of her sorry subjects he had eliminated from existence as they had raped and killed innocent victims on a Skunk Creek gravel bar.

Lucas had stood his ground with the Evil Lady as she sought his pleasuring, keeping her amused and distracted while authorities closed in for a final raid.

Lucas had seeded her sordid womb when she had inflicted unbearable pain on him, causing him to lose his concentration and pass out as her clan was taken down.

She had shot him dead and melted into the shadows.

She had birthed Lucas Jones's daughter, a fragile beauty with bright-yellow eyes just like her own, but a heart and spirit like that of her father.

She had laid the infant after birth and suckling on Lucas Jones's grave, knowing that the village would step up to her care and well-being.

Yes, most knew every detail. It was the stuff of lore and legend. It was the Hardlyvillain folktale that would define a generation. And it was all true.

What no one knew, at least until now, was that she had returned for her only heir, to train and raise in her own image of evil.

And that she had devised the most horrid of schemes to secure possession of the innocent young girl.

In addition to the older siblings, Lettie had conceived a boy with Lucas just prior to his death. In her shock at Lucas's loss and in honor of his memory, she had bestowed Lucas, Jr. on that newborn, thinking it would be her final touch of Lucas. Such was not to be. When Sheriff Sephus Adonis and Pierce Arrow presented the tiny baby with bright-yellow eyes to Lettie as Lucas's final gasp of life, Lettie had gathered the warm bundle into her arms as her own, without question or hesitation. Those eyes spoke directly to her from beyond his grave. Lettie named her Vixen in tribute to her wild circumstance.

Lettie's transition to Vixen's mother was swift and sure. After recovering from the initial blow of the strange story of Lucas's demise, Lettie loved the little girl from the moment she held her. Theirs was an almost animalistic attraction that bonded both ways. When Lettie looked into the bright-yellow eyes she saw not Vixen's natural mother, who Lettie knew nothing of, but a kindness and unconditional love that only certain parents, and most dog owners, grasp. Vixen's strong grip on Lettie's thumb as she first nursed had Lucas Jones written all over it. That Lettie was nursing Lucas's last child with her at the same time she was suckling his last gasp of life on earth melded and cemented a merged sense of love and passion. That both infants shared mother's milk as near-twins bound them as well. It was almost as if a sacred circle embraced the two around and beyond Lettie's arms.

Lettie's subsequent conception of baby Mona and this precious surprise baby without a name in her belly with Pierce filled her dance card to the brim.

But there could be no mistake about it. Vixen was Lettie's and no one else's. She was raised as such.

No one would take her away, not while Lettie breathed life on earth.

Countdown

Hardlyvillains were not aware of the drama playing out beneath their gaze. They did not know that the Evil One was back, and that, as before, several of their precious young ones were at risk.

Only Sheriff Sephus, wife Airreal, Jimmy Jones, Pierce, and Lettie were in the loop at this moment, and all agreed their closed circle should remain inviolate.

Sheriff Sephus recruited and swore in two occasional deputies to guard Jimmy Jones's house. Without providing specifics, he ordered each to hide in bushes at respective front and back entrances and shoot to kill anything that moved. The general nature of his orders was confusing to both men, but an order given was an order received. They took up posts immediately, cocked their weapons, and placed cut greenery on their heads above their camo hunting gear. Neither were particularly well disguised though both thought they were. Jimmy Jones laughed out loud when he peeked through drawn curtains. Then again, this was his last line of defense. He sat with his infant, Sally still sedated, and waited nervously.

A couple of hours later, two shots rang out, standing Jimmy Jones straight up and setting the baby to wailing. A dog barking outside rounded out the chorus. Jimmy peeked through the front window to find Ol' Dill's dog Muffle chewing on the front door guard's pant leg with anger and ferocity. The occasional deputy had dropped his gun and was running around the front yard squealing as Muffle ripped and tore into his pants and occasionally flesh. Jimmy popped open the front door and ordered Muffle to cease and desist which the small half-breed did at his command. The occasional deputy kept running away, cursing Muffle and the horse he rode in on.

Muffle lay at Jimmy Jones's feet begging forgiveness, blood leaking from a bullet graze on his flank. The back door guard, who had already fallen into a comfortable nap, leapt up, circled the house, and drew down on both. He was severely confused in that he thought it was Jimmy Jones he was supposed to be guarding, but orders was orders and he cut loose a round, sending Jimmy and Muffle diving through the front door for cover. Fortunately, he was a lousy shot. Jimmy screamed at the idiot to go home and shoot at someone else. Which he set out to do until a strong arm trapped him against a tree and he looked with terror into burning yellow eyes for the two seconds it took the other hand to cut his throat with a long, old, knife he barely saw. All this in the woods just in front of Jimmy Jones's house.

While Jimmy was on the phone screaming at the sheriff to get his stupid occasional deputy under control, the latter bled slowly to his death, able only to gurgle through the blood.

She slipped unnoticed to Jimmy's front door amidst the chaos to drop a second ransom note on the porch before melting into the long shadows and loping silently away.

At about this time that fateful day, Booray Abdul was launching his dream, or at least an adaptive version of it.

When Booray had moved to Hardlyville to wed Li'l Shooter and raise a family, he was intent on opening a restaurant featuring the food of his native Lebanon. All who had sampled Booray's cuisine marveled at his sense of spices and natural gift for melding flavors into one-of-a-kind taste treats. Booray never used recipes or cooked the same thing twice. Each dish was a piece of non-replicable abstract art.

Booray's initial dream stumbled on the reality of Tiny Taylor's market dominance at Greasy Spoons Grill and Bar. Hardlyville was not large enough to support a fine dining oligopoly and Tiny clearly controlled the market. Her barriers to competition included the quality of her offering, her ridiculously low price points, and her beloved status in the community.

So Booray Abdul calmly shifted gears as any insightful entrepreneur might do. He would not compete with Tiny head on.

He would slip in the back door and open Booray's Market, a place to acquire foodstuffs and supplies, as well as prepared Lebanese delicacies.

Hardlyville had never in recent history enjoyed the luxury of a grocery store. Most fresh vegetables and meats were home raised and stored, and when market shortages existed, bartering filled the voids. It was supply and demand economics in its most efficient iteration. A few Agenda 21'ers derided it as Marxist communism, but few citizens complained.

Booray sensed opportunity for a middleman who would not compete with Tiny Taylor directly, not disrupt the traditional barter economy, and yet provide Hardlyvillains with more options, including incredible Lebanese delicacies to be re-heated and devoured in the comfort of home.

Booray Abdul picked one hell of a day to launch his new business.

Sheriff Sephus Adonis was piecing together the chaotic early moments of that morning. One occasional deputy reported directly to him after the vicious dog attack, resigning on the spot unless Sheriff would cover his medical bills and offer hazardous duty pay.

Ol' Dill' stopped in to confirm that his faithful dog Muffle had gotten into a glass of his Absinth the night before and reacted as he always did . . . crazed . . . running madly about looking for animals, any animal, of the opposite sex, oblivious to pain, powered by pleasure. He wondered if Sheriff had received any complaints about the poor beast?

"Bring the yellow-eyed one to my rock fortress east of town at ten tonight," the note had simply read. "Wait for me in the natural rock amphitheater where she was sired by your worthless Lucas-One before I ended his miserable existence on this earth. You will come alone." Again, drafted in blood.

It was eleven thirty in the morning before Jimmy Jones discovered the note. As he ran to deliver it to Sheriff Sephus's office, infant strapped into his backpack, he tripped over the dead body of the occasional deputy who had been hired to defend him and his family, had instead fired at him and dog Muffle, and finally gone running into the woods as Jimmy had screamed after him.

Jimmy screamed again and tried to keep his screaming baby out of the occasional deputy's blood. Wife Sally came running out of the front door toward them, drowsy, drugged, and confused, drawn instinctively to her baby's cries. What she saw set her to screaming too.

A neighbor's call sent Sheriff Sephus racing to the Joneses' house, siren blaring, which garnered a larger crowd anxious to know what all the screaming was about.

Sheriff dispersed the crowd, knelt next to his occasional deputy in disbelief, then hustled Jimmy, Sally, and the baby inside to try to grasp the implications of it all. The note Jimmy handed him only added to his sense of panic.

They had less than twelve hours to figure this evil shit out.

Swap Down

The natural rock amphitheater shimmered in moonlight. The limestone fortress rose behind and around. The gaping cavern opened backstage. The sound of running water added mood music.

Lettie Jones and Pierce Arrow slowly mounted the stage where Lucas Jones had lost his life years back. Each held a hand of the little girl with the big yellow eyes who climbed between them. Lettie whispered to her to be brave, to not be afraid. Lettie herself was terrified.

Jimmy Jones and Sally followed directly behind, Jimmy helping Sally stagger up natural step indentations.

Sheriff Sephus Adonis followed immediately behind. His pistol was drawn and cocked. He would shoot if given a chance. He had stationed several of Hardlyville's surest shots around the perimeter with their deer rifles. Shoot to kill Her but only if no child was at risk was all he ordered.

The sheriff's watch read 10:00 exactly. All waited quietly in the unknown of what was to come.

An hour passed, and then another. All sat quietly except Sally who sniffled uncontrollably, wanting only to get her Girl back.

And Lettie, who slipped out for a quick morning sickness deposit and returned immediately.

The uncomfortable conversation which had passed between them just hours earlier lingered in their memories. Things like why one child should be traded for another when both might be killed, is one child's life more precious than another, why should one mother sacrifice for another, why did this choice even have to be made? Brutal questions that cut to the core, and splayed open the deepest of self-serving emotions, even among best friends. Questions of the heart that had no answers.

Collegiality, civility, compassion, and even brotherly love fell victim to powerful urges of survival and self indulgence. Pierce Arrow had stared straight into Jimmy Jones's eyes with the question of how could he expect Lettie to make the ultimate sacrifice, the baby she loved more than life itself. Jimmy Jones's eyes answered with because Sally feels exactly the same about her first born.

If left unchecked, their impulses could have degenerated into you have five, soon to be six, to our two and can surely sacrifice one in the interest of parity. Neither let it go there. Young lives as poker chips.

And then tiny Girl Jones stepped forth from the shadows into the moonlight, prodded by a long stick, whimpering. Sally gasped out loud and rose to run to her daughter only to be tackled from behind by Jimmy. "Girl, Girl, Girl," Sally wailed. The little girl with the big yellow eyes looked on in fear and confusion.

Sheriff Sephus read midnight on the lit face of his watch.

Little Girl Jones was tethered by a rope harness attached to a ghostly presence stage right. A wild head of hair framing glaring yellow eyes peeked forth with the screech of a wild animal then immediately withdrew to cover. The barrel of a long gun flashed in moonlight.

Sheriff Sephus silently cursed his gunmen for not taking a shot, then recanted in fear of what could have happened had they missed. *We sit at the gateway to Hell,* Sheriff closed his curse with. What next rested solely in the hands of the Demon Lady herself.

The evil one pulled little Girl Jones back into the shadows by the attached rope. Nothing happened for another hour.

Then a gravelly and hateful voice spat out the next set of instructions. The little girl on the leash would be allowed to return to center stage. The fat sheriff would be allowed to join her there if he would place his weapons on the ground as he rose to the stage. He would bring the yellow-eyed one. No one else would join them.

The fat sheriff would attach a second rope harness to Vixen before removing the first from the one currently ensnared. His every move would be slow and deliberate. The fat sheriff would then leave the rock stage with the freed one and lead the others out the way they came in.

Anyone who fucked up would be shot dead, including the snotty-nosed little kids. The Demon Lady punctuated the latter with a single round salute to the sky.

Jimmy Jones took offense to this description of his daughter and shouted back that his Girl did not have a snotty nose. Two more shots fired into the air overruled his objection.

Sheriff Sephus was sick and tired of "fat sheriff." He had lost nearly fifty pounds since his wedding to Airreal, as called for in their wedding vows. He wasn't yet svelte, but he sure as shit wasn't as fat as when he had gotten it on with this evil one. That was a long time past and a story in itself, and he cringed at the memory.

Sheriff Sephus Adonis looked haltingly at Pierce Arrow and Lettie Jones. It was their daughter now.

Pierce held tiny Vixen in his arms, Lettie clinging to both. Jimmy and Sally were similarly embraced, longing for daughter Girl to rejoin their circle. All knew this was wicked and unfair. No one had a better suggestion.

The evil one began a countdown from twenty. When she reached fifteen Pierce handed Vixen to Sheriff Sephus over Lettie's screams of objection. By ten, Sheriff had wrestled the child into his arms. He then mounted the stage, Pierce restraining Lettie from following. Jimmy and Sally were sobbing out loud. Sheriff laid his pistol on the rock foundation and walked toward Girl Jones. Vixen began to whimper in confusion. Girl Jones stood silent and afraid.

Sheriff gave thought to rushing the evil one but let it pass, at least for the moment. She would surely shoot him, Vixen, and drag little Girl back before anyone could touch her. And then she would be gone into her cavern sanctuary of many passages. Little Girl would be disposed of as cruelly and brutally as possible to send a message. Then another young one would vanish. It was a closed circle of hate and the Demon Lady had all the crayons.

Sheriff Sephus asked if the evil one would settle for him and let the two little ones go. She cackled in disbelief. What could she possibly use a lard ass like him for? Sheriff reminded her that he had once brought her great pleasure. In his dreams, the Demon Lady laughed before firing at the Sheriff's feet, nicking his left boot. Her countdown resumed at five, four . . .

The sheriff placed the sobbing Vixen in the confines of the second harness, freed Girl Jones, and led her back to Sally and Jimmy.

The Devil Lady reeled Vixen toward her like a hooked fish as Lettie screamed in agony and Pierce tried to hold her. She slugged Pierce in the face causing him to lose his grip. Sheriff Sephus grabbed one of her legs as she tried to mount the rock stage and dragged her back. Then Vixen was gone into the shadows with the Demon Lady.

Sheriff would later recall that moment as the only one in his life where everyone hated everyone, dear friends, neighbors, and all.

PRESIDENTIAL POWERS

Billious Bloom had been devastated by the break-up with Chuck Hendricks over her pregnancy. Just because she had screwed the president of the United States out of a sense of history, duty, and public service and just because she had birthed his only child, unbeknownst to him, did not seem an adequate excuse for just blowing her off.

Billious thought Chuck had loved her and that she loved him. Things happened before you got married and, in her case, a pretty damn important thing indeed. He clearly did not reciprocate her love or he would have stood by her side and claimed credit for a son. Even if it did grow up with an extraordinarily small pecker.

Billious found it hard to rekindle her old love life. Of course Ol' Dill was ready to spark, but that had not been part of their paternity deal. Tiny found his crowing funny and romantic in an odd sort of way.

To put it simply, Billious loved being a new mother, she loved her job as executive director of the Rosebeam Foundation, she loved teaching Sex Ed, Diversity, and Latin at Hardlyville High School, but she missed sex. There were no prime—or even subprime—prospects in town or the surrounding small communities. And she couldn't travel far because of Presley, as she had affectionately named the lad.

It was in this time of mini-crisis that her friend Lettie called with a real one. A genuine mind-blowing, gut-sucking, life-and-death crisis of the highest order.

As tearful Lettie explained the kidnapped kiddie swap from start to finish, her desperation to find tiny Vixen, and her immediate need for Billious Bloom's assistance, Billious could only nod yes without asking what.

Lettie needed Billious to go to Washington, DC, with her the next day for an appointment of the highest urgency with the president of the United States. Lettie needed the president to bring forth the full powers of the Federal Government to track down the Demon Lady and rescue Vixen. She needed Billious to help her convince the president of the righteousness of such a commitment of force.

She swore Billious to secrecy, noting that no one would be informed of any of these proceedings in the immediate future.

Lettie shared her conversation with the president of the day before. He had given her his direct cell number with the admonition that he would always be ready if called. Lettie confided that she was pretty sure the president knew that his amorous Hardlyville friend was not Lettie, but he never let on.

She requested a personal meeting with him as soon as possible. When the president asked if his good friend retired congressman Pierce Arrow would be accompanying Lettie, she could almost feel the chatter in his teeth with her reply in the negative. He immediately offered lunch in the Oval Office the day after tomorrow if he could just get rid of the Emir of Displace, a newly-formed middle eastern protectorate of the United States that was critical to combating world terrorism.

But, that was his problem. That the Oval Office had been the venue of his previous attempt to root around with Lettie implied more of the same. Lettie was afraid to tell him anything else for fear he would suddenly find himself too busy, so she simply accepted.

Lettie needed Billious Bloom's help to bring the president of the United States and all the powers accorded him to bear on the rescue of Vixen. She didn't know what that would require of either of them from the chief scoundrel of state, but her gut said tell him all and hope for the best. And Billious could fill in the blanks that Lettie couldn't.

Billious asked if that meant she would be having sex with the president again.

Lettie didn't know.

Billious followed with the obvious question about sharing the news of his son.

Lettie didn't know.

Billious finally wanted to know what Lettie would do if the president insisted on her or both of them as pleasure ransom for executive action.

Lettie didn't know.

Lettie only knew that she was not going to tell Pierce Arrow of her plans, and would explain that she had to get away for a day or two to deal with the grief of giving up Vixen while Pierce, Sheriff, and Jimmy formulated their plans for tracking down the Evil Demon. She also knew she would do anything to get Vixen back safely.

Billious told Lettie that she felt the same.

Billious immediately called her travel agent to book the two women on the next flight to the nation's capital, with two rooms reserved at the old Ebbitt Hotel near the White House for whatever needs materialized over the coming lunch.

Lettie and Billious, clad in their most conservative business suits, appeared at the front guard's desk at the White House at eleven forty-five.

The guard confirmed Lettie's ID and noon appointment but refused to allow Billious Bloom to accompany her. Lettie in turn refused to proceed to the Oval Office without Ms. Bloom by her side.

This set off a security scramble that ended only when the president' s principle aide appeared, whispered into her cell phone that it was another attractive woman, and that she had been searched from tip to toe. With a nod, both were cleared to follow the president's principal aide. She greeted Lettie with friendly chatter and asked who her friend was and what might be the purpose of their visit. Lettie could only whisper about something personal which brought a smirk to the principal aide's lips. She knew a great deal about the president's personal matters and preferences, serving as one herself. She also wondered silently if Miss Lettie's baby bump could be the "personal?"

While this drama was playing out at 1600 Pennsylvania Avenue, the wheels of panic were spinning in Sheriff Sephus Adonis's office in Hardlyville.

Immediately following the hostage swap, Sheriff Sephus Adonis, Pierce Arrow, and Jimmy Jones all sat wringing their hands around the Sheriff's back office conference table. Pierce was still bitter that Jimmy and Sally allowed the swap to take place, but he buried it as deep inside as he could. He couldn't stand Lettie's heartbreak and had quickly concurred with her need for a couple of days of privacy. Jimmy was up to his nostrils in guilt but grateful for Girl's return and Sally's regained sanity. He was committed to righting this wrong even if he wasn't the one wronged.

Sheriff Sephus could sense the tension between the two near-brothers and knew he had to bring Vixen home safe or Hardlyville would never be the same again. That said, he hadn't a clue as to where to begin.

Jimmy muttered something about needing to ask Cousin Lucas what to do next and seemed to wander aimlessly away.

It didn't take Jimmy long to reach the garden.

He quickly rolled back the disguising boulder, tied rope to tree, and descended into the dimly but constantly lit paradise below. He had stumbled onto the spirit of Cousin Lucas on his most recent visit. Or, probably it was the other way around. Visual contact was limited but spiritual interaction was not. The reconnection with Cousin Lucas had given Jimmy strength and hope in a time of need and probably had saved his life more recently.

Lucas was Vixen's blood father. His last earthly deed had been to fertilize the Evil One while trying to engage her attention as state troopers descended on her coven. He had fallen short of entrapping her, but not impregnating her. Lucas's last sigh on earth had breathed life into the little girl with the big yellow eyes that his widow Lettie ultimately adopted as her own.

Jimmy knew Lucas would want to know that his precious baby girl, the one he never had a chance to meet, had been taken by her evil mother. Jimmy hoped that Lucas would know what to do.

If Jimmy could only find him. After all, it was a pretty big paradise down there.

Jimmy returned to the winding side passage where he had first encountered Lucas. And there he was, sitting on a rock, tossing a coin, his back to Jimmy, just like before.

No words were spoken, but thoughts were shared. Communication was quick and simultaneous.

As Jimmy laid out the whole tragic scenario from kidnap to swap, he could sense a sadness rise in Lucas, almost like a dark cloud rolling over him and his rock. He presumed Lucas knew of Vixen, but neither had ever acknowledged her presence on earth, so he wasn't sure. Lucas sat in total stillness, still facing away. Come to think of it, Jimmy had never seen his face in this sanctuary. He saw a hand slowly rise and brush across the front of his head where his face should be, like wiping away a tear.

Lucas appreciated Jimmy's report, but shook his head slowly.

He couldn't leave the garden to help. This was his spirit's precious resting place, the mansion in his Father's House. If he left, he couldn't return. He didn't know why or what would happen in that case, but the terms of his arrangement had been made clear since the moment he chose the garden for eternity.

Jimmy asked if it hadn't been him, Lucas, who had visited him in the hospital with the jolt of rebirth that saved him from death? Hadn't it been his strong hand on Jimmy's shoulder that had jump-started Jimmy's recovery? Lucas acknowledged his input, but termed it metaphorical or metaphysical or some other large word that Jimmy was embarrassed to ask more about. Lucas smiled at his confusion before sinking back into silence.

Jimmy asked Lucas what he should do? He was riddled with guilt over sacrificing Vixen for his own daughter Girl, he knew Pierce and Lettie would never forgive him for the ultimate self-serving act, and he feared for Vixen's life and future. What if the Evil One could reboot the sweetest child Jimmy had ever met into a vicious clone, a dark shadow of the smiling toddler, a horrid postscript to the life Lettie and Pierce had provided her?

Lucas had no answer. Now it was Jimmy's turn to cry. He sobbed out loud that he had no right to his daughter's happiness at the cost of another's innocence. Lucas sat motionless, without communicating. Then he slowly rose and walked into the waiting shadows.

The doors to the Oval Office swung slowly open. The president presented in a much more professional executive way than on Lettie's prior visit for seduction. Where was his silk robe with the red, white, and blue stallion logo? Lettie could smile at the memory now despite the arrogance it embodied back then.

He hugged Lettie warmly, patted her slight belly protrusion in confusion, then gave her his signature pinch on the butt. He then shook hands with Billious, slowly surveying her body from stem to stern. He invited both to sit, buzzing for lunch and wondering to what he owed the pleasure of a visit from two such lovely ladies.

Lettie was straight up, as she had been on the previous call. She thanked him for seeing them. She expressed appreciation to the president for what he saw in her. She then apologized to the president for misleading him. She introduced Ms. Billious Bloom, Executive Director of the Rosebeam Foundation in Hardlyville as her surrogate lover.

The president nodded his approval with a soft smile and urged Lettie to continue.

Lettie told the president that she was desperate. Her beloved toddler Vixen had been kidnapped by an evil lady several days past and she was here to seek his help in recovering the child.

The president wondered if that was the child Lettie had nursed in this very office several years past, savoring the recollection. Lettie complimented him on his memory saying that she had enjoyed that moment of shared intimacy as well but that Vixen was a little older than Mona.

Juices starting to stir, the president stared straight at Billious without saying a word. Lettie confirmed that Ms. Bloom was with her to provide moral support. Lettie was surprised to see Billious actually wink at the executive in heat, who blushed and smiled broadly.

Lettie drew the president back into her realm with the observation that he was the most powerful person in the world and surely had resources at his fingertips that could be called into immediate covert action. Lettie emphasized covert because of the risk full disclosure entailed, but added all necessary background information would be provided by the president's good friends, Pierce Arrow and Sheriff Sephus Adonis.

The president closed his eyes and calculated briefly before responding with a promise to help. He did control a crack SWAT squad, something even his national security advisor was unaware of. He called it Code Spode and could order its leader Black Jack and his band of five to Hardlyville under cover of darkness this very evening to meet with Pierce and the sheriff. No questions asked. He would report directly to the good sheriff for immediate action.

Lettie's eyes leaked tears.

The president of the United States dialed a two digit number on his cell phone, received and answered after one ring, and advised the responder to report to Sheriff Sephus Adonis in Hardlyville by zero two hundred in the morning. Jack should follow every order given by the sheriff unless it put the United States of America at risk. He would report back to the president when the mission was accomplished. He closed with the warning that a very special child's life was at grave risk.

Lettie sobbed her gratitude out loud, before adding that they might discover the village under the name of Donny Brook on their GPSs. The president provided this correction and signed off with "God Bless America."

The president noted that their lunches had gotten cold and wondered if they might instead join him for an early dinner in his private quarters and spend the night at the White House. He could arrange individual accommodations for both.

Lettie looked at Billious with a "you don't have to do this you know," kind of message. Billious gazed back with a mischievous "been there, done that, been kind of slow lately, what's another page in history," response.

Billious Bloom then smiled that she would be honored to dine with the president and spend the night in his house.

The president of the United States buzzed his principal aide and asked her to cancel all appointments after five that afternoon, and then escort the lovely ladies to the Blue and Lincoln Rooms respectively. Only Lettie saw the principal aide roll her eyes and sigh deeply. The president and Billious were too busy basking in the glow of each other's sense of history, time, and place.

THE HUNT FOR EYES OF YELLOW

Sheriff Sephus was stunned when Lettie called from the White House. She swore him to secrecy, noting that Pierce must not know where she was and adding that she was not alone, that Billious Bloom was with her, and that Pierce didn't have to worry. Sheriff knew what this was all about and extended his promise.

His shock was amplified when Lettie shared that Black Jack of Code Spode would be reporting to his office at two AM. She had no idea how that would transpire but urged the sheriff to be ready.

Sheriff Sephus gathered Pierce and Jimmy to advise them of the president of the United States's offer of intervention, beginning at two in the morning. Pierce knew intuitively what was up and felt the familiar rush of anger that had accompanied Lettie's heroic stand of several years back. Sheriff sensed his pending explosion and suggested that Lettie and Billious had everything under control. "Greedy bastard," was all Pierce could mutter. Jimmy Jones wondered if Pierce was talking about him.

At precisely two AM there was a knock on Sheriff Sephus's office door. He opened it to find a small muscular Caucasian man clad entirely in black, who introduced himself as "Number One." He proceeded to introduce numbers two through six and each emerged from the shadows as his number was called. Sheriff could call him by number or by his proper name, Black Jack. He was commander of Code Spode, the president's personal security team. They were there at the president's command to find a little girl named Vixen who had been recently kidnapped.

Commander Jack added in closing that neither he nor his men existed. They were figments of everyone's imagination, including the sheriff's, and were authorized to reveal themselves to only two others, one Pierce Arrow, and one Jimmy Jones. No one else in this God-forsaken community or corner of the world would ever see or know of them.

The sheriff called Pierce and Jimmy out to complete formal introductions, noting that Commander Black Jack and his Code Spode team were neither real nor there. Jimmy was confused and poked his finger into Commander Jack's arm, finding flesh and bone if only briefly. A quick grasp from the shadows bent Jimmy's arm behind his back and elicited a yelp of pain. "Okay," Jimmy screamed, admitting that Code Spode was not there.

Commander Jack apologized but cited national security reasons for everything Code Spode did. Not only were they never here, but they were never wrong, and rarely failed to accomplish their mission—which they needed to learn more about now, before anyone got hurt.

Pierce Arrow regained his senses more quickly than the others and began to talk. It was his little girl who had been snatched. He would spare Code Spode all of the gory background details but he knew who took her, she was evil, without conscience, and had a strange compulsion to raise his little girl in her own image. Both the girl and her cursed mother had big yellow eyes. The mother had and would continue to murder with her weapons of choice, long knives and a pistol.

Commander Jack advised Pierce that he was aware that Pierce was withholding information, probably to protect someone's innocence, but that he had provided adequate data to launch the recovery effort.

He asked Pierce where the kidnapping had taken place. Pierce, the sheriff, and Jimmy led Commander Jack and Code Spode to the rock fortress under cover of darkness. Jimmy worried that they would discover the garden and tried to steer them to the catacombs behind and beneath the natural amphitheater. Code Spode spread out like a grease fire and returned within an hour.

They could prove that someone had been residing therein for at least a month. They spot carbon dated ashes, bones of animals, black and blonde hair follicles, and other miscellany discovered in several subterranean rooms.

"These guys are really good," Pierce whispered to sheriff, still wondering in the dark bottom of his mind if Lettie had to give up anything to obtain their services.

But no Vixen. No sign or indication of any immediate presence. The Demon Lady must have moved on with the child immediately after the hostage exchange.

What next? wondered Sheriff Sephus. Code Spode wanted to know the location of similar environs close by. When Pierce confirmed there is generally one around every corner in the Ozarks, Commander Jack shrugged and ordered numbers two through six to fan out in each direction and utilize their pocket satellite imaging devices to locate and explore every cavern and cave in their path. He would remain hidden in Sheriff Sephus's office and they would report back within twenty-four hours. If they sensed a presence along the way they would send a "gather forces" message and provide surveillance until a critical firepower mass could be assembled.

Commander Jack assured Sheriff Sephus that if the Evil Lady and her victim were within range, his men would find them.

When they returned just past midnight of the following day, number three was missing. It took Commander Jack and his remaining warriors only two hours to locate their colleague with his throat cut all the way to the spinal cord. Commander Jack was apoplectic and promised to avenge this travesty. In all of his years as commander of Code Spode, Commander Jack had not lost a soul under his command. Not when they had swooped in to grab the Secretary of State from an Arab terrorist group preparing to disembowel her on a YouTube video. Not when they intercepted a suicide bomber aboard Air Force One. Not when they rescued a captured aid worker held captive by a rogue revolutionary army in the Republic of Congo.

Not one casualty. Not one. Until now, in this vermin infested, God-forsaken, evil encrusted, hillbilly humping corner of the uncivilized world. The Ozarks, the friggin' Ozarks. Commander Jack would get his revenge.

At least Vixen is still in the neighborhood reasoned Pierce, finding little comfort in the thought.

THE SCENT OF LOGIC

Banker Jamin Bennell's recovery had been slower than he anticipated. He had lost a lot of blood and was never a particularly hearty man. Even with Mabel and Captain Happy by his side, he lingered in big city hospital for over a week.

Banker Jamin was worried about his depositors. He knew all the FDIC rules and regulations for insured deposits. He knew that the federal government would reimburse up to $200,000 per depositor, and since only Jimmy Jones kept that much in the bank everyone else would be covered. He worried about Jimmy because he often had more than that on account. Jamin knew not from where Jimmy's deposits came, nor how he spent his money. He had heard stories about Jimmy's weed business and his constant acquisition of more land on which to grow, but none of it was his affair. He would make sure Jimmy Jones did not lose a penny even if he had to cover it himself personally. That's what good community bankers did. He knew for a fact that is what his own grandfather did during the Great Depression in his small town.

He also worried about Jimmy's daughter Girl, who was a personal favorite of his and Mabel's. She had, in fact, been in his care when the shooting started and he hadn't done a very good job of protecting her. He should have locked her in the vault or something. It all had just happened so fast.

He would establish a reward for information that might lead to her return. Maybe even a ransom account to entice the kidnappers.

More disturbing was that for the first time in his short but distinguished career in Hardlyville, banker Jamin didn't have a clue about what was going on. He was out of the information loop. He didn't know that there was only one kidnapper. He didn't know that it was the Demon Lady herself. He didn't know that she wanted Pierce and Lettie's Vixen. He didn't know that a hostage swap had occurred. He didn't know that the president of the United States had sent in his personal SWAT Team to intervene. He didn't know that one of the latter had been murdered in cold blood.

That said, it didn't take banker Jamin long to get back into the flow. Everyone in town trusted him. When he expressed guilt to Jimmy Jones, who came in to ask about his cash, about failing to protect Girl, Jimmy whispered that he should worry about Vixen instead. When he asked Pierce Arrow about Vixen, Pierce confided in him about the She Devil's cruel and vicious kidnapping hoax. When he asked Sheriff Sephus about how he might help fund a reward or ransom fund, Sheriff let him know about Code Spode, which incidentally didn't even exist. On a follow-up visit about his cash, Jimmy let it slip that he had been conversing with the spirit of Cousin Lucas in a special private Garden of Eden.

Before all was said and done, banker Jamin knew everything and more. This was a good thing because banker Jamin could apply a depth of logic to this tragic situation that no one else could muster up. That was what good community bankers did.

Banker Jamin sat and thought a while. He then asked to meet with the sheriff, Pierce, Jimmy, the spirit of Cousin Lucas, and Jack Black of Code Spode. Of course, since the latter didn't exist, he would have to only imagine his presence. As for spirits, he guessed they too could bring something to the table of logic, even if they were indiscernible from a smudge of dirt on the floor.

He hosted the meeting in the bank's board room. Captain Happy called the meeting to order, believing that all were present. Certainly, the sheriff, Pierce, and Jimmy were there. There was also a little guy in a black jumpsuit hiding behind the curtains who wasn't there. And every now and then a glass of water on the table would move, seemingly without reason. Jimmy tried to explain that Lucas's couldn't leave The Garden for fear of never being let back in, but the whole situation was confusing enough as it was.

Banker Jamin's logic flowed as follows, as expressed by Captain Happy.

"The Evil Lady has seized the daughter she and Lucas had conceived. She will do anything in her power to create a monster of good-hearted Vixen. We all think the She Demon has supernatural powers of some sort or another."

"What would those be?" the black jump suit behind the curtains who wasn't there whispered.

"Things like extraordinary strength, intuitive communication, an unnatural way with wild animals like cougars and panthers, an affinity for living in the wilderness, an unholy sexual appetite, and the meanest streak anyone has ever witnessed.

"It stands to reason that if the She Demon has supernatural powers, so does Vixen. And if Lucas has spiritual gifts, so does Vixen. In short, one plus one equals two. Two is greater than one and Vixen has more going for her than the Demon Lady herself.

"We know Vixen has yellow eyes but is not inherently mean. Beyond that, only potential. What if Vixen has those intuitive communicative powers of her mother? What if Vixen has a spiritual connection to her father. What if we could help her unlock these genetic gifts to roam free and lead us to her?

"Or her to us?

"And if Lucas's spirit cannot leave his special hiding place, how might we draw the Evil One into his realm where his powers could be brought to bear?"

The water glass shook violently at this suggestion. Clearly Lucas's spirit wanted to get in the game.

"What if this ungainly alliance of human, paramilitary, and other-worldly could come together to chase down evil with the help of an innocent, but gifted, little girl?"

Banker Jamin's logic was almost formulaic.

DEAD ENDS

Lettie and Billious slipped quietly back into Hardlyville. Lettie's tired but relieved smile told Pierce all he needed to know about her fidelity. Billious's glow completed the equation. Hardlyville history had been well served by both.

Pierce brought Lettie up to speed about her precious Vixen. She was likely still in the area, hidden deep in the bowels of the Ozarks, as evidenced by the grisly murder of one of the president's men. He shared banker Jamin's logic about drawing on Vixen's potential to intuitively communicate her location to Code Spode as one course of action.

He then trod gently into the realm of Lucas Jones's spirit. Lettie knew about the garden, though neither she nor Pierce had ever descended into it. Pierce then dropped the atomic bomb. The spirit of Lucas was dwelling there into eternity. And probably the best shot of getting Vixen back was to lure mother and child onto his playing field, his eternal home court. One hoped good would prevail over evil in such an apocalyptic encounter.

This was too much for poor Lettie.

Here she was, pregnant and living with and loving on a man other than her deceased husband, whose spirit roamed in an other-worldly cavern just up the road. And they wanted his daughter, who she was raising as her own, to lure her evil mother and his last sexual partner into an underground Ozarkian paradise so good and evil could duke it out in eternity.

Lettie simply couldn't track all of the moving parts or comprehend the twisted logic. Mix well natural and spiritual, throw in a pinch of supernatural, add her daughter as leavening agent, bake in hell for eternity, and cool what's left to room temperature. All she wanted was sweet Vixen home, safe and happy—not a recipe for the ages.

Jimmy descended back into the garden, after making sure none of commander Jack's men were on his tail. He needed to communicate with Lucas as soon as possible.

Lucas sat on his familiar perch, turned away from Jimmy. He seemed distant and disturbed. Jimmy wondered if Lucas had listened in to Banker Jamin's strategy session? Lucas nodded his head slightly. Jimmy reviewed Banker Jamin's impeccable logic, namely that Lucas's daughter Vixen probably had more power than either the Demon Lady or Lucas himself as a result of their merged gene pool and respective circumstances. Lucas nodded again.

Jimmy himself was leery of the strategy that seemed to be gaining favor, that of luring Vixen and her mother to the garden for a final shoot-out between good and evil. Jimmy feared for Lucas. What if he lost? Jimmy feared for Vixen. What if the Evil Lady got onto her game and cut her throat like the others? And Jimmy feared for the garden. What would an epic battle of mythical proportions do to a precious habitat? How many Hellbenders and blind crayfish would survive?

Jimmy wondered if Lucas could communicate with Vixen without the Evil Mother eavesdropping. Lucas wasn't sure but was game to try. If they could take the battle to her, the garden and Lucas's home in eternity could be spared. It would be Code Spode at risk, doing what they were trained to do.

Jimmy finally broke down and cried, apologizing for trading Lucas's daughter into danger to save his own. He would do anything to get her back. Lucas nodded again. He would try to reach Vixen and learn her location. He urged Jimmy to sit tight.

An hour later Lucas shrugged in defeat. None of his intuitive communication channels were registering response. He didn't know if it was the inherent limitations on real-world activity that constrained him or the naiveté of his targeted recipient? It didn't much matter which because he simply wasn't getting through.

Jimmy urged Lucas to try again. Lucas sat for another hour or so, seemingly in deep concentration, then shrugged again, head down, shaking slightly. He slowly rose and wandered off into the shadows with a silent sigh of something between sadness and concession.

Meanwhile, Code Spode methodically searched every cave and cavern they could find in the Ozarks. They found a lot of interesting stuff, but no little girl with yellow eyes.

There were secret convents of nuns, small hippy communes, bear and cougar dens, copperhead snake pits, moonshine stills, snake handling clans, and even a couple of ancient soothsayers. But no little girl.

Code Spode turned to hunting in pairs so as to avoid additional casualties. This limited their reach but enhanced their safety. And, no little girl.

All reassembled in Banker Jamin's bank board room. The reports were devastating in their simplicity and hopelessness.

Code Spode could find nothing, not a trace of the Demon Lady and the little girl with the big yellow eyes. Jack Black had never been so skunked in his life, though he hadn't even been here.

Jimmy Jones confirmed that Lucas had tried and failed to connect with his daughter. The limitations on his worldly reach were real and beyond appeal.

Sheriff Sephus had called on his trackers again but Sarcoxie Combs had refused to turn them loose after the Aimless Bevel fiasco had cost her one of her finest for no apparent reason at all.

Pierce Arrow had nothing to contribute beyond his "better angels" theory again. Eyes rolled at that one, again.

It was clear that this crisis defied logic and plan-full solutions.

Jack Black had reported to the president the full range of Code Spode efforts and the loss of one of the president's men. Though they hadn't really been in Hardlyville, he was requesting orders to return Code Spode to their secret quarters at the CIA under cover of the next night's darkness.

The president of the United States called Lettie before signing off on Commander Jack's request. He apologized for their failure to find Lettie's daughter. Lettie was devastated and the president at loss for words to comfort. He did invite Lettie and her friend Billious Bloom to visit the White House whenever they wished, confirming that Ms. Bloom now had an open invitation similar to Lettie's.

Always groveling, thought Lettie as she thanked him and the U. S. Government for their efforts to find little Vixen.

The president then authorized Code Spode's return to Virginia. Jack Black made no pretense about his joy in leaving this armpit of the world that he had never visited. Sheriff Sephus was not unhappy to see him go either.

Sheriff Sephus Adonis had simply never run into so many dead ends in his entire career in law enforcement.

And the little girl with the big yellow eyes was gone.

UNDONE

As word spread through Hardlyville of Lettie and Pierce's loss, they were swept up in a community embrace that sought to comfort and encourage. Hardlyville was good at this, and Lettie knew from previous group hugs that it helped. It was just that little Vixen was so innocent, so precious, and so loved. Lettie cried often. Doc Karst worried that her grief was being shared with the baby in her belly, but had no remedy for that.

Pierce Arrow tried to comfort as best he could, but his shoulders were not broad enough, his arms not wide enough, his heart not full enough.

He knew that the community needed to regain its focus on the future and move on for now. He and Lettie were desperate for the same. So he struck, in the interest of momentum and hope.

Nothing positive had come from the sale of Hardlyville. Nothing good had happened since they started calling it Donny Brook.

In actual fact, no one called it Donny Brook anymore except the syndicated investors who hadn't a clue where or what it was and an occasional tourist visitor. Business had not been what was projected. Investors were unhappy. Hardlyvillains were unhappy and almost resentful of becoming somewhat of a welfare state.

This was not consistent with their culture or their values.

Sure, they were receiving their annual payments. But they were less than promised and most spent the money on stuff they didn't need. Things like iPads and iPods and trouser lizards (small lizards kept in pants pockets) and an occasional SUV began to litter the Hardlyville landscape. Jimmy Jones bought one of the latter and after a month traded it back in for the very same pickup truck he had offered in the initial deal. Doin and Goin had even left their posts as managers of the new motel, which sat empty most nights.

It was simply time to unwind the transaction that Pierce somehow associated with all that had gone wrong since they had closed on The Deal, as it was now referred to with derision. He had been opposed to it from the beginning. And, he had been right. You can't sell something that's not yours—not history, not lore, not community, not kindness, not neighborly concern.

Pierce knew exactly where to turn. He called his long ago acquaintance from back east, attorney Clyde Shade, Esq. Pierce had never liked Shade much. It started with his name and ended with his methods. But Clyde Shade was a damn fine attorney, which was what Hardlyville needed right now.

Pierce had gone to college with Shade. He was the party animal that Pierce longed to be. He made the A's that Pierce couldn't fudge out of a B+ mind, no matter how hard he studied. He dated the women that Pierce couldn't quite get his arms around. And he went on to law school and an immensely successful career as a trial lawyer.

The law didn't bother him. What was important was his take on the law and how he explained it to juries and judges. He was not into wasting time on commas and periods, or whereases and wherefores. He measured success by tears shed in the dock. He loved to have liberals in his juries. He could break them down, male or female, with a phrase, a descriptive, even a tear of his own. And whomever he was defending or attacking, guilty or not, generally received a lifetime payday, of which Clyde Shade got a large share.

Shade was so rich he could buy or sell just about anything. He owned an island in the Caribbean, a vintage Air France Concorde aircraft, a trout stream renamed after himself in Montana, and a university in New Hampshire, also bearing his name. This was just the tip of his balance sheet.

So why not a village in the Ozarks, which he could donate back to its citizens and receive a large tax write-off wondered Pierce?

It took Pierce a week to make contact with Clyde Shade. He finally had to explain to Shade's secretary's secretary that he had a big business deal to run by Shade, a former classmate in college. Shade's actual secretary called Pierce back and said that Clyde Shade barely remembered him but would meet with him at Shade's Midwestern office in Chicago on Michigan Avenue the following Monday afternoon at four. Pierce Arrow confirmed that he would find a way to be there.

Pierce gathered up the Donny Brook closing documents from Banker Jamin's vault, his college yearbook, and a photo of Hardlyville from the good old days, packed his suitcase, and kissed Lettie's latest tears goodbye.

He arrived an hour early for the appointment and sat fidgeting in the most garish office he had ever sat in. Trophy animal heads ringed the waiting room with a full size lion patrolling the path into the back offices. Must be one hell of a big game hunter Pierce concluded.

Good thing Pierce was an hour early as he got to wait another two hours before the pompous receptionist motioned for him to join her. He was on a first name basis with most of the dead animal heads by this time.

He passed down a long tall hall to a closed ornate birds-eye maple door which the receptionist opened slowly. Shade Esq. was on the phone but waved Pierce in, pointing to a large leather chair across from him. After a half hour conversation in which Pierce sensed an unhappy female friend, Shade slammed the phone down in frustration. He insulted the disconnected party on the other end in graphic and derogatory terms with a few sexual innuendos thrown in before turning his gaze to Pierce with a "Good God Arrow, you've aged!" He confessed to remembering Pierce more personally than barely, recalling several shared experiences that left Pierce squirming with embarrassment.

Pierce complimented Shade on his assortment of animal heads and obvious prowess as a hunter. Shade laughed out loud at this and said he hadn't killed a one of them. He puts them there to remind him how many human idiots there are in the world and to personally thank each of them for making his life so comfortable.

Pierce was lost in either the simplicity, the depths, or the contradictions of his analysis, not unlike college days.

Shade addressed the obvious glaze over Pierce's eyes. "Why would anyone," he asked Pierce, "pay gazillions of dollars or pounds or rupees or Yuan to kill a poor stately animal under intensely controlled circumstances and double down to hang clouded plastic eyes and empty horns on their wall? What return on investment? A blank stare divided by thousands of dollars equals zero.

"On the other hand, when a client invests in me, it costs them a lot up front but their return on investment is exorbitant. I never accept a case unless I know I can win. For me. For my client.

"Hanging heads incentivizes me to win, and win, and win. Heads wins. Tails lose. Ever seen a rear end mount?" Shade concluded.

"Hard to wag a dead tail."

Pierce Arrow immediately remembered why he had come to see Clyde Shade.

Banker Jamin convened the Reconstituted New Committee to Sell Hardlyville (RNC) in the bank boardroom. It had been reconstituted after the first failed syndication several years past. Pierce Arrow, Undertaker Bob, Chuck Hendricks, and Billious Bloom had all been retired, each for a different and unique reason.

The core remained. Banker Jamin was the main man, because of his analytical brilliance and genuine trustworthiness. As always, Captain Happy was along to help communicate. Civic Leadership, as represented by the Mayor, who spoke only in platitudes and smiled incessantly, J.P., Hardlyville Postmaster General, and Steele, wife of Rifleman and Chair of the Hardlyville Chamber of Commerce were seated in order of lack of authority. They were joined by Tiny Taylor, Jimmy Jones, and Pastor Pat to add entrepreneurial energy and moral turpitude. Ol' Dill added a unique sense of historical grounding.

Pierce Arrow was the featured presenter, sharing his self-appointed emissary role with Clyde Shade, internationally known trial attorney. Pierce was gentle with his fellow citizens, not mentioning his prior and heartfelt opposition to selling out. He spoke only of the need for Hardlyville to move beyond the tragedies of the past few months and find fresh beginnings. He did not criticize The Deal. He focused on missed projections and unmet expectations. He did not blame all of the bad and evil that had befallen Donny Brook on a flawed transaction. He simply observed that Hardlyville still had a nice ring to it. He concluded with the observation that he had found someone to help unwind the deal if that's what Hardlyvillains wanted.

Banker Jamin nodded for Pierce Arrow to continue.

Clyde Shade, Esq. was an old acquaintance of Pierce's who had made it big in the world of litigation. Pierce had called on him the previous week in Chicago to test his interest in helping Hardlyville unwind The Deal to the benefit of citizens as well as investors. While Hardlyville could not afford to buy Shade's next Gucci suit, there could be a way for Shade to benefit sufficiently to accept Hardlyville's case.

It might go something like this. Shade would approach the syndicated investors with a proposal to buy Donny Brook from them for a discounted value of investment. Like maybe a fifty-percent haircut. This got the Mayor's attention because he was deep into personal grooming and a fifty-percent discount would save him a lot of money. When Pierce explained that this was more of a reduction in market value than actual shearing of hair, the Mayor went back to sleep with a hearty "life is worth no more than a hair on my head," smile fully intact.

The discount would be warranted because investors were losing money on an investment that was not sold to them as a tax shelter. And given the one-dollar-buyback option guaranteed

Hardlyville, at deal's end they would reap no windfall to cover accumulated losses.

Shade, on the other hand, would look at the deal as strictly a tax play up front. He would acquire the town of Donny Brook for a negotiated price far below market, provide investors with a large current year tax write off, then make a charitable contribution of Donny Brook to the citizens of Hardlyville the following year and take a significant tax deduction for his generous gift. Folks could then name or rename the blooming place anything they wished.

The Reconstituted New Committee to sell Hardlyville had formerly decided that they had the authority to sell Hardlyville without citizen vote under the vague authority provided under the village charter—namely none in terms of either powers or restrictions. This was not unlike most small towns in the Ozarks. It was a cultural thing.

Following that line of reasoning, they certainly had the authority to approve unwinding the transaction without citizen vote. And since Shade's recompense for turning back Hardlyvillain history to a happier time would all be sans cash, there were no financial implications to consider.

"What about the annual payments to citizens?" Steele wondered.

Pierce would confirm with Shade, Esq., but common sense would dictate that since recipients had not voted to receive annual payments, that "payments to individuals" was simply a provision in the transaction, and that the RNC was the approving authority for The Deal, that the RNC could authorize undoing the whole mess. When Pierce Arrow used that last word he slapped a hand over his mouth. It was the first incendiary word that had slipped out through the whole presentation. He apologized, but no one objected. The RNC giveth, the RNC taketh away he concluded.

The discussion that followed was muted and brief. No one could disagree with the conclusion that The Deal had not worked as planned. It had not provided the village of Hardlyville with sustainable financial viability, it had not raised one individual's standard of living, and it had dented the psyche of a proud and gentle community. And, related or not, a lot of bad things had happened.

Pierce did add that it might be worthwhile to give all citizens a chance to vote on reaffirming the name of Hardlyville in the interest of civic pride. It would give folks a chance to stand for something rather than against it. It would relegate The Deal to past trash and elevate the community's proud history, from founder Thomas Hardly to now, to page one of a new chapter in the big book of Hardlyville. His suggestion was greeted with great enthusiasm.

So it was moved, seconded, and unanimously approved by the RNC that Clyde Shade, Esq. be hired immediately, no cash retainer, to unwind the Donny Brook deal in its entirety. All non-cash benefits from the transaction would accrue to Shade, Esq. personally. Hardlyville and the RNC would be relieved of any and all liability relating to anything. The mayor asked if that included his loan at Bank of Hardlyville. Banker Jamin's vigorous negative head shake and Captain Happy's observation that the Mayor was forty-three days past due with penalty interest accruing daily at ten percent sent the Mayor scrambling to the men's room with a "check's in the mail," parting flourish.

A second motion was also approved unanimously. As soon as the Shade deal was closed, a binding community vote would be held on reaffirming Hardlyville, with all of its history and glory, as formal name of the village.

The Reconstituted New Committee to sell Hardlyville (RNC) then proudly voted itself out of existence.

The vote was unanimous. The message was clear. The village would henceforth and forever be known as Hardlyville. Again. This irrevocable city ordinance could never be overturned. Not with a vote of 223 to 0, and ballot language that included the word "forever."

Not even the Agenda 21'ers voted no. Several of them had to hold their writing hand with their other to mark the "yes" box for fear of sliding naturally toward "no." But they did it.

BETTER ANGELS?

Lettie tried to live with grief. As her baby and belly grew, she knew she must move on to celebrate this latest miracle. Pierce Arrow, on the other hand, was mad as hell. He was furious at this evil She Devil who would not leave his community alone. He was murdering mad that she had taken little Vixen from brokenhearted Lettie and him. He was subterranean mad at Jimmy and Sally Jones that they got their daughter back at the cost of his.

Pierce Arrow was normally slow to anger and quick to forgive. There was no forgiveness in his heart at this time. Perhaps their red dirt baby from southern Utah would fill the void. He just didn't know.

They travelled under cover of darkness, covering miles at a time. She pushed the little girl mercilessly, taunting her when she slowed or cried, even striking the girl with the back of her hand on occasion. They avoided all human contact and when an occasional dog caught their scent and barked, she dispensed with it quickly and efficiently.

It would take them at least a month to reach the cave and acreage in eastern Tennessee, where she would begin to raise the little one in her own image, and that of her lineage. She would root out fear and sadness and replace it with unbridled anger. She would squeeze out love and fill its void with meanness. She would turn the gentle little girl with the big yellow eyes into a ruthless mercenary without heart or soul. She might even get some heathen hillbilly to teach her about sex, like her father had taught her. It might take months or years, but, when she was finished, there would be yet another mortal threat to weaselly Hardlyville and its sanctimonious citizenry. This was the sermon she preached to the little one each dawn before they crawled into a tree or under a bush to hide and sleep, child bound foot to foot by a taut tendon from a deer hindquarters.

Both wore only animal skins and walked on bare feet.

Once a hunter, sleeping in a blind, awoke to see them slipping into the shadows and shouted out. She circled back and slit his throat before eviscerating him, just for the show of it all. She slapped the little one's face with her bloody hand before shoving it into Vixen's gaping mouth. She laughed maniacally when Vixen vomited the bloody mess and what little else lurked in her belly onto the forest floor. She would turn this weak one into a force of evil before it was all over.

She only killed once more. This time a biker dude who thought he was a hot shit lover. He wasn't terrible but didn't have much stamina. She eliminated him for that shortcoming. She was disappointed that the little one slept through it all, both the sex and the death, but there would be time, there would be time.

Night after night, through rain and mud and slop they crept, like the animals the little one would surely become.

Jimmy Jones couldn't sleep at night. His conscience wouldn't let him. He had a beautiful young daughter to kiss goodnight, to awaken for pre-school in the morning, a hand to hold when they walked or ran, a laugh to share at her younger brother. Girl Jones was home again, Sally was her dirty-deed-loving self again, the weed business was booming, Sheriff Sephus was looking the other way, and all was well as Hardlyville regained its history and name.

Except Pierce and Lettie. He could hardly look at them, let alone express his deep sorrow for their loss. He simply steered clear of his friends and neighbors. He couldn't even bring himself to go to the garden to visit with Lucas. He was too ashamed. Of what he wasn't sure, just aware of the deep fog that had descended on his brain.

Jimmy Jones had to do something. He was not a thinker, he was a doer. He had to do what Captain Jack and Code Spode couldn't. He had to find Vixen and bring her home, back to the two that loved her as their own.

Jimmy took his burden to Sheriff Sephus Adonis. The sheriff understood his pain but cautioned him to just let it go. Jimmy couldn't and let the good sheriff know it.

Sheriff reminded Jimmy that even the crack SWAT team assigned to the president of the United States, Code Spode, had been unable to penetrate the She Devil's veil of secrecy. That she had slipped through the cracks of their pursuit and killed one of their own in the process. That she was an evil beyond mortal comprehension. At least now that she had what she wanted, she might leave Hardlyvillains alone. Jimmy should go home and hug his family and give thanks for his blessings.

Jimmy just shook his head. This evil woman had murdered his cousin, Lucas Jones, in cold blood and had almost succeeded in killing Jimmy himself. She had attempted to poison the whole town of Hardlyville. She had kidnapped one then another precious little girl and forged the swap from hell that tore apart best friends and families. Hers was a legacy that must be avenged. If he could rescue little Vixen, bring her home safely, and dispose of her evilness in the process, revenge would be theirs. Not recovery, not healing, not normalcy. Those would take time. Just revenge. Pure and hateful revenge. And Jimmy promised that he had enough hate in his heart to match her, pulse for pulse. Now Sheriff Sephus could only shake his head.

Jimmy asked Sheriff Sephus to check his wire for recent murders or missing persons throughout the Midwest. Against his better judgment, the Sheriff did. He reported a hunter found with slit throat near Lake Barkley in Tennessee and a week later a biker found murdered in the woods along a country road in north central Tennessee. Neither motive nor suspect could be determined in either case. A knife was the suspected weapon of choice.

That's her, they nodded to each other. Sheriff spread a large map of the United States on his conference table and plotted coordinates from Hardlyville through each of the murder scenes. It was literally a straight line from here to there. If the Devil Lady and her hostage were on foot, it followed that they would take the shortest and most direct route to their final destination. It also made sense that given the similarities between the Ozarks and Eastern Tennessee geographically and culturally, that's where they were headed. Sheriff continued his straight line, north of populated areas like Knoxville to the Smoky Mountains. "Shit, brothers," he exclaimed, "she is or will be hiding out in the Great Smokies." He was proud of the logic of his conclusion.

Sheriff made Jimmy Jones promise that he would go straight home and settle in with his family until the sheriff could alert law enforcement in the suspected area. It was his intention to fly into Knoxville immediately and work with local authorities to plot a strategy for finding her. She would surely kill again and a well-orchestrated response would have a chance of surrounding her. She might even have gathered another evil coven together to carry out her mission of death and hate grounded in sex. Possibly more hints of where she might be. They had almost nabbed her once in her Ozarks mountain fortress. They would not fail in eastern Tennessee.

Jimmy promised yes, then walked home, loaded a cooler with beer and ice, and grabbed half a wild turkey breast from the freezer and a bag of his finest weed. He pecked each child on the cheek and gave Sally a deep passionate kiss before announcing that he was going on a road trip. Sally was to tell no one because he would be returning with a big surprise for Hardlyville. Just call it a community service project. Sally made him promise it wasn't another woman before nodding in agreement. He grabbed Cousin Lucas's old deer rifle and a bag of ammo from the garage before setting out for the Great Smoky Mountains of eastern Tennessee. He should make it there in time to see the sun rise.

Sheriff Sephus tried later to call Jimmy and tell him that Tennessee authorities were anxious to collaborate and he would drive to the big city for a plane trip early the next morning. Sally explained that Jimmy was sleeping but that she would share the Sheriff's message. Internal alarms were starting to buzz but she would sleep on it before beginning to worry.

Jimmy Jones finally stopped in the furthest reaches of eastern Tennessee just off Highway 25 near the small town of Del

Rio to get his bearings and clear the dope from his foggy mind. He had beaten Sheriff Sephus by half a day.

She led the little one by the hand into the carefully camouflaged cave entrance, pointing to a bed of fir boughs for her to lie down on. Vixen was exhausted, confounded, scared, and hungry, but fell asleep immediately. The Evil One slipped into a fresh deerskin and quietly into the dusk. When she returned in an hour with a small field dressed doe, Vixen hadn't stirred. The Evil One started a small fire and carved chunks of haunch to skewer on sticks above the flames. *Welcome home little one,* she snarled silently, adding that she would teach her well in the ways of this nasty world.

Vixen lay sleeping in her new reality.

After devouring her first real meal in weeks, the Evil One lay down flat on the dirt floor and began to plan lessons for the little one. Should she start with pain and pleasure, or maybe crime and punishment, or even death and destruction? She drifted into an internal ordering of priorities.

She was awakened by a gentle touch on her cheek. She slapped the small hand that lightly stroked her skin as the two exchanged yellow stares. Tears leaked from the little one's eyes as she again raised her tiny hand to brush the Evil One's cheek. This was a sensation she had never felt in her life. It wasn't sensual, it wasn't threatening in its persistence. It was simply kind. The Evil One gulped in confusion before pointing to the cold meat fireside. Vixen sat cross legged staring at her captor with watered eyes, chewing slowly on the stringy meat.

They sat eyeing each other for the next several hours, neither moving. Not one word was spoken. Finally Vixen crawled slowly to her mother's side and rested her head in her lap. The Evil One shrugged it off to the cave floor only to feel the small head of her daughter return, a tiny hand resting mid thigh on her mom. She slapped the hand away, only to have it return in a minute or two.

The Demon Lady's mind whirled around a memory, perhaps her first. Her head rested in a soft lap in front of a warm fire. Perhaps the memory was even warm. A gentle hand had stroked her hair as her mother had sung softly to her. She had felt as one with the kind lady she called mother.

"What was that?" she muttered to herself through the recollection. What was that feeling the two shared? She stared at the curly hair in her own lap. This was her own daughter, her own flesh and blood. She hadn't asked for this but here it was.

She escaped this reality by retreating back to the memory that had forced its way into her consciousness. It was a good memory, a warm memory. Why was it intruding on her mission right now?

Vixen nodded off into sleep again. On her mother's lap.

The Evil One lightly stroked the young child's hair, not even sure of how or what to do. This was a feeling she had not felt since the time her memory evoked, a time with her mother. Her own mother. What had happened to her? She had a vague notion of violence but couldn't put an image with it. She also found the word that was missing. Love. Her mother had loved her.

The Demon Lady began to leak tears. They dripped on the little one's head. They were clear, not yellow. She had never cried before. Not in pain, nor from pleasure. Why now? What was going on in her chest? What was beating strongly and wildly?

She remembered laying her own small head against the beat in her mother's breast. What was this memory that was so confusing to the task at hand?

151

Vixen stirred slightly, nuzzling against her Mother's taut belly, drawn to the steady beat above. She reached her free hand to her Mother's and wrapped around the little finger.

"Stop it!" the She Devil roared, leaping up and shedding Vixen like a blanket. As Vixen reached toward her, the Evil One slapped her hand and tears again leaked from the small yellow eyes. The tears were clear, not yellow, just like hers, and those eyes looked right through her Mother.

She slapped Vixen again, this time in the face, to try to erase the gentle smile that was forming on her lips. Vixen's head snapped back as the Evil One glared her hatred of all things kind and good.

But Vixen reached out again and gently stroked her mother's cheek. As she drew back to strike again, the memory of her own mother's smile was reflected back in that of her daughter.

The Evil One sobbed in confusion and the pain of contradiction. Tears no longer leaked. They flowed, as her breast heaved and a low guttural moan welled up inside. She motioned to her daughter to go, to leave, to give her space to be mean and evil. Vixen's kindness was killing her. Vixen's love of her mother was pulling motherly love out of her heart and soul. She had no place for such in her life and she needed to be rid of Vixen. It was her daughter who was stronger.

The Demon Lady knew instinctively that she would either have to kill her daughter. Or free her. She would not be able to change her. The mother in her soul precluded the former. Her own mother would approve, if only on this one occasion, of her decision. The mantel of motherhood was simply too heavy for her to bear.

Vixen looked at her Mother with confusion. She again reached out to stroke her Mother's now soaking cheek. Her Mother did not strike out but drew the little one to her bosom, if only for a brief moment. She then rose quietly, grabbed her long knife, smiled through tears at her only daughter, and loped into the night.

DRAGNET

As they closed the net around the cave entrance, Sheriff Sephus pulled his pistol. He would not be slow to act this time, as he had when they waited too long to save his friend Lucas. He would go first and shoot to kill unless the Evil One hid behind the child. Then he would try to negotiate with the Devil herself. No one behind him would fire until he did.

He charged through the small opening, getting stuck for a moment before a shove from Jimmy Jones set him free.

A small fire was burning. The child looked up from her skewer of meat in surprise. The sheriff was the last person she had seen from home and the last person she expected to run into here. She didn't know quite what to say, so she smiled. Sheriff Sephus charged around the perimeter of the large rock room while Jimmy Jones rushed to cover Vixen with his body. She thought he was playing a game and began to laugh. As Tennessee State Troopers poured into the cavern, confusion reigned. Thankfully, no one fired a shot or they likely would have unloaded on each other.

Jimmy asked Vixen if the Evil One was around.

"You mean my mother," was a reply that stunned even the most cynical. Vixen proceeded to explain that her mother had left several days earlier.

Sheriff Sephus wanted to know if she was returning. Vixen could only shrug, again in confusion. He asked Vixen if she was ready to return home to Hardlyville and her parents. Vixen nodded yes with a bright smile, yellow eyes twinkling. Sheriff took one tiny hand and Jimmy the other. They led her out the cave opening to begin the long journey home.

The State Patrol set up a couple of sentries, in case the Evil One returned. But few expected that to happen. They would watch closely for unsolved murders in the area for a while.

Sheriff and Jimmy discussed whether to call Pierce and Lettie but chose not to because no one knew what they were up to. Not their wives, not their friends, not even snoopy Ol' Dill.

In fact, neither of them knew what the other was up to until the Highway Patrol had arrested Jimmy on charges of possession of marijuana and being passed out on a public road. Sheriff Sephus had arrived as he was being interrogated and asked to take custody of the boy. He concocted a wild tale about following him all the way from the Ozarks, at his parents' request, to return him home. Sheriff Sephus would vouch for the young man's character and promised to pursue proper charges, but just right now he needed Jimmy's help in finding the kidnapped girl.

Jimmy had slept as the sheriff and highway patrolman scoured county records for land ownership and found a large parcel bordering Great Smoky National Park held in the name of a religious trust. It was the name of the trust that piqued the sheriff's attention and sent chills running all through him: The Church of the Sacred Mother. He remembered the Evil One invoking the name Sacred Mother on one of her tirades about death and redemption. It had to be her, and it was.

Authorities wanted to keep Jimmy locked up as they planned and began execution of their raid. Sheriff Sephus had insisted that Jimmy be allowed to join them as he knew just how much Jimmy needed to be part of the solution if he could ever call Pierce Arrow friend again. They reluctantly agreed, and the rest was history.

Now as the sheriff and Jimmy loaded little Vixen into a trooper car for a return to the airport, Jimmy noticed her lack of attire and arranged for a stop at Walmart to clothe and shoe her. Six hours later, they were on the ground where the sheriff had left his car. Soon after that, they were headed home to Hardlyville.

Jimmy begged the sheriff to allow him to deliver Vixen to Pierce and Lettie. He needed to close the circle of friendship that had been rent apart. Sheriff concurred and drove straight to the *Daily Hellbender*.

Pierce had gone home early as Lettie had experienced a particularly rough day. Morning sickness and noon sadness translated into an "I need you Pierce" by mid-afternoon. He simply sat and held her bony frame. He worried that she was not getting the nourishment needed to grow a healthy baby though her bump was growing. He also feared that her depression would affect the mood of her fetus. He knew none of this made sense and had asked Doc Karst about it. Doc could only shrug. He didn't like to give antidepressants to pregnant ladies in early to mid term, and he couldn't force-feed Lettie. He talked to her at every monthly appointment about increasing her intake of fruits and vegetables, but to no avail. He too was concerned.

Pierce broke his hug to go take a leak and upon returning glanced out the front window. His loud gasp brought Lettie to her feet and next to him looking out. They both were suspended in time and disbelief. There—with face pressed against the window, yellow eyes gleaming, smile mashed clown-like—was precious Vixen, Jimmy Jones's hands on her shoulders.

Lettie knelt slowly down and kissed her daughter's lips through the glass. Pierce stared at Jimmy with wonder and affection. He then pinched himself to make sure all of this was real, that he was seeing his daughter kiss his wife, and his dear friend personally presenting her to them.

As Pierce processed, Jimmy scooped Vixen up and planted her on the front porch for Lettie and Pierce to wallow with on the wood floor. Vixen giggled out loud, Lettie sobbed and moaned in joy, and Pierce bawled. They simply couldn't let go of each other to come up for air.

News spread fast and many in the community came running up to join the scrum. Group hug lost all meaning. Ol' Dill took advantage of proximity to briefly fondle every female protrusion he could find. No one seemed to notice except Li'l Shooter, who had been nursing Abi and hadn't re-bra-ed. She could only laugh at the old coot.

In fact, most of Hardlyville was laughing, smiling, crying tears of joy. Banker Jamin immediately closed the Bank of Hardlyville, declaring a Vixen Bank Holiday for the next twenty-four hours in violation of every Federal and State banking law in existence. Pastor Pat pressed through the crowd to kneel in front of the ball of flesh that was Pierce, Lettie, and Vixen and thank God for bringing them together again.

A village that had recently regained its name and history, had now recovered its soul.

ANOTHER MOTHER

Billious Bloom took to motherhood like a smallmouth bass takes to crawdads. She engulfed it. Without hesitation or thought she plunged right in and was an immediate natural.

She named her little one Presley Cicero Bloom. Not that she liked that first name. She just wanted to call him Pres, which struck her as only appropriate given the lineage. At least Cicero honored her Latin grounding and responsibilities. And she recalled a remarkable fling with a like-named young man on one of her "rare" book buying ventures. And, she was proud of her last name.

Billious simply wandered around being happy and thankful. She was thankful that Octavia Rosebeam had started and funded the Rosebeam Foundation. Sheriff Sephus had once let it slip that she did so with ill-gotten gains, something about robbing a bank, but would not elaborate further. So she was thankful for at least that bank robbery. She was thankful to the Board for naming her Executive Director and giving her the leeway and funding to establish the foundation as an international player.

157

She was thankful to Pastor Pat for introducing her to sex after all those years as a virgin. He still blushed when she winked at him, as she did at every opportunity.

She was thankful to sex for opening a closed door to her spirit and passion, and releasing both to be free.

She was grateful to be free. Free of romantic entanglements. Free of guilt. Free to be a woman raising a beautiful boy on her own.

She was grateful to be teaching diversity and sex education at Hardlyville High School. She was well-schooled in both, and even took little Pres to class on occasion to demonstrate what happened when you got pregnant. It was great for her, but for a sixteen- or seventeen-year-old damsel to be responsible for a baby with no job or education? Different story. And it resonated with her classes. There had not been one teen pregnancy among recent Hardlyville graduates and Billious knew she was making a difference.

Billious Bloom had hit her full stride as a mother and woke up happy and thankful every morning.

She was due to visit the Smithsonian Institute in Washington, DC, her first trip back since she and Lettie called on the president of the United States for help in finding little Vixen. While she had said nothing to the president about his boy, who was staying with Flotilla Hendricks, she had enjoyed his attention, his ministrations, and sleeping with him in the Lincoln bedroom. She even thought she had heard someone shuffling around the bed at the height of their frenzy. The president had later confirmed it was probably just Ol' Abe "voyeuring" around. It hadn't been the first time the president had welcomed a special friend to the Lincoln Room, nor the first sense of shared presence. She was pleased that the president seemed to enjoy her for who she was, specifically not Lettie, and he had invited her to return often.

She figured it was about time for the president to meet Pres, though she had no intention of sharing that this was his bastard son. She had no idea what the repercussions of such disclosure would be, but she was sure it would not bode well for her motherhood, her son, or her freedom.

Her call to his cell phone was quickly returned along with an invitation to dinner and another overnight in the Lincoln bedroom.

She accepted without hesitation or qualification. The president had cleared his calendar on the evening in question and he was looking forward to resuming where they had left off.

She appeared at the White House with little Pres on her arm at the appointed hour, throwing the principal aide who met her at security into a tizzy. The baby was an uninvited guest who could not possibly be included in the evening. Ms. Bloom countered with the obvious—the president was expecting her, baby or not.

A quick call to the president confirmed his intentions, and they were waved through.

Security insisted on checking Pres's diaper for explosives per official protocol. They soon learned that Pres had indeed laid a big bomb and they were going to have to clean it up since Billious had already cleared Security. She couldn't come back and he couldn't go through. Again, protocol. This made for a colorful and odiferous scene with Billious passing wipes and dipes back through the X-ray machine, a young, shy, pale male security guard doing the honors, and handing the evidence to a horrified principal aide to dispose of before passing tiny Pres on to his smiling mother. A long line of guests to an informal White House Dinner hosted by the vice president were not amused by the delay. "Can't be too careful," or something like that Billious Bloom chirped.

The president of the United States ushered Billious into the Oval Office, placed her (his) son on the floor, and laid a passionate kiss on her lips. This went on until the baby started crying and Billious gently pushed the president away. She proudly lifted their son and introduced him to the president as Pres Bloom. The president inquired about his father and Billious shrugged an I-don't-know-but-I-love-the-baby response. She added that she was confident that Pres would not get in anyone's way once fed and put to bed.

The president summoned his principal aide to get a crib as soon as possible while Billious began to nurse little Pres. The principal aide would spend the night in the Oval Office with the baby so the president and Ms. Bloom could enjoy an early supper and Ms. Bloom could get a well deserved full night's sleep. Ms. Bloom assured the principal aide that Pres would sleep most of the night and that the bottle of breast milk she had pumped would satisfy any of his early morning cravings.

The principal aide was aghast. Not only did she detest babies, but the president had whispered to her after their most recent lovemaking that he really loved her. If this was love, she was through. Then, as always, she swallowed her objections and did as instructed while the president watched Pres nurse with envy.

Pres did sleep through the night and it was the president of the United States who experienced early morning cravings.

A Hero's Welcome

Booray Abdul's business was booming and his strategy had worked. Tiny Taylor's business was unaffected and she even began carrying a "Booray" special on her menu weekly. Though she always fried it before serving. Baby Abi was a joy to him and Li'l Shooter, and Grandma Steele absolutely cooed over the little one. Grandpa Rifleman, who generally fired a round from his pistol into the air whenever he got overly excited, had to stop wearing his holster on visits because every time little Abi gave him a toothless grin he drew and shot skyward. Into Booray's ceiling. Grandpa Rifleman was tiring of patching holes and paying roofing bills . . . but not of the grin.

Jimmy Jones and Sheriff Sephus Adonis were the latest in a long lineage of Hardlyville heroes. Their respective wives, Sally and Airreal, knew them for the imperfect clods they could be but were proud nonetheless.

Sally had forgiven Jimmy for not telling her the risk he was taking in going after the She Devil alone and armed only with a deer rifle. She acknowledged to most that she would have had trouble doing so if her husband and father to her children had gotten killed in the process of doing something so stupid, but he hadn't.

Dear CiCi Cobb, an old high school flame of Jimmy's who had tried every trick in her arsenal to get Jimmy into bed with her, was sniffing around again. She told Jimmy she knew how to treat a hero, at least that's what Jimmy said. Sally guessed she had been a little more specific, but Jimmy said he just laughed and told her to go find a real hero, a pretty humble response that made Sally smile.

Airreal, on the other hand was giddy over her new husband's wisdom and bravery. She had sensed it was there but had not been around long enough to witness it in person. For Sheriff Sephus to figure out the Demon Lady's general location from drawing a couple of straight lines on a map of the US had been brilliant. All the president's men, with all their technology and weaponry, went home to DC with tails between legs. Not her man. And then for him to insist on being the first one into the cave to face whatever evil lurked within spoke to deep-rooted courage. Her husband grew in stature to her, even as his bulk diminished. His diet was working and he was close to keeping his wedding vow to lose one hundred pounds.

So Sally Jones and Airreal Flambeau did what any proud spouses might do. They threw a party to honor their mates. They invited the whole town and used both Tiny Taylor and Booray Abdul to cater. Part of Sheriff Sephus's success at losing weight was due to a shift from Tiny Taylor's fried everything to Booray's middle eastern cuisine. Both would be offered at this celebration. Ol' Dill cooked up a special batch of white lightning which he contributed, at no cost, in astounding amounts. They chose the outdoor garden at the old Donny Brook Inn as venue so anyone with too much to drink to safely walk home could find a bed to crash in. Finally, a use for this relic from a sorry time that made sense.

The mayor tried to declare a holiday but got confused during his remarks and ended up wishing everyone Merry Christmas and a Happy New Year. Rifleman, of course, fired round after round into the sky.

But the star of the evening was little Vixen. She spoke softly and haltingly into the microphone held in Pierce Arrow's hand. She began by apologizing for the pain inflicted on Hardlyville by her birth mother. She begged the community's forgiveness. This caught everyone off guard, regardless of the amount of Ol' Dill's finest consumed. Mother? Even Pastor Pat, the village's ultimate reconciler, recoiled initially. But the simple profession of his own faith's central tenant in the heartfelt words of a young child conjured up all sorts of Biblical messages and contradictions for him. He would need to pray on it.

Vixen move on quickly to thanking Sheriff Sephus and Jimmy Jones for bringing her home. She praised their bravery and concern but noted in closing that her birth mother had given her up voluntarily. This was not a rescue. It was a recovery. This again set the crowd to murmuring. There was clearly more at play here than a cute little girl, albeit one with bright-yellow eyes, saying thank you.

Pierce Arrow was riveted to her every word and stunned with the depth and meaning of her brief remarks.

She loves her birth mother, thought Pierce, *and has forgiven her for the evil that possesses her. That's one big heart,* thought Pierce, as he grappled with the anger and hatred in his own. "It's almost supernatural," he whispered to Lettie.

"It is," Lettie smiled softly back.

Vixen closed by saying how grateful she was to be home with Pierce and Lettie and her brothers and sisters . . . and her Hardlyvillain neighbors whom she loved as dear family. She again thanked Jimmy and Sheriff Sephus for bringing her back, closing a circle that most could comprehend and applaud crazily for.

Jimmy had gotten a little drunk. He was wandering around hugging everyone in town, retreating quickly when CiCi Cobb threw her arms around him for a chest bump. Sally saw and approved, smiling daggers at Ms. CiCi and shoving her wedding ring in her face with a "suck this" or something similar.

Jimmy had moved on to the Freeload twins. They were relatively new to town but had gotten to know Jimmy quickly because of their taste for weed, becoming two of his best customers. Jimmy had even taken them smallmouth fishing a couple of times. On one occasion he had lamented the passing of native hellbenders in Skunk Creek because of civilization's encroachment and more specifically the Big Pig flood of several years past. As he drank more Bud Lite, caught more fish, and smoked joint after joint he became pretty loose lipped. While he couldn't remember exactly all he said he was pretty sure it was too much. Every time they saw him lately they asked when he was going to take them to that secret hellbender hole of his. When they raised the question this night he visibly shuddered and asked them to forget whatever he had told them. This only piqued their interest more and they later swore to one another they would keep an eye on Jimmy until he showed them, willingly or not.

The Freeload twins were really pretty bad news. They were stupid to begin with and stupid enough to think they were smart. They cared little about anyone else's personal property, and though Sheriff Sephus couldn't prove it, he sensed that they had something to do with a recent spate of robberies.

They also liked to shoot animals, mostly for fun. They hung deer rack after deer rack on the walls of the rented apartment they shared, and even had a coyote, a wolf, a skunk, and a stray dog up there with the rest. They shared with Jimmy that they would love to hang one of those hellbender things up on trophy row someday and hoped he would help them track one down. Jimmy was stunned and assured them he would never tell them what he couldn't remember how much he told them before, and that they should take their weed business elsewhere. He added that he would kill them if he ever found out they did such an atrocious thing. This earned a smirk from one and a leer toward Sally from the other who cautioned Jimmy that he'd better keep an eye on that pretty little wife of his. She had sure been keeping one on him all night long. Jimmy lunged toward the twins but slipped and fell at their feet. One feigned a kick while the other just laughed. Fact was, they kind of scared him, even when he was drunk.

Sheriff Sephus eventually steered Sally and Jimmy to the bridal suite, sent Airreal to their place to replace the babysitter for the night, and by two o'clock in the morning had pretty much dispersed the crowd. The Donny Brook Inn had never been so full.

With little Vixen back where she belonged, Pierce and Lettie back in the dear friend column, Sheriff Sephus singing his praises, and the Freeload twins off his customer list, Jimmy was feeling good enough about things to visit the garden and catch up with the spirit of Cousin Lucas. Jimmy was sure that Lucas would understand the shame Jimmy had felt over sacrificing Vixen and the long absence between visits. He also hoped Lucas would be proud of his efforts to return Vixen home. He just knew he needed a big dose of Lucas to catch him up on life in general.

He left after work one evening, telling Sally he had a business call to make, which generally meant a new weed customer. Since Jimmy generally didn't use on the job, she could always tell whether it was business or not.

What Jimmy did not know was that the Freeload twins had attached a radio monitoring device to the underside of his pickup after their recent run in, intent on tracking Jimmy to his secret hellbender hole. Since both Freeloads were unemployed, they were immediately available to jump into their truck and trail at a distance when Jimmy left town.

After the long drive, Jimmy parked in front of the rock fortress like he always did, spied the horizon for uninvited guests, again like he always did, and headed with his rope toward the big boulder covering the garden entrance. He rolled it aside, tied rope to tree, and descended into the otherworldly peace and serenity that waited far below. He no longer even brought a flashlight, knowing that the dim subterranean light, which source he could never ascertain, would illuminate his way. He landed gently in the cold waters of the spring branch and stood still until his eyes adjusted well enough for him to see at least four pair of hellbenders sliding to and fro around him. He smiled at his good fortune.

Jimmy then headed back into the side passage where he had found Cousin Lucas on past occasions. He rounded a bend, expecting to see him sitting on the singular big rock, flipping a coin. Nothing. Jimmy tried to think his way to him. Telepathic was what Lucas called it. Nothing. So Jimmy sat on Lucas's rock to wait a moment or two. Maybe he was taking a leak or something?

Meanwhile, up top, the Freeload twins had hidden their truck in the woods and climbed up the rock fortress path to look down on the hole in the ground through which Jimmy had descended. They had a hunch that this was the secret hellbender hole and they settled in to see what happened next. Both were packing pistols and itching for action if Jimmy Jones wanted some.

Jimmy never tired of sitting in the garden but he figured Cousin Lucas must be up to some important business elsewhere in the kingdom, and Sally would expect him home before midnight. He softly retraced his steps and climbed back up into a clear beautiful night. He pulled his rope up, untied it from the tree, rolled the stone cover back, and covered his tracks with a branch, like he always did.

The Freeload twins waited fifteen minutes after he left to pull a rope from their truck, roll away the stone, tie the rope to the tree, and descend into the darkness. One shone a flashlight down to light the way for the other, who splashed loudly into the cold water, cursing the wetness. The second descended slowly while the first lit his way down.

Both smiled when they trained their lights on the flowing water. They had looked up hellbender on the internet and what they were looking at was a whole herd of them. First one then the other drew their pistols and commenced firing at anything that moved. When the smoke cleared three hellbender carcasses floated to the silver surface of the spring branch as a blood slick began to spread.

The twins decided this would do for now, grabbed the slimy bodies to take home and mount, and made their way back up the rope. They rolled the stone back but forgot to wipe away tracks in their elevated state of excitement.

Two days later the twins ran into Jimmy at Tiny Taylor's Greasy Spoons Grill and Bar. They apologized if they had been rude at the celebration, blaming alcohol and dope for any misstatements. They would like to make amends and wondered if Jimmy would stop by their apartment later for a cold beer and discussion of how they might get back on his customer list. Jimmy reluctantly agreed.

When Jimmy knocked on their door later that afternoon he was greeted warmly. Cold beer in hand, he was led to his dismay into the mount room. He could barely look at all the cold heads and plastic eyeballs and focused his attention on the floor. As they took turns bragging on their latest acquisition, he glanced up quickly to a bloodcurdling sight. A stuffed dead hellbender hung from their wall.

Jimmy Jones screamed out loud and cursed them both. He knew where this had come from and would have them arrested for trespassing and murder. He grabbed the mount and ran for the door, the Freeload twins roaring with laughter. They hollered that he was welcome to keep the mount as they had several others to replace it. They wondered if he might even take it home to that pretty little wife of his and get lucky tonight.

Jimmy's eyes burned with tears and anger. They had obviously followed him to the garden earlier in the week and wreaked havoc on the gentle creatures down below. He headed straight to Sheriff Sephus's office.

Jimmy demanded that the sheriff arrest the two idiots on charges of murdering endangered species and lock them up for life. Sheriff Sephus tried to calm Jimmy and finally got him to focus on telling the story. Jimmy said it was a long one. If the sheriff had the time, he would share it all. Sheriff Sephus nodded for him to proceed.

Two hours later a severely shaken Sheriff Sephus Adonis could only mutter "shit, brothers." Sheriff Sephus had never heard such a story, all the way from town founder Thomas Hardly to a secret Ozarkian Garden of Eden that seemed to stir the reproductive juices of Jimmy and Sally Jones and served as final mansion to his dear deceased friend Lucas Jones. He asked Jimmy what charges he wished to file. Jimmy repeated murder and trespassing. Both seemed a bit extreme to the sheriff. Jimmy didn't seem to know who owned the land above the garden now, only that it had once been part of the notorious Skunk Creek Ranch. So if the idiots were trespassing, so was Jimmy. That wouldn't work.

Killing a federally-protected animal had a little more promise, though the sheriff would have to research the hows and whereforths of that one. He did agree to accompany Jimmy back to the Freeload twins' place with a search warrant to see if other critters were involved and seek their explanation as to possession. Since Sheriff Sephus always forged his own search warrants, they were soon on their way.

Sheriff Sephus knocked on the twins' apartment, showed the search warrant, and asked to look around. As he entered, he heard Jimmy, who was following closely behind holding the hellbender mount, gasp. The bastards had killed another one, he spewed, pointing to the now filled space he had left behind.

Sheriff Sephus walked over to murderers row, lifted the hellbender mount from its nail, held it next to the one Jimmy held, and noticed tears trailing down Jimmy's cheeks. The Freeload twins simply smiled.

Sheriff asked the twins where they had obtained such fine specimens of a federally-protected species. One pointed at Jimmy claiming it was his fault. When Sheriff Sephus asked for clarification, the twin began a long story about how, at the community celebration for the two very heroes standing in front of him, he had struck up a friendly conversation with Jimmy's wife, whose name he couldn't recall. Since they had both had a bit to drink, one thing led to another and the telltale twin found her leading him into a dark corner at the Donny Brook Inn. She talked about how lonely a lady gets when she lives with a hero because he never has time for her, and how her natural needs are rarely met. She wondered if this twin, or even his brother, might have the time and interest to help her meet her God-given requirements, which really weren't all that much?

Jimmy lunged at the twin but the sheriff intercepted him, crooking Jimmy's arm behind his back in a restraint hold and asking the twin where this story was headed.

"To bed," was his sneering response.

Sheriff Sephus wanted to know what this had to do with the hellbender mounts. Everything brought forth another sneer. Sheriff asked him to go on, telling Jimmy he would break his arm if he didn't settle.

"Well, after a pretty passionate kiss, she guessed I would do and invited me to her house next morning after the hero was at work and the kids were in day care. She was still a little hung over from party time but didn't take long to become the woman she claimed to have been the previous evening. Just say it was a long and lusty morning with a fireball of a lady."

Jimmy lunged again and the sheriff squeezed tighter begging him to slow down.

"Well, the lovely lady was so pleased when we came down, she reached into a closet in the bedroom and tossed me this stream lizard mount. Said she had another if I wanted to come back same time next week. I did, and so did she. You sure are one lucky guy, hero, if you would just stay around home long enough to enjoy it."

Jimmy growled with the lunge this time and Sheriff Sephus had to let him go or the arm would have cracked wide open. Jimmy jumped the offending twin and began pummeling him about the head. The sheriff grabbed one of Jimmy's wrists and cuffed it, finally gaining control of the other to cuff as well. Jimmy was screaming and crying that he was going to kill the fucking Freeload twins for murdering hellbenders in cold blood and insulting his wife. The beaten twin spit blood that had pooled in his mouth into Jimmy's eyes, telling him again how good his wife was in bed.

Sheriff Sephus finally dragged Jimmy to the police car, telling the twins he would be back for further questioning and to not leave town.

The Freeload twins sat chuckling and popped a beer. They then hung the third hellbender mount on the wall.

Jimmy Jones was apoplectic and blubbering obscenities when Sheriff Sephus finally got him in the cell. The sheriff urged Jimmy to calm down, he knew the louts were lying, and with Jimmy's help he would prove it. But he needed that help or he could do nothing.

He asked Jimmy to take him to the scene of the purported crime immediately to look for evidence. Jimmy re-emphasized that he had promised Pierce Arrow that he would never take a soul there for the rest of his life.

Sheriff Sephus immediately called Pierce and asked him to join Jimmy and himself on an important mission of discovery. He would share details on the way.

Pierce knew something bad was up and assumed it had to do with the She Devil so he raced to the sheriff's office, telling Lettie he may be home late. She was to double-bolt all doors and sleep with Vixen, loaded shotgun at her side.

All piled into the sheriff's car and set out on the long trek to the garden. Sheriff Sephus filled Pierce in as to what was going on and why Jimmy insisted on clearing it with Pierce. Pierce confirmed with the sheriff that he had never visited the garden either, but that this occasion warranted such action. He was secretly relieved that no mention was made of the Demon Lady and called Lettie to relieve her sense of crisis.

Pierce remarked that this trip reminded him of the one the three had taken several years back in the wake of disbanding the evil coven and in search of the "X" on Thomas Hardly's map. They had failed on that occasion but Jimmy had persisted and now they were back to close that circle.

Jimmy's first clue was that there were footprints around the boulder. He always brushed his clear with a branch and the intruders had neglected to do so. Sheriff Sephus pulled a crumpled piece of paper from his rear pocket and sketched the foot print pattern with a pencil.

Jimmy descended first and cursed what he saw. Blood spattered a couple of rocks next to the spring and another murdered hellbender had floated ashore next to it. Pierce followed Jimmy down, and Sheriff Sephus labored heavily before plopping down in the cold water. Pierce put his hand on Jimmy's shoulder with a soft "I'm sorry."

Sheriff Sephus quickly found shell casings which he placed in his pocket. And on the ground not far away was a dirty baseball cap featuring the logo of the Minnesota Twins professional baseball team. They had clearly been here, these God forsaken twins, and had committed unheard of atrocities against man and nature. The sheriff said he had plenty to seek justice against them and just hoped that they hadn't fled.

Jimmy asked if they wanted to try to connect with the spirit of Lucas. Both hesitantly nodded yes, not really sure of themselves. As Jimmy led them down the side branch and around the tight corner he advised that Lucas hadn't been here on his last visit. The rock where Lucas had sat before, with his back to Jimmy, was vacant again. Jimmy could only shrug and lead them back to the exit rope and the mission of justice.

They went straight to the Freeload twins apartment. The twins huddled behind the locked door asked if they had a warrant. Sheriff Sephus observed that he really didn't need one and kicked in the door.

He indicated he had several questions for the twins. First and foremost he wanted to know what their first names were. He laughed out loud when one answered Younger and the other Older. Younger and Older Freeload certainly fit the moment. Sheriff Sephus wandered over to the holstered pistols hanging on Trophy Wall, pulled one out, removed its load, and pulled the spent cartridges from his pocket. The match was perfect.

He then lifted a tennis shoe laying near the front door, checked its tread, compared it to the pattern he had sketched, and nodded again. Younger Freeload wanted to know what was going on.

Sheriff Sephus then grabbed a baseball cap lying on the table and flipped to its front logo. The Minnesota Twins closed the deal.

He announced to the Freeload twins that they were under arrest for trespassing, murdering an endangered species, and perjury.

He asked if they wanted to go with him peacefully or fight, knowing Jimmy clearly preferred the latter.

An indignant Older Freeload announced that the sheriff could never arrest them for several reasons, assuming victims of slander had an opportunity to tell their story in trial under oath, even in this two-bit town. Sheriff Sephus nodded for him to continue.

Older Freeload noted that he would be obligated to reveal the location of this special place the hellbender called home to any and all who would listen. It wouldn't do much for the twins but would sure as hell invite the public in to enjoy such a beautiful place. Pierce Arrow visibly cringed.

Younger Freeload followed with his version of how he found such a rare and beautiful sanctuary. He would share his personal relationship with beautiful and sexy Sally Jones and how in a moment of shared ecstasy she had promised to take him places he had never been, including a special remote secret hole in the ground to make love. Jimmy Jones charged Younger Freeload and began to pummel him. Sheriff Sephus with Pierce Arrow's help was able to finally restrain Jimmy, cuffing him to a couch.

Sheriff wondered how Younger Freeload could ever prove such a preposterous charge. Younger simply smiled and asked Jimmy if he even remembered the large black mole about half-way up Sally's thigh. Jimmy charged Younger again, this time dragging the couch with him. The Freeload Brothers were doubled over in laughter at this point. Sheriff Sephus asked Younger how he knew about this mole since the rest of his tale was clearly pre-fabricated? Younger replied that he had peeked in on her through a hole in the wall taking a leak at the Donny Brook Inn that night and it was clearly visible right about panty-line level.

Sheriff Sephus asked Jimmy if this was true. Jimmy nodded yes and charged again, ripping the handle off the couch and swinging wildly at Younger Freeload with it. Sheriff Sephus tackled Jimmy before he could injure Younger and dragged him out to his police car, locking him in.

Accusers and guilty parties were at an impasse. With the sheriff and Jimmy gone, Pierce Arrow proposed a compromise.

The Freeload Twins didn't to want to go to jail, and didn't much seem to like Hardlyville anyway.

Jimmy Jones was intent on murdering one or both of the twins, which would also not be a preferred outcome.

Why not simply part ways? If Pierce could walk outside right now and tell the sheriff that the Freeload twins would load their pickup and be out of town and beyond state borders by noon tomorrow, and would never return, Pierce guessed the sheriff would let them escape despite his warrant for their arrest. He also would bet that Jimmy Jones would not pursue his heartfelt threat of violence after them unless they should return. What in the world could they care about some dark hole in the ground when they already had their trophy hellbenders? It surely wasn't good for much else, Pierce reasoned. And since neither of them really had a thing going with Sally Jones, was there anything to miss there? No, it seemed to Pierce Arrow that a mutually agreed upon and immediate separation met the best interests of all parties. Pierce would even throw in a case of beer for their travels.

The Freeload twins asked for a moment alone to consider the transaction. It didn't take long for them to say yes and begin loading their trophy heads.

Both Sheriff Sephus and Jimmy Jones fumed at the idea of letting the idiots go free, but finally bought into Pierce's reasoning that it offered the least potential damage. No one would believe the shit about Sally but it would embarrass her needlessly, and to no end. Did Jimmy really want everyone in town to know that she had a big mole on her thigh above her bottom panty line? And no one would ever know about the garden if they could just get the yahoos out of town and headed back to Texas from whence they came.

Sheriff Sephus locked Jimmy up for twenty-four hours to keep him from losing it. He told Sally that her husband had gotten into a little spat with a couple of no-goods who the sheriff was running out of town immediately. Jimmy could come home when he cooled down a bit.

"Case closed," declared Sheriff Sephus, expressing his appreciation to Pierce Arrow for his take on justice.

A Mother's Death

In the days following, Sheriff Sephus Adonis had taken to reading the police wires out of eastern Tennessee. He didn't know why. Maybe it was to see if any other unusual murder cases surfaced in the area, something consistent with the She Devil's M.O. He doubted anything would show up. She was too savvy for that after such a close call. She would likely lay low for a while before resuming her evil ways.

It appeared she was acting as an independent contractor these days, without a supporting cast of haters. He knew it wouldn't take much effort for her to gather a group of troubled souls in some far-flung remote base to build another coven of evil. There were always those out there who could be captivated and mesmerized by a message of sex, lust, pseudo-religious doctrine, and murder in the name of salvation, all delivered by a snake charming, sassy, manipulative woman of charismatic bearing. He had seen her at her worst and feared her power over people.

Maybe she would just smolder alone for a while, a teapot of vitriol, brewing to another boil before bubbling over to burn. All Sheriff Sephus knew was that he hoped she would never set foot in Hardlyville again in his lifetime.

Sheriff Sephus Adonis did a double take on a story circulating from rural North Carolina by way of Knoxville. He read it four times before jumping to a conclusion. He called Pierce Arrow and asked if he would join him at his office for a matter of the utmost importance. He needed Pierce's counsel and advice.

Pierce was there in a matter of minutes. Sheriff Sephus printed off the brief report to hand to Pierce, his hand shaking badly.

"Officials in a remote western North Carolina county have found the body of a hard-to-guess-how-old aged woman, clad only in the skin of a deer, in a remote section of heavy woods. A long knife protruded from her heart. There is no motive nor any suspect(s) in the case."

Pierce and the sheriff stared at each other. It had to be her, they concurred. Sheriff called his new friend in the Tennessee Highway Patrol to see if he could find out additional information about the one Sheriff Sephus thought might be the subject of their hunt. Two hours later, he learned that the only distinguishing marks on her well-chiseled body were two eyeball tattoos, one to each buttock. It was further confirmed that no one laid claim to the body, which had been buried in a simple unmarked grave in a small public cemetery.

Pierce and the sheriff were stunned and unsure of what to do next. Most in Hardlyville had never acknowledged the existence of the She Devil but every soul in town knew of her and the horror she had inflicted on their village. They were simply too frightened to admit something so horrid could exist. Denial was the balm of the masses, if 257 souls, give or take a few, could constitute a mass.

Pierce and the sheriff debated whether they should share the news, face the reality, and celebrate her demise. Or would it be easier on the community psyche to just go on pretending that nothing so evil could ever exist, to bury the fear with the body, to leave the shadow lurking in the deep shade of past memory? It was a classic juxtaposition of fiction and reality, with blurred lines of intellectual demarcation.

"Which way would you sleep better at night over time?" Pierce wondered aloud.

She died a "Mother's Death," Vixen said, as simply as if Shakespeare had written it.

Pierce and Lettie had just shared the bizarre story from western North Carolina with her. Her response stunned them. Again she spoke with almost a hint of affection.

Lettie asked Vixen what she meant.

"Heartbreak. My Mother found that she loved me more than she loved herself, and had no place to go with it."

Pierce looked at Lettie with a *how does such wisdom flow* kind of glance.

Lettie tried to get Vixen to talk more about her reaction, fearing that she might be repressing something. She had wondered to herself whether the Evil One had abused Vixen while she had her. Had she hypnotized or brainwashed her?

Pierce looked at it exactly opposite. The Evil One had been touched by the power of Vixen's love. He didn't know what form or shape or words that might have taken, but Vixen loved her Mother and the She Devil had given in to it, if only enough to fracture the evil core and let a touch of affection seep in, almost like cleansing a sour well with a surge of spring water. The

Demon Lady couldn't reconcile her innate unrequited love of her daughter with the evil soul that possessed her. She couldn't bring herself to murder her daughter, so she killed herself instead. After all of those years of being in control, she lost it. To love.

Vixen understood. A Mother's Love. The strongest, most compelling earthly power of any. Beyond attraction. Beyond lust. Selfless. Instinctual. Vixen hoped she would feel it someday.

In the end, Pierce, Sheriff Sephus, and Lettie went public.

Pierce's lead editorial in the *Daily Hellbender* carried the banner "Evil Falls."

He began with the seemingly innocuous discovery of a female body with a mortal, self-inflicted knife wound. He then provided perspective, describing in detail each and every brutal act and murder the She Devil had perpetrated on the citizens of Hardlyville. From innocent float trippers, to Lucas Jones, to trackers and guards, to water supply, to bank robberies and kidnappings, and who knew what else, he laid it all out. And now, she was gone, dead gone, ding dong, hallelujah.

He summarized the historical context of her genetic connection to village founder Thomas Hardly, as recounted in the historic Rosebeam letters. Octavia Rosebeam had been the Devil Woman's birth mother by way of a brutal rape. Likewise, young Vixen, with the big yellow eyes, was her granddaughter, again by a rape of sorts, this time in reverse. He described father Lucas Jones's last stand against the Demon Lady in full graphic detail, leaving nothing to the imagination of the reader.

Pierce Arrow laid it all out for the village to ponder. There was no rug in town large enough to sweep this under.

The Evil One had existed. She had been real. Pretending she hadn't, and couldn't again, was self-delusional, a preemptive strike against fact and reason. To deny is naive. There is nothing so bad that it can't exist on this earth.

But "better angels" exist as well. Some wear them on coat sleeves daily, some carry them inside for times of grave need. Some don't know their hiding place. In this case, a better angel won the day.

The battle between good and evil has raged every day of humanity's existence, on levels we understand, and in dimensions we don't or won't. What is natural to some is supernatural to others. Where did this one fall on the spectrum? That was clearly in the eye of the beholder.

Pierce closed the most provocative editorial ever run in the *Daily Hellbender* with Vixen's "Mother's Death" synopsis: the Demon Lady had died from a broken heart, her mother's love deeper than self. If ever one could doubt that there are "better angels" lurking in every beating breast, the sacrifice of an evil self for a daughter's sake should dispel such a notion, Pierce concluded.

He intended his words to be grounding. It was to some. Discomforting to others.

GOINGS AND COMINGS

In addition to the shocking suicide of the Evil One, a few more ticks on the Hardlyville clock of time passed.

Ol' Dill went down swinging. He died with his boots on, with fur flying. Any metaphor would suffice. Tiny Taylor confirmed all of the above through a thin veil of tears. A slight smile also paid tribute to the old geezer she had come to adore. His spirit, his sense of adventure, and embrace of the impossible had lifted her out of a lifetime of mediocrity with men. Ol' Dill had fulfilled for Tiny Taylor the promise of a mutually giving relationship, keyed to respect, love, and lust. Despite the large gap in age between them.

They always pretended that they were just friends. A light touch or rapid blush passing quickly enough to avoid detection. But everyone in town knew differently. Most were even aware of the once a month Thursday night liaisons which grew to bi-weekly as Ol' Dill's time got short. He simply squeezed as much out of his late-eighty-years-old life as time and Tiny could accommodate.

Without an heir, he left the old family still on the outskirts of town to Tiny so she could expand her Greasy Spoons Grill and Bar offering. She had begun to cook with some of his more exotic concoctions, which often featured the homemade aphrodisiac, absinthe. Though the latter smelled worse than any standalone odor Tiny had ever sniffed—durian from Singapore came to mind—it blended mercifully and beautifully into Tiny's vast fried food offering. It was particularly tasty on battered wild turkey fried deep brown in carp oil. Between Booray Abdul's takeout additions to the menu and Ol' Dill's moonshine seasoning, Greasy Spoons became a destination for food snobs from around the country.

Pierce Arrow even got an old friend at the New York Times to run a piece on Spoons in the Sunday Travel Section. He regretted doing so immediately, as he could no longer get into the restaurant on most weekends.

Hardlyville's civic leader group eventually had to open the mothballed Donny Brook Inn to accommodate the influx of foodies. Some visitors would reserve blocks of rooms for several days in order to earn a seat at Spoons, which did not take reservations. Tiny felt that allowing someone to secure a spot at the expense of another without standing in line was undemocratic.

Recent Hardlyville High School graduate Pomp Peters was offered the chance to manage the Donny Brook Inn renewal and soon began to turn a tidy cash flow for city coffers.

By securing a permanent "still to table" source of product with Ol' Dill's demise, Tiny Taylor was able to assure a demanding public of a consistent otherworldly dining experience as well as commemorate her old friend and lover in a variety of dish offerings. Ol' Dill's Kick Ass Fried Frog Legs in White Lightning became the Spoon's signature dish.

Tiny Taylor would never forget Ol' Dill Thomas and she set out to assure that neither would the world of high cuisine.

Pastor Pat labored with words as he prepared for Ol' Dill's funeral.

What might he say that could possibly capture the essence of the man and his meaning? He finally settled on The Parable of the Wild Turkeys, a sermon he shared periodically with townsfolk, particularly when drunkenness, infidelity, and sexuality raised their horny heads, as they did from time to time, often in tandem.

Some people, mostly children of the sixties, blamed Richard Nixon for all subsequent ills in the world. Not Pastor Pat. He was sure it was the Wild Turkeys, plural.

The first Wild Turkey was the one you drank when you were out to get shit-faced drunk, the 101-proof bourbon gobbler. The second Wild Turkey was the sex-crazed male of the species whose annual spring mating ritual cast doubt on the presence of even the smallest of brains.

Pastor Pat's normal sermon gently pointed out through simple stories how much trouble a man could get into imbibing in and/or acting like a wild turkey. He would always begin by explaining how a parable looked and sounded, likening it to an Ozarkian Folk Tale with morals.

He adapted his signature message to Ol' Dill's demise in a kinder, gentler fashion, nearly proselytizing the old goat.

The gathered crowd, virtually all of Hardlyville, and a few outsiders who were addicted to Ol' Dill's finest, snored their approval. As his words fell on the usual deaf ears he sensed an urge to go further to honor his friend Dylan Thomas.

Gathering his black robes behind him, Pastor Pat suddenly leapt from the pulpit of Skunk Creek Church of Christ, cackling madly, fanning his robes up and back behind him, shimmering, undulating, gyrating as if possessed by a gobbler itself.

Tiny Taylor, though in deep mourning, couldn't contain herself and laughed out loud at the spectacle playing out in front of her. She wasn't sure what it had to do with dear Dill but it had certainly roused the crowd.

Famed local turkey caller Freddy Horntree grabbed a mouth call from his shirt pocket and began to turkey talk dirty back to Pastor Pat who redoubled his courting efforts, much to the surprise of Mabel Fortinator, his latest project in sexual re-habilitation, who was seated in the second row. She had never seen him in such a frenzy in their liaisons and, frankly, it ex-cited her.

Most in town knew that Mabel was Pastor Pat's latest slip from grace but that she was indeed needy after her soulless husband Sal had left her for the third time in his last three out of town sales trips for any female he could recruit to bed. He would follow their coupling by professing his undying love and slapping on a cheap engagement ring. This would insure con-tinuity of affection for the next round of calls in that particular locale.

He would separate from Mabel until he tired of his new playmates, then earn her forgiveness for his indiscretions by sharing all and promising never again.

Mabel at last finally had arrived at "never again" herself. She sought pastoral counseling and sustenance from Pastor Pat. His empathy and gentle ministrations led Mabel to won-der why she had waited so long. Most had long since forgiven the good Pastor for stepping up to help a devastated damsel in distress.

At least until this moment in Ol' Dill's celebration, when Pastor Pat advanced along the second row toward Mabel, head shaking, robes fanning up and down, arms flailing, spittle flying from his twitching tongue.

Rifleman, envisioning nothing but trouble coming like a freight train down the track, fired a round over Pastor Pat's head, stopping him in his tracks before he reached Mabel, and clipping the large gold cross on the communion table. Shaken from his self imposed trance, Pastor Pat quickly tucked his robes behind and retreated to the pulpit as Mable Fortinator swooned. At least Pastor Pat had accomplished his goal. All leaned forward to hear what he would say about Ol' Dill next, let alone try to explain his aberrant behavior.

Pastor Pat quickly asked for a word of prayer. As fever pitch settled around the hall, he wandered through the obligatory these and those for him and them.

And then he simply walked into the wooden confessional that Ol' Dill had constructed with deteriorated aging whiskey barrels from the still at Pastor Pat's request. He pulled shut the wire window, separating himself from the service and his congregants.

Suddenly Tiny Taylor understood and rose to address the murmuring crowd. They quieted quickly. She thanked Pastor Pat for his moving tribute to her dear friend's zest for the pageantry of life and love. She then complimented him on knowing when to quit, just as Ol' Dill had done. Her simple analysis of a bizarre funeral service put all at peace as she led them to Ol' Dill's final resting place in Hardlyville Cemetery, next Octavia Rosebeam's grave, and asked the pallbearers to gently place him in the ground. So there they would rest forever, the last remaining links from now back to the beginning, Hardlyville history interred and commemorated.

"Vintage Hardlyville" was all Pierce Arrow could think of to put in the next edition of the *Daily Hellbender*. Where else could a Catholic adornment provide refuge to a fallen

Protestant preacher in celebration of a life, long and well-lived. He wrote it, but would have to think about it if anyone asked for interpretation. As always, he was amazed at the village's ability to preserve yet re-invent itself, all in the same breath.

Ol' Dill's best friend, part time village jester and full time lover to the Sisters Sledge, passed shortly thereafter. Donald "Dinky" Doodle, aka The Donald, had earned his manhood the hard way. The ridicule, the whispering, the self-deprecating humor had given way to Ol' Dill's absinthe-based confidence booster and led him to a long and fruitful, if unofficial, union with the Sisters. He died between their ample and loving bodies, suffocated with affection, fully engulfed in their heart-stopping attentions. The official diagnosis was heart attack, but those who knew the trio well preferred the descriptive "heart embrace." He too died with a full smile on his face, and the village, beyond sadness at losing an irreplaceable sense of humor, celebrated rather than mourned.

Pastor Pat wouldn't even touch this one after escaping with his credibility, if not dignity, just weeks before.

To lose such legends and beloved denizens within days of each other was a stunner to most.

But, as with most of Hardlyville's storied history, the void would not last long. In this particular case, it was filled, almost eye for eye, tooth for tooth, life for loss.

Only Pierce Arrow and Lettie Jones could fully understand the magic of their new baby boy. As they calculated back to the probable moment of conception, there was only one excuse. Kokopelli. The hunchback dwarf of Hopi tradition had paid them a visit one clear, cold, moonlit night beneath a great Arch in the desert. They had danced the dance and heard his flute. And Peli they named him, younger brother to Lucas Jr., Vixen, and Mona, and sole male namesake to the Arrow name. Their house and hearts were full.

And while Sheriff Sephus Adonis and lovely Airreal had married later than most, it didn't take them long to catch up. Airreal was evidently pregnant within hours of their betrothal. Tiny Flambeau Adonis, named in honor of her mother's African heritage, was born nine months to the day after the knot was tied and vows exchanged. Ol' Dill had accused the Sheriff of having to get married. He passed within hours of Flambeau's arrival.

Jimmy returned to The Garden several times before resuming contact with Lucas. Their communication as always was a wordless transposition between two worlds.

Jimmy didn't want to pry but wondered where his cousin, at least in spirit, had been the last few visits. He saw Lucas's shoulders shrug as if no big deal and thought he picked up the human concept of vacation floating in the air. He had never seen Lucas's face on any of these encounters and this one was no different. Hard to tell whether he was serious or smirking behind the dichotomy of vacationing to get away from paradise.

He pondered the timing of Lucas's absence and its alignment with the Demon Lady's demise. He shared the implications of his hunch, that Lucas had a hand in it all, recalling Lucas's previous intimations that he couldn't leave his mansion. There were contradictions abounding. Lucas only shrugged.

Personally, Jimmy loved Pierce Arrow's "better angels" theory, for it gave so much hope to the future. Professionally, he wrestled with its reality. He had seen the Evil One at work. He sensed no angels, better or not, flying around her Medusa halo. Maybe it was just all over his head. Lucas was certainly not going to offer any help with clarification.

The thought that Lucas was somehow involved in her elimination fit better in Jimmy's good vs. evil concept of the world. Beyond this psychodrama crap of inner feelings struggling for higher or lower ground within.

Jimmy liked things pure and simple. Good things fight bad things, righteous beings battle evil witches for right and wrong outcomes. Maybe Lucas kicked her butt in an epic confrontation over control of their precious daughter Vixen. Maybe Lucas had stuck the long knife in the same place where the She Devil had shot him years before. This was justice in play. He tried that one on Lucas, again to no response.

Jimmy let Lucas know that he was glad the big guy was back, because Jimmy needed him. Lucas let slip that he was proud of Jimmy and the courage he had shown in bringing Vixen home. So how did he know about that if he had been on vacation? Again Jimmy wished he could see Lucas's face to go with the casual shrug.

COIN OF THE REALM

One early morning Jimmy was digging around in his favorite drawer for protection. We're not talking his precious Beretta in this instance. Sally had decreed no more kids. She had a girl and a boy and a good bit of her girlish figure, which she loved to taunt Jimmy with. She enjoyed his amorous advances more than ever and feared that too many pregnancies could cost her pounds and attention. She adored her Girl and her Lucas Jr. II, and she loved Jimmy dearly. The fact was, her love platter was full.

So Jimmy faithfully robed up whenever the opportunity presented. This particular one had resulted from a pre-dawn nuzzle followed by a quick and thorough pat down.

When Sally wanted to know what was taking so long Jimmy held up a couple of silver coins that had surfaced as he had rummaged around amongst broken fishing lures, old roach clips, and unused Trojans. They hadn't seen it or talked about it in years on the counsel of Pierce Arrow. And while it sucked seduction right out of the room, the silver orbs stirred memories and fixed attention.

Sally threw her nightie back on and Jimmy sat down next to her on the bed, handing his original find to her while stroking the one Cousin Lucas had flipped to him on a previous trip to the garden.

They were 1803 U.S. Treasury-minted silver dollars, according to Pierce Arrow, who with Lettie, were the only other living human beings to have seen one. Across one side was a skinny looking bird that looked kind of like a crossbred eagle and wild turkey. Had to be tails Jimmy reasoned because on the other side was an amply bosomed, long haired, beautiful lady. Definitely a head shot.

Jimmy had found one on their first visit to the garden and received the other one from Lucas. He had a sense that they were of significant historical and monetary value. He recalled Lettie tying them to the brutal murder of village founder Thomas Hardly in the late 1800s through some dude named Garth, but couldn't remember the details. He remembered Pierce Arrow specifically warning that if there were more, and he surmised there were, a mini version of the California Gold Rush would most certainly condemn the garden to extinction.

Jimmy wanted nothing to do with that and decided to think short term, offering to trade his to Sally for her nightgown. She bit on the deal and they picked up where they had left off before history had intervened. Jimmy made a mental note to revisit the silver dollars with Pierce Arrow but quickly lost it in the splendor of the immediate moment.

Paul Michael (Pomp) Peters was on top of the world. He had secured a full time job that he both enjoyed and was good at. That had been the parting advice from his high school Sex Ed and Diversity teacher Ms. Billious Bloom and he had followed that dream since graduating.

Pomp was now the permanent General Manager of the previously defunct Donny Brook Inn.

Pomp Peters had no interest in college. In fact he had little interest in anything beyond finding a way to lure his one and only love Uvi Abdul, Booray's baby sister, back to Hardlyville to earn her hand in marriage. They had met at Booray and Li'l Shooter's wedding, an unlikely merger of Bedouin and Hillbilly culture into a shivaree of unforgettable proportions. Both were young and innocent but smitten with each other immediately.

Uvi was pledged to another at an early age in her homeland of Lebanon. She was also expected to be delivered as a virgin. That was the custom and evidently there was a waiting line.

When Pomp heard through Uvi's brother Booray that she had forgotten about the virgin part, that her marriage had been annulled immediately after that fact was discovered on her wedding night, that she had been branded as a harlot reducing her market value and potential suitor pool substantially, and had cried to her parents constantly about missing her brother Booray in Hardlyville, his heart soared.

She had slapped the "Pomp" name on Paul Michael as a badge of affection and he had from that moment refused to answer to anything else. She had explained simply that it was the very first English word that came to mind when she saw him waving wildly to her from a welcoming crowd in Hardlyville.

Uvi's mother and father loved their daughter with all their heart and felt that her being ostracized was a silly miscarriage of tradition and justice. Yet she was indeed branded in her own country and would likely end up with a lesser husband because of it. They grieved over that and the potential for having a prick as a son-in-law.

Pomp passed a note through Booray to his parents asking if he might call on them in Beirut and seek the hand of their daughter in marriage. He of course needed to know from her whether even a hint of romance and affection existed before making such a trip and dramatic gesture. He was sure of his love for Uvi, had a good job with steady income, and promised them he would treat her kindly and produce many children.

Their welcoming response set wheels in motion that had never turned in Pomp's short life. He was a simple, if impulsive, young man, more literal than nuanced. His bold outreach had earned him an invitation to visit the Abdul family in Lebanon. He had no idea where that was or how one went about getting there. Booray told Pomp that he would have to get on an airplane. He had no idea what that was or how one went about getting on one.

Booray also suggested that Pomp be prepared to get married on the spot if indeed he asked for Uvi's hand. There had been enough embarrassment to the family to last a lifetime and Abdul Abdul and Kiri would likely want to seal the deal immediately for their beloved daughter before risking another failure. This would require at least a suit, dress shirt, tie, and shoes. Pomp knew what these were but didn't own any.

Pomp needed objective help, so he turned to his only mentor in town, Ms. Billious Bloom, for advice. As was her bent, Ms. Bloom took charge immediately.

She first had to ascertain whether Pomp was really serious. Marriage was a really big deal and Ms. Bloom was the local poster child for living a happy family life without one. Her questions to Pomp were direct and invasive. His answers stunned and inspired her. He clearly possessed a reverence and deep respect for Uvi, the basis for most successful marriages. He also thought she was beautiful, clever, intelligent, cute, and sexy. He had discovered all of this in the brief two weeks of her visit to Hardlyville.

The mention of the SEX word opened up a whole new line of inquiry. Ms. Bloom started with Pomp's own sex life. He simply said he had followed Ms. Bloom's formula of PMPS=B throughout high school which had resulted in 1.6 partners rounded up to 2, and had always used protection. He had sipped from the cup several times since but had found only physical not emotional comfort. Ms. Bloom nodded her approval, kind of amazed anyone had listened to her in Sex Ed class.

She moved on to Uvi. Pomp was comfortable with her not being a virgin, because that was the only attribute which had given him a shot at his true love. She had allowed him to feel her juvenile and fully-clothed breast on one occasion during their prior visit, and that was enough to send electric shock waves and earthquake tremors throughout his whole body. He had refused to wash the offending hand for weeks after, causing his Mother great concern as it took on the blackened cast of gangrene.

So Ms. Bloom quickly concluded that the love/sex quotient was in a range of proper balance. So she moved on to more mundane matters.

She explained that Lebanon was located in the Middle East, that there were wars going on all around it, but that it was safe to fly into on an airplane. She ordered Pomp one round trip ticket and a separate return for Uvi online and promised him she would get him to the airport and on the first flight. He would be on his own after that.

There also was the matter of a passport. Pomp didn't understand why any foreign country couldn't just look at him and conclude that he was Pomp Peters from Hardlyville, just like he said. Ms. Bloom explained that it simply wasn't that simple, with terrorists, madmen, secret agents, spies, and the like flooding the airways.

Pomp asked if he should pack heat given such dangerous circumstances and Ms. Bloom assured him that to do so would cause considerably more problems than risking it unarmed. She submitted an expedited passport application complete with passport photo. Pomp proudly paid for everything from his substantial savings account at the Bank of Hardlyville.

And then it was off to the big city for clothes. Ms. Bloom was an invaluable fashion consultant for Pomp. She convinced him to buy both a suit and a blue blazer with gray slacks to make it appear to Uvi's parents that he owned a substantial wardrobe. Pomp remembered wearing a borrowed Arab robe at Booray and Li'l Shooter's wedding and wondered if he needed to buy one of those. Ms. Bloom doubted that they could find one in the Ozarks and assured Pomp that the family would see to local custom.

Meanwhile Booray Abdul was beside himself at the thought of his baby sister Uvi moving to Hardlyville, even if it was as the betrothed of that lovable hayseed, Pomp Peters. He actually had taken a shine to Pomp, out of respect for his work ethic and unadulterated affection for Uvi. He assured Pomp that he would be welcomed and cared for by his family, that a true Bedouin wedding would be an experience he would never forget, and that his return to Hardlyville with Uvi as his bride would bless both them and the village.

He cautioned Pomp not to do the dirty deed with Uvi in his parents' home as that would tarnish their local standing. He suggested that they wait until they returned to Hardlyville, but if they couldn't, he might try the bathroom stall of the large 787. Booray had never done so, but had heard from several who had that sex at forty thousand feet was unforgettable. Pomp assured him they could wait.

When departure day came, it was Ms. Bloom at the wheel with Booray along to build confidence and offer emotional support on the way to the big city airport. As they waved goodbye from the security ropes, Booray slapped himself for forgetting to tell Pomp he would have to take off his shoes and belt and give up his wallet.

Pomp figured he was about to be robbed and took a swing at the offending TSA guard who responded with a kick to the groin that dropped Pomp on the spot. As agents rushed in, Booray and Billious screamed to be allowed to explain. They were admitted into a small interrogation room where Pomp was still gasping for air and clinging to his privates. Their intercession eventually worked and Pomp was allowed to race for his plane which was in the final boarding process.

Ms. Bloom and Booray Abdul could only hope that he made it in time.

Jimmy Jones paid what had become his quarterly visit to the garden for sustenance and grounding. The spirit of Lucas was his rock and his sounding board. He didn't bring Sally anymore because she was afraid she would get pregnant, if even from breathing the air. That meant that he was Cousin Lucas's only constant contact from what he ridiculed as civilization. Only Sally, Pierce Arrow, Sheriff Sephus, and the scuzbag Freeload Twins had ever set foot in this sacred spot, and the latter two would never visit again.

As Jimmy slipped into the dimly lit space, his eye caught two things in the water. First, and of great relief, was the presence of at least two juvenile hellbenders, flopping along behind their mother, peace restored to their surroundings. The second was more disruptive to the pristine spring water. It glinted in a dull kind of way, and tracked upstream to another, then another unnatural spot of color.

Jimmy reached down and pulled three of the silver dollar things from the water. He knew they had to be of the same vintage.

As he looked further upstream he saw more subtle sparkles and followed them to trails end, pocketing more than twenty along the way. He looked high and low for the source but saw nothing of note until a slight indentation in the rock wall caught his eye. He plunged his hand in without thinking and was rewarded with a prick and two fang holes.

Holy shit he murmured to no one in particular, realizing that he had been struck by a snake. The bite began to swell immediately and pain him greatly. He stuck the hand in cold spring water but realized that would offer only temporary relief. He needed to find Lucas fast.

As he turned into the narrow passage and followed the feeder spring around the tight corner he breathed a sigh of relief. There sat Lucas, back facing as always, flipping a coin. He screamed in pain as the snake bite took on an ugly color and throbbed with each step he took.

Lucas communicated that he should pull near. He reached behind his back to grab Jimmy's hand and squeezed it tightly before dipping into the healing waters. Pain and swelling vanished in an instant and the bite holes closed. Jimmy's hand was its old self and Lucas had probably saved his life.

Jimmy and Lucas exchanged thoughts about what his discovery might mean. First, it was likely that Jimmy had found the mother lode of silver dollars. Second, at least one or more poisonous snakes, probably copperheads, stood watch over the cache of coin. Third, it was likely that whatever bag or container that contained the old coins had finally lost its holding power and capacity. Finally, as more coins leaked out it was possible that some might make it out of the garden through natural outlets; a reveal that could prove disastrous.

Jimmy looked to Lucas for advice. Lucas nodded to a large rock in the spring and suggested that Jimmy jam it in the hole from which the old coins had leaked. He cautioned Jimmy to watch out for the guardian reptiles, and even pen them within if possible.

Lucas then turned to Jimmy for the first time in their many meetings. His face glowed with rapture and there were no signs of the entry wound that had taken his life. Jimmy could only sob and reach for his best friend ever. Lucas backed away with a gentle smile and some sort of transmission that said "off limits." He promised that Jimmy would understand some day but he hoped not soon. Such was out of the realm of his relevance.

Lucas confirmed that he would be here forever, for Jimmy, for Hardlyville, and to safeguard the grand silver dollar reserve account that would be the financial safety net for Hardlyville into eternity. He promised Jimmy he would check on the subterranean vault which housed the coins periodically.

Jimmy asked Lucas if he ever ran into Ol' Dill or Dinky Doodle among others.

Lucas just smiled that radiant smile and communicated nothing beyond it.

Jimmy bade Lucas goodbye, climbed out of the Garden with two perfectly functioning hands and twenty silver dollars, and headed straight to Pierce Arrow at the *Daily Hellbender*.

He shared with Pierce his discovery of more of the antique silver coins and the likelihood that their hiding place was now secure and protected. He added "guarded by Lucas," as well.

Pierce liked the idea of a hidden cache of monetary reserves securing Hardlyville's financial future, kind their own Federal Reserve Bank. He cautioned about the risk of inflation if the Hardlyville Fed were to unleash such liquidity into the local economy but wondered whether introducing a few of the valuable coins into the marketplace during hard times might stimulate local spending and speed recovery. Jimmy didn't have a clue what Pierce was bouncing back and forth in his self-contained conversation. Pierce Arrow blamed it on a Brit named Keynes. Pierce said he was in over his head and told Jimmy it was time to bring in someone who understood monetary policy. While it meant adding another to the small list with knowledge of the garden, Banker Jamin was totally trustworthy, brilliant, and understood financial matters. They headed immediately for the Bank of Hardlyville.

When Pierce advised Banker Jamin that he had just been elected Chairman of the Hardlyville Fed, even the shy, normally humorless and speechless country banker laughed out loud. When they explained what they meant he became speechless again, and rang for Captain Happy to join them for interpretive purposes. Not another insider moaned Jimmy.

Two hours and a full explanation later, Banker Jamin had formally established the Hardlyville Fed account at Bank of Hardlyville with a zero balance. He, Pierce Arrow, and Jimmy Jones were listed as sole signatories, with two of the three signatures required for withdrawal. Each had a designated heir in case of death, again subject to the approval of the other two. While it was unlikely the account would need to be funded and tapped, it was vital to have a credible process in place to access funds if needed.

Banker Jamin wasn't sure what he, or Captain Happy, would explain to the bank regulators. How could they begin to grasp the concept of a fully-funded, subterranean piggy bank, guarded by poisonous snakes and a dead man, which would serve as stimulus to the local economy in times of economic need? How could he convince them that he had never seen the Village of Hardlyville's liquid reserves but knew them to be real and accessible? He couldn't.

So he would simply advise them that the zero balance Hardlyville Fed Account was just that. Nothing. An attempt at humor which made the townsfolk chuckle. Nothing more. Nothing less. Hopefully they would simply write it off as a bunch of local hayseeds playing jokes on one another. What else could they do?

HARDLY YOGA

"Om . . . Om . . . Om . . . Shanti, Shanti, Shanti," Uvi began her evening meditation. Despite her yogi master status and five-hundred-hour teaching credentials, she was struggling for focus and inner peace this night. Her dear Pomp was on his way to wed and would arrive about midnight. Her life was about to change forever.

Pomp had never been more embarrassed in his life. From the beginning, this trip had been a disaster. From getting kicked in the privates by a security guard before he even set foot on an airplane, to having to beg on his knees at the gate for the aircraft door to be re-opened, to the serious thunderstorm the plane took off into which caused him to vomit all over his new clothes, to peeing his pants because they wouldn't turn off the seat belt sign due to severe turbulence, it had been an unmitigated disaster. And this only sixty minutes into a twenty-plus-hour flight.

Pomp was miserable, he was embarrassed, and he stunk. He might as well just go ahead and shit his drawers to complete the misery equation.

At the hub for international destinations, he had a two hour layover and tried to clean up. Unfortunately one of the patrons in the men's room went screaming for help when he removed all of his clothes and began to wash them by hand in the sink. The intervening security officer assured Pomp it was illegal to run around naked in any part of the airport, including rest rooms. He ordered Pomp to fully reclothe immediately or face charges. Pomp promptly put every wet, hand-soapy article of clothing back on and resumed waiting for his flight to Beirut via London.

Over the next twenty hours, Pomp was shunned, ridiculed, threatened, and generally dehumanized. His clothes began to dry three quarters of the way across the Atlantic. That was before another bout of plane-tossing turbulence got him going again. This time was better because he hadn't eaten anything since leaving Hardlyville. Nothing came up, but his loud dry heaves left about a quarter of the rear section cringing in dreaded anticipation.

The layover at Heathrow International in London was memorable only in the sense that he met a Bobby. Pomp Peters had no idea who the guy in the funny outfit was when he approached, but put on his best smile and manners. He then had no idea what the guy in the funny outfit was saying in a language he had never heard before. "Don't you understand English," finally registered and Pomp responded with a vigorous nod in the affirmative. It seemed that a fellow traveler in the terminal had observed Pomp urinating in a potted plant in the concourse. Pomp nodded and began to explain that he had fallen asleep for the first time since beginning his journey and had awakened with an urgent need to bleed the lizard, smiling at his attempts at levity. "I just couldn't wait to look around for a toilet so I did what I always do at home," Pomp confirmed. He added that his sweetie was "waiting for him in Beirut, Lebanon, and that he just couldn't afford to pee himself again."

Now it was the Bobby who was looking for a translator. When he could find none, he simply shook his head at Pomp and warned him that a second offense would land him in the "pound." Pomp took this as a verb and threat of bodily harm from a weenie in a funny round hat. He prepared to defend himself.

As the Bobby drew his nightstick, a kindly old gentleman identifying himself as a fellow traveler from the American Midwest quickly inserted himself between the potential antagonists and shared with the Bobby several of the details of Pomp's disastrous trip that he had observed, how the poor boy had never been out of the hayseed Ozarks, and that he didn't understand the nuances of international travel. He begged forgiveness on Pomp's behalf and, to Pomp's confusion, promised to take him under his wing for the remainder of the journey. "I will not let him get into any more trouble, kind sir," the gentleman promised with an earnestness that carried the day. With a loud and frustrated "hrumph," the Bobby holstered his nightstick and marched away.

The elderly gentleman upheld his end of the deal through re-boarding, though Pomp Peters could never figure out what that meant and how it related to some funny-looking and somewhat rude dude named Bobby. All he could do was say "thank you."

Pomp's adrenaline kicked in as they approached Beirut-Rafic Hariri International Airport. He was going to meet his true love and ask for her hand in marriage. He had been promised that all parties would consent. All he could think of were the dark flashing eyes and the smile that seemed to dance from several years back. They were young but he knew in his heart this would work.

Tires squealed on the tarmac and suddenly he heard a loud pop. The airliner swerved to the left and skidded off the runway, coming to rest with a beautiful ocean front view out Pomp's window. He had never seen anything so spectacular, at least until he would gaze in Uvi's eyes in a few moments, which became a few hours. He was numb to the sirens of emergency vehicles rushing to the plane and the cries and wails of frightened passengers. He could only smile.

This got security's attention again and earned him a formal pat down.

A visit to the men's room as he waited to clear customs finally wiped the smile off his face. He looked like shit, like roadkill, like death had visited and lost interest. He smelled even worse. All he could do was act pitiful, which would not be difficult.

Twenty-six hours, one crash landing which he later learned was either the result of a blown tire or a terrorist bullet, and two sink baths after leaving Hardlyville for the first time in his life, he peered shyly into the airport lobby. And there she was, in a flowing red tunic, fresh flowers in her hair, smiling broadly at his pitiful countenance. Her parents gasped their shock as she raced to embrace without pause. Her hug settled all scores and lit the poor country boy up like a roman candle.

Later in their elegant town home, apologies complete, Pomp bid goodnight to all and headed off to his room for a bath and sleep. As he lay in a semi-conscious state soaking in warm water, drifting in and out of awareness, he felt a small hand begin to soap his body. All over.

Uvi cleaned him, toweled him off, led him to bed, and loved him.

It was too late to stop when he remembered what Booray had warned him about.

He awoke to another tender touch on his cheek and a steaming cup of jasmine tea in the other tiny hand. He couldn't remember her leaving during the night. Maybe it had just been a dream. Their encore quelled that rumor. Pomp had never felt so close to anyone in his life.

He approached Uvi's father in his study to pop the question. Would he and his wife honor Pomp Peters with the hand of their youngest daughter? Abdul Abdul nodded their assent and inquired as to what came with the offer. Pomp wasn't sure what he was looking for, but again promised happiness, financial security, and many babies. Abdul Abdul shook his head in the negative.

Pomp then recalled that Booray told him in passing that Abdul Abdul had offered Rifleman and Steele a camel as their wedding present. He suggested that maybe he could shoot a black bear on their next visit to Hardlyville, provide a feast of black bear stew, and pay for a taxidermist to stuff the poor bugger for shipment to their home in Lebanon. Abdul Abdul liked this idea for it would give him a genuine Ozarkian talking piece for his study, which was where most of his friends and customers called on him. He offered his formal approval and urged Pomp to be gentle with his daughter on their wedding night, implying that they wouldn't have to wait until they got home as warned by Booray. Since they had already not waited, Pomp felt cleared for more passion and joy.

It was then on to Uvi to seek her "yes." She spoke of the love she had held for him since they first met, of the constant throb his teenage touch on her breast had left, and with admiration of his tenderness as a lover. He apologized for his lack of experience but she assured him that her abundance of the same would more than offset.

She then said there was but one condition on her acceptance of his kind offer. She must have a yoga studio of her own in Hardlyville.

He asked her to spell it for him, acknowledging that this was a new concept for him. He was sure it would not be a problem but he did need to understand what this yoga thing was before he could promise anything.

Two hours later with his mind whirring around chakras, pakimama, flying squirrel and lizard positions, and cactus juice stimuli he promised to build Uvi her own studio in the Donny Brook Inn, complete with a cast of snobbish foodies from back east who would surely appreciate the sophistication of her offering.

Since all this talk of strange and unusual poses which Uvi demonstrated flawlessly along the way had aroused the proposer and proposed to, a brief love-in was required before Uvi's final yes.

"Namaste," she whispered to him before they reclothed.

Pomp hadn't a clue what that meant but he knew he wanted some more of this Namaste.

The next week of celebrations and traditions flew by. Pomp had trouble recovering from jet lag because most of his sleeping time was used for Namaste. When Uvi tried to explain what it meant, he nodded vigorously that he got it.

The wedding ceremony itself lasted three days and probably would have carried beyond if the date on their plane ticket hadn't brought closure. Abdul Abdul and Kiri promised to come visit as soon as they had reason to, namely a grandbaby, and Pomp promised them a quick invitation, not aware that the process was already underway. Uvi's idea of birth control with Pomp was—none. She loved Pomp and wanted to carry his child. She was well on her way there when they boarded the jet for her new home.

Most of Hardlyville was out to meet the newlyweds at the city limits. Booray and Li'l Shooter picked them up and snickered at the mess on Pomp's new shirt. Uvi had sponge bathed him after each violent eruption, but the sour odor was beyond expunging. She held him so closely that the scent of her sweet perfume mingling with the putrid odor of his stale vomit sent Booray barfing out the driver's window.

Neither cared. Pomp only knew that he never wanted to board a plane again.

It was the same old routine. The mayor gave an inane welcoming speech, something about refugees of foreign wars were always welcome in Hardlyville. Rifleman fired round after round skyward. Sheriff Sephus led the motorcade past cheering crowds through the middle of town to Pomp's modest cabin beyond. Diversity in Hardlyville and the baby in Uvi's belly continued to grow.

The next morning, Pomp proudly showed Uvi around his new domain of authority, The Donny Brook Inn. She quickly saw where the yoga studio should be—first floor, southeast corner, morning sunlight. It would require construction and the sacrifice of two first floor lodging rooms which Pomp assured her could work. He would have to get Banker Jamin's approval, but figured the lure of a construction loan and Uvi's charm would carry the day.

Pomp wondered what she would name her studio. Her customer base would consist principally of guests, many from larger cities around the country, who came to Hardlyville to dine at "Spoons" as it had evolved, leaving "Greasy" and "Grill and Bar" behind. Everything pointed to a somewhat sophisticated audience deserving of a provocative branding statement.

Uvi doubted that Hardlyville Yoga would cut it.

She did announce that if they were going to sacrifice two rooms she must make love to Pomp in each of them to assure a succession of good fortune. The thought of more Namaste thrilled Pomp.

And, *Hardly Yoga* had a nice ring to it.

A Pig in a Poke

His hands trembled when he saw the envelope while sorting his daily outgoing mail.

Postmaster Bond's mind flashed back to the day of the Big Pig flood. His senses were flooded with memories of the smell, the filth, the solid waste, the bloated carcasses. He recalled standing on a wooden bench, just above the fouled waters that had seeped into the old post office, hoisting his mail bag above his head, and wondering how the mail would get through that day. He guessed he would have to cancel for only the second time in his storied run as Hardlyville's Postmaster General. He had stood on that bench for almost twenty four hours, leaning into the building for a nap or two, mailbag wedged between his body and the wall, trying to breathe through the fetid air, waiting for water and waste to recede. It was the most difficult time in his life. And as later accorded by his community, the most heroic.

He read the mailing address again:

> The Village of Old Chatham Planning and Zoning Commission

Old Chatham, New York

re: the matter of Pornopoly Rosebeam's estate

But that's not what made him cringe.

The Hardlyville return address bore the corporate name of Fine Swine Farms located at #2 New Pig Road, neither of which Postmaster Bond had ever heard of, though the handwriting looked vaguely familiar? "What the hell is going on?" he screamed to no one in particular? "Have the bastards snuck in the back door again?"

Postmaster Bond ran to Sheriff Sephus Adonis's office in full-scale-panic mode. When the sheriff saw him running up Main Street, waving the envelope wildly, he assumed anthrax or some similar plague had been mailed to Hardlyville and locked his office door. Postmaster Bond begged to be let in, and the sheriff finally relented after assurances that he would not be fatally infected. In fact, Postmaster Bond opined that what he held in his hand was even worse.

It didn't take long for the sheriff and Postmaster Bond to concoct a scenario in which someone was again trying to sneak large herds of porkers back into the Skunk Creek valley, despite the presidential designation of the Skunk Creek Watershed National Refuge which prohibited large scale animal CAFOs into perpetuity.

A quick call declaring emergency status to Pierce Arrow had him running to the sheriff's office soon thereafter. Pierce's blood was boiling before he even made it past the return address. Pierce pronounced that Fine Swine Farms was an oxymoron in itself. Postmaster Bond knew the meaning of the second half of that big word and concluded that Pierce Arrow was hurling an insult at him. He threw the letter on Pierce's lap and stormed out of the sheriff's office.

Suddenly Pierce Arrow began to smile. He recognized the long, flowing strokes of an old-style fountain pen. He knew where to go to solve this mystery and asked Sheriff Sephus Adonis to accompany him to Billious Bloom's office at the Rosebeam Foundation immediately.

Along the way, Pierce couldn't help but think back to the last time pig panic had gripped the community, not many months prior. It caused him to laugh now. Not then.

An elaborately disguised corporate farmer from Iowa had approached banker Jamin to see if he had any repossessed farm land for sale. He posed as a retired executive seeking to fulfill a dream from his childhood in retirement. He had always wanted to be a farmer.

Banker Jamin didn't. Generally, everyone in town repaid their bank loans on schedule. For those struggling, banker Jamin would work out alternative amortizations and temporary interest rate relief. He had rarely lost a penny lent to a Hardlyvillain.

He referred the gentleman to Jimmy Jones who was always wheeling and dealing in farm land these days, and Jimmy ended up selling him thirty acres with a small farm house due west of town at a premium price.

Jimmy didn't think much more about it until he and several of his neighbors received notice through the mail that Dinkleberry Farms of Iowa would be filing a request for a large scale piggery permit with the state natural resource agency. The notice continued that the permit would seek approval for establishing a swine breeding operation for twenty thousand pigs on the thirty acres recently purchased from one Jimmy Jones.

"This is the same damn regulatory path the state used to approve that Skunk Creek Ranch permit several years back," lamented Jimmy to wife Sally, "without due process, without environmental impact analysis, without Hardlyvillains even being aware of the project." It had all been done behind closed doors and in the shadow of dollar bills, Jimmy recalled, agency approval sanctioned in the end by the state authority on clean water, the State Oversight Board (SOB.) The Big Pig Flood that devastated Skunk Creek and Hardlyville followed shortly thereafter and thankfully led to the establishment of the Skunk Creek Watershed National Refuge to prevent forever a similar atrocity. "And here they are at it again," moaned Jimmy, with himself as principal accomplice.

The notice confirmed that all waste would be handled by third party contractors well versed in every aspect of managing pig shit. Dinkleberry Farms was simply being a good citizen by advising its new neighbors that they had nothing to worry about.

And by the way, the notice concluded, the two barns envisioned to hold all these pigs and all this waste would be positioned just to the west of the precise boundary established by the National Refuge and would not infringe on the community's precious Skunk Creek watershed.

Jimmy Jones was beside himself. He had been conned by the "gentleman" retiree into selling his property to an Iowa corporate farm. No wonder he was willing to pay a little more. Jimmy ran straight to Pierce Arrow.

Pierce was stunned by the brazen arrogance of the notice. "What can we do?" Jimmy had asked. Pierce didn't know but would find out as soon as he could get to the state capital and meet with staff members of the state natural resource agency.

A week later Pierce presided over a town hall meeting in the gym at Hardlyville High School. He explained with anger and sadness what he had discovered.

First of all, there was not much the citizens of Hardlyville could do to stop the piggery. The state had very few restrictions on the location, size, financial viability, waste discharge, site design, construction plans, or general impact on local waters of confined animal feeding operations (CAFOs). Big Pork had seen to that. Their lobbyists had key state politicians in their back pockets, or better yet, the latter had their hands in the formers' wallets.

Skunk Creek and Hardlyville had so far been spared the invasion of corporate refugees from Iowa and Illinois by its National Refuge designation. Other state counties and waterways hadn't. Cheap land and lax regulations were honey to the bees, nectar to the corporate sucklings fleeing high prices and tightening rules. Only so many fouled water tables, cancer deaths related to nitrate poisoning, and putrid smell days could be tolerated in the name of economic development before victims fought back and regulations were tightened. This had happened with increasing frequency in adjoining states.

Pierce Arrow kicked himself for not noticing what was going on around him, for not writing about it in the *Daily Hellbender*, for nestling in the Skunk Creek Watershed National Refuge cocoon, oblivious to the encircling threat. He had assumed that they were protected forever by presidential decree. He had discovered instead that they had been surrounded by the scourge and that the hogs of hell were at the gates of their fortress.

There was only one hope in the bleak regulatory landscape and it was a forlorn one, the State Oversight Board. It was the final stamp of state approval, if needed, in the case of opposition. The very same entity that had provided the final "yes" for Skunk Creek Ranch.

He called on his fellow Hardlyvillains to stand up to this deceitful effort to sneak in the back door of their sanctuary. They would start Friends of the Skunk (FOTS), hire an attorney he had met in the state capital, and fight Dinkleberry Farms to the death.

Jimmy Jones was so incensed that he took to the small stage with one of daughter Girl Jones's old piglet dolls and burned it in effigy.

And stand up they did. As expected, the state natural resource agency granted the permit. There was nothing else they could do as there were few regulations for them to enforce. FOTS's attorney then lodged a formal appeal with the state appeals board, which upheld the permit, because there was nothing else they could do either.

This put the final decision in the hands of the SOB. Pierce marveled at how the state's clean water commission could be brought into the butt end of the process rather than at the beginning, but it seemed to fit with everything else that was going on.

A sense of doom enveloped the village. This was the same SOB that had permitted Skunk Creek Ranch years before. This was the same SOB whose Chairman had gone to jail for accepting bribes and money laundering. This was the same SOB which regularly rolled over for corporate interests in the name of jobs which rarely materialized and political donations which escalated with each successful permit issued.

Or, as Pierce had later discovered, maybe it wasn't.

As Hardlyvillains stewed, FOTS rattled cages, and their attorney adopted any stalling tactic he could dream up, a funny thing was going on at SOB. It had begun with the appointment of several commissioners who took their charge to protect the waters of the state seriously. It grew as they shared concerns about the expansion of CAFOs in the Wild-Wild-west regulatory environment evolving in their state. It solidified in their focus on the case of Dinkleberry Farms v. FOTS.

No one at SOB seemed against CAFOs per se—in an appropriate location, of scalable size, with proper environmental impact studies, defined waste disposal and water sourcing plans, and proof of financial wherewithal beyond a shell corporation.

The very edge of the Skunk Creek Watershed National Refuge, twenty thousand smelly porkers on thirty acres, a five-thousand-dollar capital injection into a paper corporate entity, and the lack of any studies or plans did not meet several commissioners sniff tests of appropriate, scalable, proper, defined, or provable.

In fact, as Pierce Arrow learned later, three of five commissioners stated their intentions to vote to revoke the permit in private session. They knew it would cause a firestorm to conclude that their own mother state agency had erred in issuing the permit in the first place and that they were invoking a higher power, protecting the waters of their state, over following the letters of the law, of which there were few. They had concluded that there was nothing about Dinkleberry Farms's proposed CAFO that was good for the waters of the state. These three would vote their conscience and let the pieces fall where they may.

Their decision to revoke would likely send the case into the court system, beyond the corruptibility of the legislative process, and potentially subject to higher standards evolving in other courts around the country.

It would also make a statement that state lands and waters were not the happy hunting grounds for corporate CAFOs that they were perceived to be. Kind of a "keep your shit in your own back yard and send your chops and ribs if you want our business" message.

Ironically, two days before the earthshaking vote was to take place, FOTS's attorney convinced a circuit court judge to block the vote on grounds that several of the commissioners had toured a pig CAFO and were permanently corrupted by the propaganda of its owners. That the commissioners had done so that they might better understand how a CAFO operated and add public credibility to their stand against this one was never considered. "Improper conduct" FOTS's attorney termed it, ringing up billable hours faster than a roadrunner crossing a glade. "Eye opening and further reinforcing my opposition to the permit," countered one commissioner in the aftermath.

"Talk about snatching defeat from the jaws of victory," Pierce later laughed to Lettie. "Here we were about to win a very important victory and we were suing to put off the very decision we were seeking. What a mixed up jumble of shared opposition." Pierce laughed again. He remembered it all so well. And yet no one could talk in the heat of battle. Gag orders prevailed amidst commission members while the FOTS attorney continued billing by the hour.

Fortunately the misaligned combatants prevailed in the end. Commissioners were forgiven their naiveté rather than penalized for "improper conduct," by an appeals court. The citizens of Hardlyville finally tired of the FOTS attorney's delaying tactics and dismissed him. The final straw was when he talked another circuit judge into recusing the entire SOB, both supporters and detractors, for conduct unbecoming volunteer public servants. Even Pierce, who served as chair of FOTS, gagged on that one.

In the end, the SOB commissioners voted their conscience over the objections of corporate attorneys and lobbyists and rejected the permit by a vote of three to two, sending the warring parties to court at the expense of the corporate farm where the case died a slow, drawn out death, beyond bribes, beyond clandestine contributions.

State legislators beholden to Big Pork immediately passed legislation eliminating the historical requirement for citizen representation on the State Oversight Board. "Citizens in charge of protecting our states' waters?" had thundered one legislator who had lots of Big Pork money in his pocket. And Big Chicken for that matter. "What do citizens know about jobs and economic development? What do they know about who puts food on their table and wages in their pockets?"

The governor finally vetoed the last minute add-on amendment to a legitimate bill, and the veto withstood an attempted override.

"State politics at its grossest level," observed Pierce to Lettie in disgust. Both could only shake their heads as they ate their Iowa bred and butchered pork chops.

Most importantly, there were no sows breeding on the outskirts of Hardlyville. It had been a happy ending to a convoluted fiasco, and Hardlyville had ultimately prevailed. A stand had been taken and a battle won. The war would continue.

Pierce Arrow reveled in the memory as he knocked on Bilious Bloom's office door. He might have to write all this down some day.

Fact, in truth, can sometimes be stranger than fiction, he mused.

Ms. Bloom was indeed in and stunned to see her letter in Pierce's hand. She needed for that letter to be delivered immediately in the interest of selling a piece of property willed to Ms. Rosebeam by her Aunt Pornopoly just outside of NYC. Ms. Rosebeam had lived with her Aunt while studying at the prestigious Center for Latin Studies in her youth. Aunt Pornopoly had held her hand and heart as she had recovered from a brutal rape, and subsequent abandoning of the result at moment of childbirth to a foster parent. Ms. Rosebeam had returned to live out her life teaching Latin in Hardlyville but never forgot her aunt's many kindnesses and corresponded with her frequently, even visiting on occasion. The property left to Ms. Rosebeam and her estate sealed their bond.

Billious explained that the letter was all part of a ruse to convince a greedy planning and zoning commission in Old Chatham, NY, where the property was located, that indeed the estate of heir Octavia Rosebeam, deceased, was into large scale pig farming. Unless they rezoned the property in question to residential, Fine Swine would expand its corporate farming business to their fine community.

Old Chatham P & Z wanted to acquire Aunt Pornopoly's property at sub-market rates due to its current agricultural land status and convert it into a swank gated community adjoining Old Chatham Country Club, further benefiting the community's rich and famous. They would change the zoning only after acquisition. It was a nefarious and self-serving plan. As Executive Director of the Rosebeam Foundation, the Rosebeam estate's sole beneficiary, it was Ms. Bloom's fiduciary responsibility to assure a highest and best sales value to further expand the foundation's endowment.

Pierce and the sheriff nodded their approval of the scheme and marveled at Ms. Bloom's ingenuity. Even they knew that upstate New York residential property would carry value in many multiples above farmland. They quickly returned to Postmaster Bond with an explanation which relieved his fears and expedited handling of Fine Swine's letter.

Each marveled in their own way at the deep wounds and fragile scabs which remained from the Big Pig Flood. It had almost destroyed their village and the precious waters of Skunk Creek that had always run alongside her. All agreed it was important for subsequent generations to inherit that sense of panic and near-tragedy if they were to stand tall in defense of their water legacy.

After Ms. Bloom's successful strategy added hundreds of thousands of dollars to the Rosebeam endowment instead of just thousands—and with her permission—Pierce Arrow editorialized in the *Daily Hellbender* about the need for eternal vigilance over Skunk Creek, the literal and historical lifeblood of an always vulnerable village and way of life.

A Float Trip

Twenty years have passed in a wink. As keeper of this narrative from Thomas Hardly to now it will soon to be time to sign off. But, not quite yet. I have one good float trip left in me . . .

Skunk Creek glistened in the spring sun. Red bud peaked at near psychedelic and dogwood splattered hints of white amidst a greening canvas. Clumps of dainty, blue flowers popped up from new grass and a few white ones followed. Tan stands of morel mushrooms broke through the scattered branch-covered forest floor. Turkey gobbled, barred owls hooted, and doe wandered unafraid with fawns at their side. Great blue heron nested high in the sycamores. Spring in the Ozarks is like no other time, nor place. It grounds, it inspires, and it launches cycles of life that never cease.

Jimmy Jones gathered his troupe for final instructions. They would set out to float Skunk Creek in its entirety over the course of the next eight or nine days, depending on rain and water. From headwaters to the big water below, stopping briefly in Hardlyville mid-course to re-provision.

"They" would be, in birth order (with Mother), Otis Hendricks (Sabrina), Lucas Jones, Jr. (Lettie), Vixen (Lettie), Girl Jones (Sally), Mona Arrow (Lettie), Lucas Jones, Jr., II (Sally), Abi Abdul (Li'l Shooter), Pres Bloom (Billious), Peli Arrow (Lettie) and Flambeau Adonis (Airreal.)

Other young ones had come and gone along the way, but this was the core lineage, the next generation, the spring buds of the village. Rifleman would join Jimmy in the john boat, which would be filled to the brim with beer, ice, and other forms of nourishment.

Vixen was the only living blood relative of town founder Thomas Hardly and wife Petunia, by way of Hardlita Rosebeam, Octavia Rosebeam, and Lucas Jones and an Evil Lady with piercing yellow eyes. All were long gone including, most thankfully, the latter.

Vixen was engaged to be married to Pres Bloom, who had just been elected the youngest mayor in the history of Hardlyville.

Some thought he had higher political ambitions. She was simply the sweetest, kindest soul in the heart of the Ozarks.

That there were two Lucas Jones, Jrs. spoke to the deep affection most held for the memory of the town hero himself, the one who died at the hands of the Evil One, defending the village and its children to his last breath. Lettie, his first wife, claimed initial naming rights, but graciously allowed Jimmy Jones, his cousin and best friend, to copycat. Young Lucas and L.J. were, naturally, best of friends too.

Much had changed over the past twenty years. Water supply more than water quality had begun to dominate regional water concerns.

Skunk Creek still flowed fast and pure, as did its tributaries, including Swine Branch from which the disastrous Big Pig Flood of decades past had sourced. Of course, that disaster resulted from large scale industrial farming in a watershed that should never have happened. The Skunk Creek Watershed National Refuge designation would protect from such idiocy far into the future.

Just four hundred miles to the west, the water table from which wells supported life was drained and dry, and most residents had moved east. Scrub foliage and badlands had crept over time into the very edge of the Ozarks. Tornados and other weather extremes had swept away life and ground cover. Most blamed it on something called global warming, but die-hard property rights folk named it "California Swarming." And, indeed, as California had dried to a bone and transitioned into harsh desert, many had fled back to the lands they had abandoned for gold rushes and sunny beaches centuries earlier. This influx of migrants, many of whom had lost their fortunes when mansions couldn't find enough water to prime toilet flushes or source a shower, crowded into small cities and towns, overwhelming services and cultures, and driving up surrounding land prices to near prior-West-Coast levels. They wanted water and the Missouri and Arkansas Ozarks still had it in great abundance. Family farmers could not afford not to sell their land for quick riches. They soon moved north for access to privacy and water resources they had previously taken for granted.

Colorado's subsequent demise fueled further encroachment. The western half of the United States had become a great desert moonscape, unable to support much beyond lizards and rattlesnakes, which were also at risk of extinction due to loss of rodent food supply.

A relatively stable high pressure weather ridge had generally protected the Ozarks from extremes with a few exceptions. Most notably was the seventy-eight inches of snow that fell on Hardlyville and surrounds during one winter week, several years back. Once again, the Hardlyville birth rate soared and assured that the new generation of Hardlyvillains would leave their mark beyond themselves.

Hardlyville itself was spared the epic land rush and accompanying price inflation. City mothers and fathers wisely agreed that under no circumstances would any property be sold to outsiders. Straight and simple. If you lived in Hardlyville and you died, your kinfolk took your property or the community ponied up to buy it, at traditional—not inflated—prices. Nothing was ever put to writing, but the tacit agreement held. Hardlyville had sold out once and would never do so again. It was the grand lesson of Donny Brook. The history, the name, the village would live on.

And on this bright spring day, with Skunk Creek at full throttle, five canoes and a john boat would put in to celebrate and close a number of circles.

Jimmy Jones was now a community elder statesman. Along with Booray Abdul, Billious Bloom, Rifleman, and Steele.

Ol' Dill, Dinky Doodle, and Doc Karst were long gone. Their respective ladies survived as an old wives club. Village lore had it that Tiny Taylor, the Sisters Sledge, and Lois had sexed the old goats to death. This was counted as the happiest of all endings.

Pierce Arrow had passed ownership of the *Daily Hellbender* to Ms. Billious Bloom who was grooming son Pres, her only child, to become editor-in-chief, while continuing to spread the glory of the Rosebeam Foundation collection of Latin antiquities around the world.

Pierce spent most of his waning years lounging around in dirty pajamas, writing soft porn romance novels that always starred the legendary Florence Hormel as consummate giver and receiver of passion and true love Lettie Jones as the ultimate heroine. Lettie just kept on giving as she always had. To husband Pierce, to her many children of varied lineage, and to the community she so loved.

The former president of the United States visited every now and then. He always left with a word of praise for the community's conservation ethic, and a smile. He and Billious romped more openly now, but the secret son remained just that. To the former president, Pres Bloom was just a smart, good-looking kid grown into an ambitious young man. The former president offered to mentor him in the intricacies of politics, not knowing his genetic markers were already at play. He and Billious would always be casual lovers and fast friends, but no more. Hardlyville always welcomed the former president as an honorary citizen and creator of the Skunk Creek Watershed National Refuge, which had restored and protected the village's most precious resource.

Jimmy Jones had sold his weed business to an up and coming young entrepreneur who reminded him of his younger self. Actually the young man could only afford to buy a special seed stock and lease the land from Jimmy at this point in his career, but he invested all he had.

Jimmy had transitioned his enterprise into "medicinal marijuana" after reading about all the health benefits accorded his favorite recreational drug. He learned that cannabis had been around for thousands of years, extolled for its curative, as well as happiness, quotient.

Back in the day when the good old US of A federal government had started spreading rumors about demon weed with cartoon sketches of crazy people with long hair and scraggly beards, right wing politicians demanded that marijuana be categorized as a Class 1 dangerous drug and banned from public access.

This didn't much affect domestic consumption and just drove it underground for entrepreneurs like Jimmy Jones to exploit for profit. Those most impacted were probably public figures, those running for office, or awaiting congressional approval for high position. It required that they lie about prior usage in high school and college or face the voters' wrath. At least, that's what their political consultants advised, despite the fact that most of those voters had toked at least a time or two during their ill-advised youth. *What's one more lie,* the politicians reasoned.

One famous nominee for some high court position who told the truth about prior usage was ultimately forced to withdraw his candidacy.

What Jimmy read was that marijuana not only made people happy and hungry but also provided relief from seizures, pain, nausea, and other significant maladies. It was also credited with inhibiting the growth of certain cancer cells. None of this was admissible into the public realm because of our national war on drugs and focus on incarceration and character assassination.

It just made Jimmy Jones rich by Hardlyville standards and gave him a sense of helping humanity.

The "medical" moniker gave Sheriff Sephus Adonis room to look the other way, as well as show respect for the community leader Jimmy had become. Jimmy generally had about five small businesses going at any one time, from cow patty recycling to wild turkey feather art. It kept him busy, earned a little cash, and when he tired of one, he shut it down and did something else. Oddly enough, everything Jimmy Jones touched these days was nearly legal.

Pastor Pat continued to minister to the community from the pulpit of Skunk Creek Church of Christ. He still strayed on occasion, generally with a widow these days, but stayed true to his mission to pray forgiveness for all villagers, including himself, regardless of race, religious belief, sexual appetite, or sexual preference, and to have a damn fine time doing so. His was a truly ecumenical vision.

Banker Jamin was raising one of his ten or twelve kids to take over Bank of Hardlyville. His gaze had settled on his and Mabel's only daughter Uvella, who had an unusual way with numbers, not unlike her father. On the other hand, she was gregarious and energetic like her mother. She would need both traits in that Captain Happy would also soon retire as bank spokesperson. This was a good thing in that he took fewer and fewer baths every year, and they now numbered in the single digits annually.

The only aberration in this generational transition was Ol' Dill's dog Muffle who was now, per most counts, about twenty years old and still siring offspring. He did not appear to have aged a day since Ol' Dill's demise. Some called it a reincarnation of the famous Hardlyvillain lover, some blamed it on a rogue batch of absinthe-laced moonshine with the power to stop time, others just smiled and left a bowl of dog food outside their back door.

Jimmy had organized this trip in honor of all who had gone before and the hope that those to follow would bring a like passion and love of place and neighbors to the table. He also wanted the young ones to see the Skunk Creek he had grown up with, nearly half a century before. He wanted them to "get it." He wanted them to know what its clear, cold waters meant to their home town, their little corner of the Ozarks, and—in a broader sense—to humanity in general. With all that was going on around them, they would need every ounce of passion and energy they could muster to preserve Skunk Creek, despite its protected status. If that could be their legacy to their grandchildren, life in Hardlyville and the Ozarks would continue to be good.

He thought they understood, but only he among them had floated the whole river course, and then just once with Cousin Lucas. It had both humbled and inspired him, if such can be explained. He knew it would them as well.

Rifleman agreed to join Jimmy in the supply john boat to paddle only when asked to and to protect floaters from all harm, be it natural or unnatural. Jimmy made him promise to hold fire until there was a clear and present danger. Rifleman's persistent habit of free-firing rounds in the air anytime he got excited would surely slow the fishing. Jimmy didn't want him over paddling either. Jimmy's strong rudder of his sturdy john boat covered most contingencies.

Jimmy asked floaters to carry their own camping gear, fishing equipment, and one warm case of beer each. This would assure a constant supply of the latter to dump into day coolers for the john boat to ice down.

Floating without cold beer broke some commandment—he couldn't remember if it was the twelfth or thirteenth. At least, that is what Cousin Lucas had said. Even Pastor Pat had sanctioned this exception to religious orthodoxy, reasoning that, like the Constitution of the United States, the Holy Bible could accommodate an amendment or two in the interest of modernity and marketing to a new generation.

The old "you've got to go to church or you will burn forever in hell," or "just because I say so," generally fell on deaf ears these days, and Pastor Pat was not going to accept a decline in membership without a fight. His creativity had worked to perfection so far and his pews overflowed with parishioners, old and young. Serving real wine instead of grape juice didn't hurt.

Providing an adequate multi-day supply of ice-cold beer for an army of young beer drinkers was a most daunting challenge. Jimmy's years of experience served him well. He would line up eight large coolers, gunnel to gunnel, the length of the john boat. One would be filled with enough food to get the party to the midway resupply chain at the Hardlyville bridge, as supplemented by fresh catch along the way. Seven would be filled with ice. Two of the seven would carry large loose bags to tap the first two days out. The other five would contain a block of dry ice with loose bags stacked around and atop, and duct-taped shut. One of those would be opened on each of days three through five for transfer to each canoe's day coolers, and get the entourage to Hardlyville bridge for more ice. That left two full coolers in reserve for extreme emergencies. Warm cases of beer were stuffed into any remaining nook of the john boat cavity. No, Jimmy Jones and his party would not be without cold beer on this trip.

And then there was the gallon jar of Float Trip Pickles. Jimmy couldn't leave that behind and would save one corner of a cooler for Hairdog Herminson's tasty concoction. Cousin Lucas would never go on a float trip without them, and Jimmy had always stayed true to the ritual.

It was said that Hairdog and his brothers Homer and Boomer would toss cucumbers, jalapeño peppers, onions, and shavings of skunk bladder into a vat of aged moonshine, then let it "rest" for exactly ten days. There were a few other ingredients added that Hairdog would never identify or admit to before transferring his product to gallon jars. The label read "Float Trip Pickles," with the byline "Set your gut and libido on fire." Hairdog had learned about that big foreign word in Ms. Bloom's class on Sex Ed at Hardlyville high school. He had flunked her course because he couldn't follow her rigid rules limiting "fornication" as she called it. He guessed it was just too much of that libido stuff, but despite his failure, the word stuck with him. And when he figured out that his foul-smelling pickles led to heartburn as well as hanky-panky, he knew he had a winner. Hairdog marketed his pickles as a foodstuff as well as an aphrodisiac, another big word Ms. Bloom had taught him. Jimmy could vouch for both and had gotten in trouble on occasion when eating more than two pickles at one sitting.

Jimmy knew he would have to keep a close watch on the float trip pickle jar with all the young and as yet unmarried floaters around. Not that he doubted that at least several of them sampled the joys of young love from time to time, it would just be irresponsible of him to "prime the pump," so to speak. He would limit his float trip charges, and probably himself, to one pickle per day.

A word about john boats. Unique and traditional to Ozarks waters for at least a century, these wood planked behemoths were buoyant enough to slide over shallow gravel shoals, yet strong and stable enough to hit a boulder head on and somehow remain upright. They could carry more gear than a pickup truck bed and somehow spread the load for balance and grounding. Canoes had become lighter and more steerable over the years. Johnboats hadn't changed.

Sally and Steele drove Jimmy and Rifleman to the headwaters put in. It was a long and dusty trek for the old van and canoe trailer. Jimmy had been there only once before with dear Cousin Lucas and got lost several times along the way. Booray and Li'l Shooter ferried the remaining floaters, eating the van's dust every time Jimmy had to turn around and set out in a different direction. They finally arrived at a washed out low water bridge that marked the beginning of their journey.

Cici Cobb, who was still trying to horn in on Jimmy Jones's marriage after all these years, was waiting at the put in, flashing shots of her sagging body anytime Jimmy even glanced up. Jimmy kept his head down for the most part, slipping an occasional smile at Sally who kept flipping the universal finger of disgust at Cici.

She had gone ahead and married her storefront boyfriend Quarter Bogus and popped a few kids, but still harbored a dream of bedding poor Jimmy, who had always remained true-blue to wife Sally.

Canoes loaded, paddlers gathered for the traditional launch photo and pre-float toast. Jimmy cited the long list of his elders who had preceded them on Skunk Creek, lingering over Lucas Jones's name longer than the rest. He hoped they might even find a hellbender along the way. As his toasts dragged out, most grabbed a second cold one to extend honors. Long float trips begged for a name. Things like "Breakeven Float," "Just Say No Float," "Got Lucky on this one Float," "Cottonmouth in the Tent Float," "Big Pig Float," "Voyage en Bateau Float," seeped through Jimmy's memory. But the best he could come up with for today was "A Float Trip." And indeed, it would be.

And then they were off, Lucas, Jr. the first not second, with Girl Jones in the bow took the lead. They had actually dated in high school, found others to enjoy along the way, but were back together again. Otis and Mona followed, Pres and Vixen and the others trailing slowly behind. Jimmy and Rifleman would bring up the rear to maintain a steady pace and preclude unwarranted activities. Warranted was considered okay by the elders and was defined solely in the eye of the beholder.

A Float Trip . . . Continued

Pierce Arrow and Lettie Jones had wanted to attend the launch party, especially given their direct interest in so many of the participants. But Pierce's eyesight was failing badly. He took pride in the role he and Lettie had played in restoring precious Skunk Creek to previous glory. He could see the sparkling waters and moonlit rapids in his mind's eye, if not his real ones. Lettie did not want to leave him behind, so she passed.

The famous Pulitzer Prize Committee had considered recalling Pierce's Pulitzer, earned for reporting on the Evil Coven, due to the smut he had drifted into writing. Lettie had appealed successfully to the committee chair to forgive and ignore the naive indiscretions of an old man. She had further promised to edit every distasteful paragraph of unneeded cringe words from every final draft, though she found herself laughing out loud at most before striking the delete key. She guessed that was why she and Pierce had lasted so long, a shared sense of weird, off-color humor, and of course the proverbial messin' around. The latter didn't happen much anymore though it didn't keep him from trying. Laughing at Pierce early one morning as he got a little handsy in the dark, she informed him that he was no Ol' Dill Thomas and should wait at least until sunrise. This hurt Pierce's feelings but he complied with her edict. Unfortunately he slept through sunrise and awoke mid-morning to find Lettie gone. She left a big red crayoned heart on the kitchen table with IOU scribbled across it.

Lettie Jones's love of Pierce Arrow was deep and pure, with enough space to share with first husband Lucas, whose last name she still carried. Pierce had filled a void of sorrow with laughter and joy when she needed it, and Lettie would forever be grateful.

That Lucas, Jr., Vixen, Mona, and Peli were all floating together for the next couple of weeks under the tutelage of Jimmy Jones filled her with some anxiety, but in her heart she knew they would be okay. Lucas would be with them. Her two older children by Lucas had moved on to college and jobs beyond Hardlyville, among the first of their generation to do so. She felt her younger ones being drawn into the cocoon that had protected her over the years and was in no hurry to tamper with their perspective.

The first night out for floaters was vintage perfect. Large full moon, blazing campfire, slight chill in the misty air, burgers, brats, and beans on the grill. Jimmy even added a dozen sweet, fresh-caught goggle-eye fillets, sautéed in butter, as an appetizer. Skunk Creek literally glistened. Some slept in their tents, others simply lay down next to the rushing water, covering their bedrolls with tarps to keep off the dew.

The second and third day and night were similar. Jimmy had rarely seen a more beautiful run of weather and water. He urged the young ones to soak it up as it would turn, sooner or later. It always did.

It ended up being sooner. A strong front swept through late one afternoon with severe lightning-laced thunderstorms, dumping buckets of water and washing out dinner. The beer was cold, bags of shelled peanuts were passed and all stayed well if not dry. Jimmy cast a wary eye at Skunk Creek and sensed she was beginning a rise. He stuck sticks along the water's edge and urged anyone who awoke during the night to check the creek level. He liked this particular gravel bar for its bluff-facing beauty and small gravel, but wished it was a little bit higher and deeper on a night like this.

It was Otis who hollered for Jimmy first. As Jimmy exited his tent into the rain he could see they were in trouble. His wood stake markers were nowhere to be seen, either washed away or buried beneath a surging current. He shined his flashlight toward the creek and saw only brown roiling water where glimmer had once ruled. He noticed that Pres and Vixen's tent had water lapping at it and ran to wake them and help carry it further back and up the gravel bar. The entire tent city soon followed. Water chased them still higher twice. This was not to be a peaceful night of sleep. Skunk Creek was clearly on a major rise, and with rain still pouring sporadically and who knew what happening upstream, their sizable strip of gravel was rapidly shrinking.

Jimmy surveyed the thick woods behind and decided it was time to evacuate to there. All collapsed their tents on wet sleeping gear and dragged them back into the soaked undergrowth. Canoes were pulled up next. Everyone shivered in the chill, and Jimmy briefly felt a deeper shudder, as memory served up the horror of the Big Pig Flood so many years past that had reordered Hardlyville history through several generations. He advised everyone to hunker down in rain gear to wait it out, and sat as a silent sentinel to an ever-rising and raging dark torrent of water.

Rifleman awoke with dawn, as he usually did, to a sliver of light along the horizon. Storm clouds had lifted, shrouds of fog hung heavy as sunrise attempted to peek through. He laughed at Jimmy Jones sitting straight as an arrow, his dripping cowboy hat drawn low over his brow, sound asleep. Skunk Creek raged below, but seemed to have crested. Logs and debris cluttered its course and coffee brown was its color of choice this morning.

Several hadn't slept during the night and huddled together for warmth in the cold dank woods. Those who gradually came to kept asking each other what in God's name were they doing out here. Warm memories and thoughts of the prior days' joys had washed far downstream in a surge of roaring water. Yin had been Yanged with no apparent interdependency. This was simply miserable.

Flambeau was the first to speak—she wanted to go home.

"Shit, so what do we do now," wondered Rifleman to Jimmy?

Jimmy didn't know. "I've never, ever been here before," was the best he could come up with.

Jimmy figured they were at most a day above Hardlyville, probably less with this much water feeding velocity. They could stay here another day and night, hope the sun would show up and no more rain fell. There was nothing warm or comforting about this option. And the beer would get warm, as most ice was gone. He had dished too much out when the dishing was good and had tapped the very last taped dry ice cooler last night to keep beer cold for his hungry mob. No, it would be a long couple of warm beer days if they sat it out.

On the other hand, they could load up and hop on the roaring crest for probably the ride of their young lives. Most everyone, with the exception of Flambeau and Peli, had grown up on the creek with paddles in their hands. He could put those two in the canoes of the most experienced and tell them to sit low, don't touch paddles, and hang on.

Jimmy Jones was a doer not a sitter. It had both gotten him into, and out of, trouble in the past. This was an adventure. They could plow down to Hardlyville, re-provision, maybe even spend a night at home before returning to complete the full float of Skunk Creek. He would put it to the floaters and let them decide. He knew what they would choose. His only role was prohibition if he thought it was too dangerous to proceed at current river levels. He didn't. Paddlin' and adrenaline would warm them up, and beer was probably cool enough to be palatable.

An hour later canoes were lined up beside the current. Gear was wadded and stowed in varying stages of disorder. Canoe partners had been reordered to assure a strong and experienced paddler in every stern. This time he and Rifleman would take the lead to be able to warn of obstacles or particularly difficult water. There was a sense of excitement tinged with fear underlying it all.

Jimmy and Rifleman shoved off into the churning, flooded waters of Skunk Creek. As the current pushed them wherever it wanted, Jimmy had a slight moment of second guessing. But it was too late now. Canoe after canoe followed, Lucas, Jr. and Girl Jones bringing up the rear in honor of floating seniority.

This would pretty much be a rush to the Hardlyville bridge, muttered Jimmy to himself. There was no safe way of getting off this raging torrent until the backwater pool behind the bridge columns that would hopefully smooth their exit. To his left Jimmy saw a submerged piece of wood the size of a fireplace log suddenly launch skyward from a swirling eddy, propelled by a subsurface force he couldn't identify. This was another "never seen that before" moment. Jimmy glanced behind at Hardlyville's future and hoped to heck he had made the right call.

It didn't take long to confirm he hadn't. As Rifleman peered around the third bend after put-in, anticipating a narrowing in channel and subsequent escalation in velocity, he gasped out loud. A huge sycamore had fallen across the stream during the night, a victim to washed out roots. The entire channel was blocked, a leafy wall to the left, a giant root wad right, the large trunk connecting. There was no place to go. If ever a recipe for capsize and entrapment existed, he was looking at it.

Jimmy made the flash decision to plow straight forward and try to clear the partially submerged, white-barked tree trunk. He screamed back at the others to pull over and wait, but there was no place for them to go. The high mud bank on their right would bounce them back like a ping pong ball and the flooded woods to the left provided half-submerged trees to flip them.

Jimmy and Rifleman lined up the john boat for a straight hit on the tree trunk, then paddled with all they had to try to catapult over. The johnboat got lodged amidships, bow dangling six inches out of water. Rifleman dropped his paddle and grabbed both gunnels, trying to keep balance and avoid even the slightest turn into the current which would dip the side and flip the boat on top of them. Jimmy followed Rifleman's lead. They needed to buy time to exit the john boat on their own terms, not pinned to the tree, trapped in leafy limbs beneath, or buried under a capsized boat.

The view from their shaky perch revealed a multitude of crises.

Jimmy could see four heads bobbing under life jackets, canoes abandoned and quickly submerged. He shouted to swimmers to clamber aboard the old sycamore if possible, knowing that they could just as easily be sucked under into a dark abyss from which they might not exit.

A quick glance beyond revealed two canoes headed into the flooded woods left with occupants grasping for limbs to cling to as their canoes disappeared into the brown churn. At least they were free of the main current which pushed the final canoe toward the downed sycamore at warp speed. It was all happening so quickly, without order or reason, nature's fury fully unleashed.

Jimmy could see the fear in Lucas, Jr.'s and daughter Girl Jones's eyes as he ordered them to hit the downed sycamore head on, in hopes of finding a fragile resting place next to the john boat. They veered slightly on impact, dumping Lucas, Jr. and Girl into the brown roil. Lucas, Jr. was able to grab a limb to hoist himself up on the tree.

Girl Jones got trapped against the tree by the partially sunken canoe, head barely above water, screaming in pain and fear, just beyond Jimmy's reach. He tried to shove the canoe away to free her from its death grip and at least give her a long shot at survival under the tree and through buried branches to daylight. The canoe wouldn't budge. He watched her slowly slide toward submersion, his only daughter begging him in desperation to save her.

He caught movement to his left. A small athletic body was leaping toward them, clearing limbs, slipping and sliding along the main trunk, yellow eyes blazing.

Vixen grabbed the canoe just as Girl Jones slipped beneath the muddy surface, planted both feet, and with an extraordinary burst of strength moved it from Girl's submerged body, nodding to Jimmy to go get her. Jimmy hollered his exit to Rifleman and dove under the tree, feeling for his daughter. He found her entangled in a limb and fought to pull her free, placing his mouth on hers to share his remaining oxygen. He flipped upside down to use the full tree trunk as a lever to push them down. This rid them of the limb and carried them down-stream as Jimmy struggled to find the surface in an upside down, topsy-turvy rushing world of darkness.

Rifleman exited the john boat as it teetered then flipped on its side to be cracked in half by the sycamore.

Vixen eyed the brown water downstream of the tree and thought she saw Jimmy's head bobbing just below the surface. She dove after him, hoping against hope that he had his daughter with him.

Tiny Vixen found both and hoisted them above her for air. Jimmy was sputtering and coughing. Girl Jones was dead weight. Vixen had to get them ashore to try to clear Girl Jones's lungs.

Fifteen seconds of other-worldly kicks carried the three-some to a rock shelf which normally would serve as the mid-point of a beautiful bluff. Vixen stuck the fingers of one hand down Girl Jones's throat while pumping her chest with the other. A sea of vomit and water spewed forth, followed by a faint cry for help. Another surge of solid exhale freed Girl Jones to cough and gurgle lifesaving breath. Jimmy could only squeeze his daughter's hand and pray.

Vixen saw Rifleman dip below the surface. He had not worn an orange life jacket and was preparing to pay the price. Vixen passed Girl Jones's heaving head to Jimmy and dove into the swirling brown mess to grab Rifleman's shirt collar and slowly drag him back upstream to their rock ledge perch. Jimmy could not believe what he was seeing. A forty horse motor could not have dented that current.

Vixen literally tossed a gasping Rifleman on top of Jimmy and surveyed the litter behind her. Three of the young ones still clinging to trees upstream. Five more sat astride the giant sycamore. Girl Jones was coughing and crying in father Jimmy Jones's arms. Rifleman was on his hands and knees spewing brown water on them both.

All present and accounted for. Except for five canoes, one john boat, gear, beer, and float trip pickles.

It took two hours of status quo for Skunk Creek to begin to drop.

Vixen left Jimmy, Girl, and Rifleman to fend for themselves. Girl Jones cried from the pain of what Jimmy assumed were broken ribs. At least she could cry.

Vixen worked her way upstream to the three hanging on to branches. She ferried them, one by one, to a solid rise far back in the woods. She convinced the five log-bound to stay put as their best chance of survival.

An hour later Vixen led five of her stunned and shivering best friends along the tree trunk, through large leafy branches to the far bank and left them there. She returned upstream to lead the three high-grounders back down to them. She observed that they had a quorum with a wry smile. She then walked back across the downed tree, crawled over the muddy root wad, and scrambled downstream to help Jimmy, Girl, and Rifleman down from their increasingly isolated rock perch. She led them back over the root wad and tree trunk to the others, Girl whimpering in pain all the way.

Their reunion, albeit cold and wet, was cause for tears and celebration. All hailed Vixen for the quick thinking and fearlessness that had saved at least some of them from death by drowning. Unsaid was their shared awe for the supernatural power and strength she had displayed. None would ever look at her in the same way again.

Vixen's evil mother had used her gifts to maim and kill, to terrify and demoralize, to wreak havoc on humankind under the guise of religion and sex. Vixen's powers would be used for good.

As the sinking sun began to break through the evening haze, the brown waters of Skunk Creek continued to recede. Jimmy suggested that they all huddle together for body warmth and try to rest for an early morning "walk in the woods" home as he called it. Jimmy reckoned they were at least a good eight miles upstream of Hardlyville, and that they could surely cover that in a day.

Sheriff Sephus sat with Li'l Shooter, Booray, Sally, Airreal, Billious, Steele, Pierce, and Lettie, wondering what to do. The savage storm system that had flooded Skunk Creek had passed through, dropping a couple of tornados in the watershed and leaving a wide swath of damage. All were worried about how the float party had fared. Each had a child or more out in the mess somewhere between the headwaters and Hardlyville and felt helpless to assure their wellbeing. And, each in their own way, was questioning their sanity in allowing their precious children to attempt such an undertaking. Only Sally Jones was confident of her husband's judgment and experience to keep them safe. He had promised to camp high and take no risk. He generally kept his promises unless his judgment was clouded by beer or weed.

Sheriff Sephus felt the water had dropped enough to form a search party and head upstream in an outboard-motor-powered john boat. Pierce didn't think he could make it but Lettie would go given their exposure of four young ones. Booray would join them.

The ride up Skunk Creek was wild and wooly. Several trees were down and had to be portaged around. Debris littered the creek surface.

Hearts sunk when Lettie saw a familiar looking canoe sticking up from under a huge tree. It had been Lucas's favorite and Lucas, Jr. had insisted on taking it on this historic float. Another was found jammed in a bank of logs above the creek's edge. Jimmy Jones's mangled john boat was lodged beneath a large downed sycamore. There was no sign of life beyond the critters that were returning to their perches or kingfishers and woodpeckers darting about to find food.

Sheriff Sephus pulled into an eddy and contemplated options. His best guess, and hope, was that they had been caught on a gravel bar by the rise, abandoned canoes and gear for higher ground, and were slowly making their way downstream by land. If that was the case it would be a waiting game. This did nothing to alleviate Lettie's and Booray's intense anxiety. It didn't do much for the Sheriff's either as he kicked himself again for letting Flambeau, at her young age, tag along.

The sheriff suggested that they drift downstream, motor off unless needed, screaming at the top of their lungs, and firing an occasional round into the air. He hoped they could flush the float party out and at least run a couple of them in at a time. He was sure they were cold and wet, at best.

About halfway home, they heard a shout back from the left bank. They pulled in to the only skim of gravel that showed and waited, yelling all the while. As thrashing sounds in the woods grew closer, they held their breath and prayed in their own way.

Vixen was the first to break through, followed closely by Pres. Lettie leapt to hug first one then the other, almost afraid to ask about the rest. Vixen's broad smile said all as they stumbled up in twos and threes, Jimmy cradling Girl Jones at the end.

Lettie and Booray hugged their own and gave up seats to Jimmy and Girl for a rush run back to town for treatment. No one said much, because there wasn't much to say. Vixen had asked that none of the floaters share her rescue efforts because she didn't want that kind of attention. Who of all she had saved could refuse that request? So they all kind of stood around, smiling and shivering. It had been that kind of trip.

PEACE IN THE VALLEY

Hours later, with most at home and in bed, Jimmy Jones crouched on his haunches in the settling dusk, staring into a rapidly clearing Skunk Creek. He had survived the single worst decision he had ever made in his life. He would never do something so stupid again, even if it meant warm beer. Skunk Creek had won this one, he smiled, but he would be back.

Jimmy thought about Skunk Creek and her precious surrounds. He mused about the shallow ocean that had covered the Ozark Dome three hundred million years earlier, about the thermal heat that had driven tectonic plate movement to uplift soluble limestone and non-soluble chert skyward, about the physical and chemical weathering, the raging river flow, the give and take of time, that had carved the striking bluffs and rugged rock faces he stared at today. He contemplated the karst on which he squatted at this very moment, the Swiss cheese underlay to inhospitable surface cover that sped the hydrologic cycle through underground passages at speeds too fast to filter tainted groundwater.

A brief flashback to the Big Pig Flood of his youth confirmed the idiocy of placing corporate farms and confined animal feeding operations anywhere near such a timeless and fragile ecosystem as self-evident and immoral. The risk was simply incongruent with any rate of return.

He knew that if left alone, Skunk Creek and her tributaries would pump clear, cool water through subterranean arteries to cleanse and nourish the veined infrastructure over time. He marveled at the complexity of it all and sensed a higher power's hand in system design.

He had learned all of this technical jargon from a retired university professor, another who cared deeply about the Skunk Creek watershed, if only from afar. The rest of his train of thought derived from common sense.

In the end, he wondered whether the stunning magnesium teardrops on his favorite sheer bluff upstream leaked joy or despair.

A song slipped into the back door of his memory. Lucas used to slur out the words after too many beers as they drifted downstream, casting bank to bank, boom box blaring. The Ozark Mountain Daredevils or something like that. They were pretty old, as he remembered.

Something about "beauty in the river, beauty in the stream."

And "a brighter day round the corner" popped to the top. That had been one of Lucas's favorites. He used to shout it out with joy. Again and again. Over and over.

Then a little later, guitar, fiddle, base pounding, harmonica chirping in and out like a cricket, something about "standing in the water," that everybody had to do it, because "you can wake up from the dead." He remembered this part specifically, "and roll away the stone, you can roll away the stone." It was more than a Biblical metaphor. Jimmy thought that was the big word they used back in English class. The river is life itself, it is birth, it is rebirth, it is resurrection, it is the portal for more life to come. Skunk Creek was all of that to him, and more.

And so it was in Hardlyville as spring leaned into summer with no pigs perched east and upstream of the village, no Demon Lady lurking in the shadows, no dead bodies floating down Skunk Creek, no history or heritage for sale, and new hope for the children of the creek. Life in paradise was fragile, and would always be dangling by a slender thread.

—THE END—

BUT WAIT! THERE'S MORE ...

**Don't miss books One and Two
in the Ozarkian Trilogy!**

Available in print and ebooks.

SKUNK CREEK

~ BOOK I IN THE OZARKIAN FOLK TALES TRILOGY ~

Who knows what lurks in the deep, dark corners of the Ozarks?

A gruesome murder on the banks of Skunk Creek leads to a mystery and a rollicking adventure story. Populated by the crusading editor of a small town newspaper, an oversized Sheriff, a lovable band of merry misfits, and an evil cult, an Ozarks village is steeped in beauty, tragedy, love, and lust.

Hardlyville and her colorful, unforgettable Hardlyvillains bring laughter, tears, and celebration of life at every turn as they seek to prevail over natural and unnatural threats to their way of life.

Warning: Do not read if you blush or tire easily. Skunk Creek grabs readers from page one and rushes on through each disaster and fiasco. In the end, love of place and people carry the day to an unlikely conclusion.

Skunk Creek is rowdy, ribald, insightful, and grounded in Ozarks waters and history. It confronts and entertains amidst the vexing questions of our times.

READ A FREE CHAPTER NOW AT
WWW.PEN-L.COM/SKUNKCREEK.HTML

245

SWINE BRANCH

~ BOOK II IN THE OZARKIAN FOLK TALES TRILOGY ~

Who knows what lurks in the deep, dark corners of the Ozarks?

The residents of Hardlyville! And what do a local environmental disaster of unprecedented proportions, a series of ghastly murders, corrupt state politics, a bedouin shivaree, crooked investment bankers, and Noodler's Anonymous have in common? Skunk Creek!

For Sheriff Sephus Adonis, congressman Pierce Arrow, and his true love Lettie Jones, justice is no longer an intellectual concept, it's a matter of life and death. From Hardlyville city hall to Washington, DC's halls of government, to the international stage, resilient Hardlyvillains wage a fierce battle to protect their precious waters and way of life. Hilarity abounds in their madcap and unorthodox rush to remain alive—and relevant.

Swine Branch is rowdy, irreverent, insightful, and grounded in Ozarks waters and history. It confronts and entertains amidst some of the most vexing questions of our times. A worthy follow-up to *Skunk Creek*.

GET YOURS NOW AT
WWW.PEN-L.COM/SWINEBRANCH.HTML

246

ABOUT THE AUTHOR

TODD PARNELL began writing nonfiction during his years as a banker and educator, including published books *The Buffalo, Ben, and Me, Mom at War,* and *Postcards from Branson.* He is an award-winning author inducted into the Missouri Writers Hall of Fame in 2012. He tried his hand at fiction upon retiring as president of Drury University and hasn't stopped writing since, completing the Ozarkian Folk Tales Trilogy, published by Pen-L Publishing, and is hard at work on a second trilogy, Children of the Creek.

In his own words, "I've had great fun writing about the Ozarks and tackling important contemporary issues in that rich and captivating context!"

Parnell is a civic leader, environmental advocate, co-founder of the Upper White River Basin Foundation, and retired CEO of THE BANK in Springfield. He recently completed his term as Chairman of the Missouri Clean Water Commission. He holds Masters degrees in Business from Dartmouth University and History from Missouri State University, and is a graduate of Drury University.

Born in Branson, Missouri, Todd is a sixth-generation Ozarker. He resides with Betty, his wife of forty years, in Springfield and is blessed with four children and five grandchildren, so far.

CONNECT WITH TODD AT:
www.ToddParnell.com
Facebook: Todd.Parnell.7

247

Dear Readers,
If you enjoyed this book enough to review it for Goodreads, B&N, or Amazon.com, I'd appreciate it!
Thanks, Todd

Find more great reads at Pen-L.com